I0667674

WHAT HAPPENS AT THE BEACH

ANTI-BELLE BOOK 5

SKYE MCDONALD

Anti-Belle

Copyright © 2024 by Skye McDonald

All rights reserved.

No part of this book may be reproduced in any form or by any electronic or mechanical means, including information storage and retrieval systems, without written permission from the author, except for the use of brief quotations in a book review.

JOIN THE COMMUNITY!

Click here for a free story when you join Skye's newsletter community! Or scan below:

For everyone who can't resist an innuendo joke.
You are my people.

WHO'S WHO?

A brief list of the key players in the Anti-Belle world & how they are connected to this book.

Celeste (Greene) Addison: CPO for *Chat Me Up!*. Wife of Ben Addison/ sister-in-law to James Addison. Cousin of Nick Field.

Ben Addison: Celeste's husband. James Addison's younger brother. Liv Milani's ex-boyfriend. COO of *Chat Me Up!*

Melody "Mel" Thomas: Wife of Nick Field. Author. Former media manager to international pop star, Jesse Storms.

Nick Field: Mel's husband. Music producer—produced Jesse Storms's debut album. Cousin of Celeste. Son of Jen & Alex Field.

Olivia "Liv" Milani-Langer: Teacher. Wife of Will Langer. Aunt to Maddie, Juliette's daughter's friend. BFF to Megan Riley. Close friends with the *Chat Me Up!* creators. All-around badass.

Will Langer: Liv's husband. Friend of Luke Paris.

Megan Riley: Liv's BFF. Engaged to Luke Paris. Billionaire and primary investor in *Chat Me Up!*.

Luke Paris: CMO for *Chat Me Up!*. Megan's partner.

***

Lesser Players/Teasers for future releases:

David Underhill & Kira Ireland: Aka "You & I," a successful musical duo husband and wife.

Jack Spencer: Front man for the local band Cellar Door. Friend of the group. Single... for now.

Sarah Rose: Celeste's friend from *NSFW*. Receptionist at TennStar... at the moment.

Jesse Storms: International pop superstar. Formerly engaged to Mel Thomas. Not doing so great these days...

1

JAMES

She was following me again.

Shameless flirt. I lifted a hand and waved. Not that she gave a shit. She wanted one thing from me, and I knew what that one thing was.

My meat.

And we both knew she'd get it.

She darted ahead, trying to play it cool, then doubled back. I moved to hide her prize before she got to me, but she knew I was bullshitting. I couldn't resist her charms.

She plucked the lionfish off my spear in a flash.

Damn shark. I exhaled a bubbly laugh through my regulator.

The nurse shark rolled and swam away, but I knew she'd be back as soon as I caught another. "My" shark had a scar on her dorsal fin. I'd noticed her in the group of nurse sharks who followed the lionfish hunts about a week ago. Nurse sharks were rarely aggressive toward humans and loved to eat lionfish—they just didn't know how to catch them themselves. So, they often followed divers who hunted the invasive species. This particular one seemed to have picked me as her special helper.

Back on the boat, I compared my haul with the other divers. Three today in my container. Those, plus the two my shark had snarfed, meant a pretty successful haul. But I didn't keep the fish I caught. I gave them to the marina and let the crew take them home and cook them. The resort I'd called home for longer than anticipated kept me well-fed. For me, this was for sport and to help the marine ecosystem.

When we docked, I left my dive gear with the crew, confirmed I'd be on the sunset tour that night, and walked up the beach to the resort. One thing I loved about this place was that scuba excursions left from the hotel's dock. It was why I'd chosen this hotel in Aruba. Getting to dive nearly daily was also one of the reasons Aruba had become my home for so long.

After a morning underwater, my head was fuzzy with hunger. I made it to the café before they closed to snag a late lunch. A tour of the pool deck offered nowhere to sit, and my mouth watered more by the second. So, I hurried down the walk to the first empty chaise I found on the beach. Sitting back and gulping water, I pushed on my sunglasses. The shushing waves filled my ears.

This is the freaking life.

With a deep breath and the sun warming my skin, I picked up the sandwich and took a huge bite. I was so hungry that this thing would be destroyed in moments.

"I have a plan."

I paused mid-chew and glanced to my left. A woman in a black bikini and white cover-up sat on the neighboring chaise. Her short, toned legs were pale and bent at the knees. My gaze flicked from those legs to her face. A wide-brimmed hat shaded her eyes, but she had a sly little smile trained on me, confirming she'd just spoken.

"Hmm?" I said as I swallowed my bite.

She pointed an aqua-colored nail at me. "You have extra fries. And extra ketchup. I just checked in. The kitchen was closed by the time I got to the café. So..." Her wrist drew a circle as if the point was obvious.

"So... your plan is to steal my fries?"

Her hat flopped with a decisive nod.

I gaped, mute, while she stood up and straddled the end of my chair. Part of me wanted to laugh. The other part wanted to ask her what the hell she thought she was doing as she dragged a fry through the ketchup and popped it in her mouth.

"This feels like a lopsided plan," I said at last. "What am I getting out of it?"

Her lips formed a circle. Slowly, she slid a fry in and out of her mouth before eating it. "What would you like to get?"

My jaw unhinged.

Her posture tensed at my lack of reply, but she kept eating. I eyed her carefully. Her swimsuit was sexy enough. It certainly did a good job showing off her cleavage, but it wasn't risqué by a long shot. Nothing about her said prostitute, but what the hell else was I supposed to think?

"Um, I don't-or, better to say, I'm not... looking."

"Looking?" She cocked her head.

"Listen. Not to be rude, but I'm not buying what you're selling. So please move on. Okay?"

She choked on a fry. I stared at her for a long moment before realizing I should hand her my water. When she recovered, her face was dark red.

"Oh, my god. I didn't mean I was *selling* myself!" she hissed.

"What the hell did you mean then?" I hissed right back. The last thing we needed was to make a scene.

"I... I meant... I was trying to be... sexy." She lowered her gaze to the chair.

I stared at the top of her hat and fought the urge to reach for her hand. My pulse was up for no good reason.

"Why?" I asked at last, gruffer than intended. It had been a long time since I'd chatted with anyone outside of work calls and dive boat banter. This stranger had caught me totally off my game. Before a month in the islands—before the disastrous relationship that ended days before I left—I would've taken her little move differently.

She tipped her chin up again. That impish smile returned, a bit more strained than before. "Because usually when I flirt with guys, they enjoy it. Because this is paradise, and I'm here to be wild, free, and sexy. Problem with that, pal?"

A smile began to tug at my face. "Not at all, love. Not at freaking all."

"Good. So, what can I do to thank you for the fries? Also, can I have some fruit?"

I chuckled and handed her the bowl. "Bold. I like it."

"Bold. That's me." She plucked a pineapple ring and took a bite. A bead of juice ran down her chin.

"No need to repay me. I can't abide leaving a lady hungry."

She snorted. "Could've fooled me."

"Mm. You've got juice on your chin."

She wiped the wrong side. Deliberately, if the smirk she wore meant anything. "Did I get it?"

I shook my head and leaned forward. "Allow me."

My thumb stole the drop. I sat back and licked it clean, gazing at her from behind my shades. Her lovely throat bobbed with a hard swallow, and suddenly, I was on my game again.

"Here. Have a bite." She thrust the remaining piece toward me.

I took one without touching her.

Her nose scrunched. "Have some more, silly."

"Yes, ma'am."

I grasped her gently to steady her hand. The tendons in her wrist tightened when I pulled her fingers through my lips to take the fruit. I released her quickly with an appreciative hum. "Delicious."

She huffed a laugh and looked out at the ocean for a moment. Then, she picked up another pineapple. "I thought this would be easy," she murmured to herself. Louder, she asked, "Where's your girlfriend?"

"Excuse me?"

But she shook her head, finished the fruit, and stood up. "Tell her I said hi. Enjoy the beach, sailor."

"My girlf—" I began, but she was already walking away.

Alone, I leaned back in the chair and stared at the empty plate. *What the hell just happened?*

No time to ponder, though. I had a conference call with the partners and a nap to catch before getting back to the boat.

2

JULIETTE

I thought this would be easy. Dammit. I thought girls could just turn on the charm and have a guy eating out of their hands. A prostitute??

I groaned and fell back on the bed. The last half hour would not stop replaying in my mind...

My stomach fluttering while I worked up the nerve to talk to him—and then continuing to flutter the whole damn time, no matter how airy I pitched my voice. The stunned expression on his face. The absolute horror of him thinking I was a hooker.

I groaned again and kicked the bed. It wasn't like hookers were bad or anything. But selling myself had not been the vibe I meant to give. Cute and flirty were my intention.

Rubbing my eyes, I tried to power through that moment and replay the rest.

His smile, which I *finally* won like a prize. The wicked shiver that shot down my body when he licked my fingers. The silence after he did because what the hell was I supposed to say? But also, he didn't say anything. Didn't try to keep us chatting.

The moment I accepted that that guy wasn't interested in me. Girlfriend, wife, whatever. Maybe he was single, and I didn't know how to flirt properly. Not that I'd had much practice ever.

This trip is supposed to be your hot girl summer, all in a weekend. You've got to do better if you want to be wild, free, and sexy. Bold, like he said. Not a word I think of often, but sure. Vacation Me is bold. Stop lying on this bed and have some fun for once.

I chewed on my lip, knowing my mental boss was right. I would go to the pool. Order a fruity drink. Explore what the resort offered. Try to flirt again. A drunken one-night stand should be my goal. It would be enough. I could say I'd had a fling once in my life at least. I could go back to the real world and never wonder what I was missing out on.

The real world...

I grabbed my phone. Mom answered on the second ring.

"Why are you calling?" Her tone was sweetly sassy. "Is the resort on fire?"

I chuckled. "No. Just putting on some sunscreen before hitting the pool. Wanted to check in."

"Your check-ins are not welcome, missy. This is your getaway, and you should take it. I may never feel this generous again, you know."

I laughed again. "Oh, I know. And thanks again for—"

"Pfft. Stop it and go to that pool! We talked about this." Her tone softened. "Seriously, baby. I want you to have your escape. Do everything you want and not worry one bit about home. We are fine. And I have your number if I need it."

My heart swelled. "Thanks, Mom."

"Of course."

"Okay, I'll go. But, is Ivy there?"

"Napping."

I nodded. "Great. Well, then I guess the pool beckons. Talk to you later."

"When you get home," she pressed gently.

"Yes, ma'am. Love you both."

She blew a kiss, and we hung up.

This is my fairytale. This is not real life. Go live out your wildest dreams, girl.

I hopped off the bed and hit the pool.

Why had I thought single people would be everywhere in the islands? I'd heard of resorts that catered to singles. Of course, I had not counted on going solo when I'd booked this trip. Nor was I picturing a wild, sexy time. More like romantic and relaxing.

An hour at the pool somehow managed to stress *and* chill me out all at once. The glittering water and perfect hot weather were too delicious to ignore. But I was the only lounge chair for one in sight. This section of the resort was adults only, but everyone was coupled.

I was starting to contemplate how I felt about a ménage when one of the staff walked up holding a clipboard. He smiled down at me. "Afternoon, Miss. We are going out on a sunset snorkel cruise tonight. Would you like to go?"

"Well, I hadn't planned on..."

"Oh, but you should come! Everything is provided, and the reef is magical at that hour."

Drunk hookup tomorrow night, magical adventure tonight. I smiled and nodded. "Sure, sounds fun."

He took my name and room number, gave me the basic info, and said he'd see me in two hours. After that, I laid back in my chair and took a nap. For some reason, saying yes to that adventure finally quieted my brain.

Just before six, I stood on the dock in a line of people. My little gear bag in one hand, I glanced down to make sure the zipper on my one-piece was all the way up. No need to give the crew the same impression I'd made earlier.

The guy who'd signed me up was the ship's captain. He beamed when I shuffled to the boat. After checking my name off the roster, he took my hand and guided me on board, nodding at the bag in my hand. "Hey, you have your own gear."

I flashed a tight-lipped smile and clutched the bag. This mask, fin, and snorkel set was a gift from my father on my eighteenth birthday. I'd used it so much less than I'd planned when I got it, but it was precious to me. It represented dreams. Goals. A different path of life.

And the nice captain did not need to know any of that.

There were divers on the boat, too. I sat on a bench and watched with envy as they worked to set up the BCDs on the tanks which stood ready for them. They moved with such confident precision as if all those super-technical, life-supporting skills were the most natural thing.

"Get your ass on this boat, man! We are leaving without you!" The captain shouted.

"Haha, yeah, yeah. I know. Sorry."

My shoulders tensed as the last passenger jumped on. Out of the corner of my eye, I glimpsed a man in a t-shirt and board shorts.

A very familiar man in a t-shirt and board shorts.

I swallowed a groan and rubbed my forehead. *Did not need to run into him again.* "Oh, hi. Promise I'm not here to steal more of your food or proposition you."

Mom's directions floated back up. Have my escape. I could do that. He hadn't seemed angry at me earlier. No need to even acknowledge each other, really.

Besides, he was setting up his dive gear.

The little crew of snorkelers sat on the empty benches in the front of the boat. Toward the rear were the dive tanks in their holsters. I put my elbows on my knees and bent my head to appear casual. But really, I watched shamelessly as he snapped his BCD vest onto the tank and tested the regulator to ensure air flowed through the hoses. He stepped into a wetsuit and tugged his t-shirt off.

Damn. I mean... damn.

My first glance at this guy earlier made me think he was attractive. Sitting across from him on the chair confirmed how right I was. But seeing him stand in the middle of a boat, wetsuit hanging off his hips, bare-chested and practically glowing in the golden light?

That was some other level of hot.

He pushed his hand through that shaggy hair, and I nearly swooned. Unconsciously, I put my finger to my lips. Ooh, the shiver I'd gotten when he licked me this afternoon was perfectly wicked.

The boat lurched forward, jostling all of us. It shook me out of my thirsty reverie just in time to look away before he caught me staring. We cruised out into deeper waters. The sun hung low on the horizon, casting an orange glow over the water. Passengers began to wander around and mingle. I busied myself with my gear bag. I'd just pulled on my boots when someone slid onto the bench beside me.

"I have a plan."

I cringed and tried to ignore the chills his voice gave me. Biting my tongue to keep a neutral face, I glanced over.

Holy literal smoke.

He'd worn his shades this afternoon, so this was the first time I got a full look at his face. His gunmetal gray eyes were unlike anything I'd ever seen. Worse, they glinted with humor, reminding me of the underside of a cloud in a sun shower.

"Excuse me? Do we know each other?" I asked with feigned ignorance.

He had the audacity to hit me with a blinding grin. *Rude. How am I supposed to ignore you when you smile like that?*

"Oh, we go way back. And I'm offended you'd pretend otherwise."

"You're not familiar. Perhaps you've mistaken me for someone else?" My tongue was going to be severed at this rate. No one else in the world would classify a line like that as flirting, but I heard the tease in my voice.

The way his smile deepened made me wonder if he did, too. "Come on, love. It's me. Your knight in shining... ketchup."

I couldn't keep my smile from twitching or my voice steady as I said, "Oh, it's *you*! Sorry, Sir Knight. I didn't recognize you without your ketchup."

"Hmm, and it took me a second glance to confirm it was you without pineapple juice all over your face." His gaze flicked to my mouth.

This silly banter was turning me on far too much. The fact that he seemed just as entertained didn't help.

We stared at each other. Finally, he breathed a laugh and shook his head. "Didn't expect to find you here."

"Why?"

His brow arched. "Fair point. Better to say, very nice to find you here."

Is it? I pushed past my doubts and flashed a coy smile. "That's what people usually say."

"I have no doubt that's true." He gestured to my bag. "Snorkel, not dive, though?"

I nodded. He reached out and took my mask from my hand. I fought back an irrational urge to snatch it and clutch it to my chest as if he'd break it. But the guy just looked it over, nodding slowly.

"This is a nice mask. You get great panoramic views with these open sides."

"Um, thanks. Yeah, it's great."

The boat began to slow down, so he handed it back to me and flashed another smile. "Have fun. We'll talk on the ride back."

"About what?"

He winked. He actually *winked*. And somehow, this guy made it look sexy. "About everything, M'lady." With a tip of his fingers to his forehead, he went back to his gear, zipping up the wetsuit as he went.

I barely heard a word of the safety review because the divers were headed off the boat. It took everything I had not to gawk at the way they stood on the edge, popped their air regulators into their mouths, held their masks in place, and disappeared with a giant stride into the ocean. My heart ached to join them, to know how it felt to sink into the gorgeous blue water and just breathe down there.

Thanks to time, a series of unplanned events, and money, I would be watching the ocean world from the surface.

Not a bad consolation, to be sure.

And this sunset tour was indeed magical. We had flashlights to illuminate the coral in the dusky light. Creatures seemed to be waking up for the night shift as I kicked along, delighting in the lobsters and eels I saw scuttling over brain coral and rocky shelves.

The snorkel group was free to do its own thing. Groups and couples explored the area. Being solo, I didn't worry about where they were. That freedom was nice, I realized as I explored a reef wall. Not having to think of another person's whereabouts, interests, or needs for freaking once.

I grinned around my mouthpiece.

When it was almost totally dark, I headed back to the boat's beacon. The whole group had returned at nearly the same time and were holding the anchor line, waiting their turn to get back on board. I floated in my life vest, in no hurry to end this moment. Two divers surfaced, and I waved them ahead of me while I flipped to my back and stared at the starry sky. My legs were bent at the knees, arms stretched wide to hug the expanse.

Weightless. Free. Freaking magical.

Until something tugged on my fin.

It was a sharp, quick pull that made my blood run cold. *Oh, god. I'm about to get eaten by a shark.* Adrenaline seized my muscles at the second tug. A scream lodged in my throat.

My "knight" broke the surface right beside me. He yanked his regulator out of his mouth and laughed. "Recognized the blue stripe on your fins. Did I scare you?"

I opened my mouth, and my blood-curdling scream came out as a pathetic little, "Ughh?"

He had the courtesy to dim the smile. "Aw, I did. I'm sorry."

Kicking so that I was vertical, I sucked in a deep breath and tried to shake my head. "No big deal. Just thought I was about to be a shark's dinner is all. Happens all the time."

"Sorry, sorry. Couldn't resist teasing you."

Couldn't you? Why? Why are you talking to me? Didn't I make a fool of myself today? "You can make it up to me later."

I had not intended that to sound as suggestive as it did. My mind had been on dinner, but I resisted the urge to clarify or tone it down.

His smile turned into a smirk. "With pleasure."

And even in the cool water, a zip of fire ran through me.

"Come on, you two," the captain called, so we kicked for the boat.

"See anything good?" he asked. I told him about the eel and lobster. "Nice. After you."

I gripped the ladder's handles, but the captain shook his head. "Fins off first."

"Oh. Right." *Totally not my first boat tour or anything.* One hand on the ladder, I fumbled for a fin, increasingly aware that I was making the entire boat wait.

My knight grabbed his regulator. "I've got you. Hang on."

He bit down on the mouthpiece and disappeared below the water. I felt him gently grasp my ankle. The next moment, one foot was free, and then the other. In a blink, he returned to the surface and handed my fins to the captain. I scuttled up the ladder and accepted a towel from a crew member while I watched him haul up. The captain grabbed his back and guided him to sit on the bench. The tank snapped into its holster, and he instantly set about removing his gear.

Stop. Staring.

I took my fins and returned to my stuff. Good thing I brought a dry bag with sweatpants in it. The night air was warm, but I was chilly from an hour in the dark water. I pulled on the pants and found a fresh towel to wrap around my shoulders while the boat lurched into motion.

A glance down the deck revealed my knight sitting alone, elbows on knees. He still wore his wetsuit. That shaggy, sun-kissed hair hung on his forehead. *I thought we were going to talk.* I frowned at the thought and how disappointed I felt about not getting more time with him.

Leave him alone. He's not part of your plan.

3

JAMES

Diving chilled me out and gave me time to process the afternoon's meeting. The topic of another product had come up, sending my brain into a creative spiral. One of the perks of diving was that it was Zen as fuck but also required attention to detail. I could let ideas flow without obsessing for a while.

Back on the boat, though, I put my mind on planning for a different reason. I'd spotted her as I was gearing up, and all thoughts of work had flown out of my head. A little redemption seemed called for after giving my best impersonation of a sentient rock this afternoon. But the last thing I wanted to do was bother this woman, and going to her now seemed a lot like pestering.

I gave up trying to plan and glanced up—only to find her watching me from her spot on the bench. She looked away but just as quickly turned back. I cocked my head to the left. She copied me. I switched to the right. Again, a copy.

With a chuckle, I crooked two fingers toward me. She

hesitated for a moment before standing up with a towel wrapped around her shoulders.

"Are you cold?" I asked when she sat beside me.

"Chilly."

"Want the best view in the house?"

She put on that sly smile from this afternoon and gestured to her towel-wrapped body. "Pretty sure you've already got that honor."

Well, fuck me running. This girl just took my line. My next words were going to be, *then let's get you a mirror.* Never in my life had a woman stolen a line out from under me. I blinked at her, scrambling to recover. Finally, I had to admit it. "You, uh... took the words out of my mouth."

She rolled her eyes and shook her head.

Oh, no, love. Don't you dare downplay that feat. She couldn't know just how epic a moment that was for me. I was a connoisseur of pickup lines. Sometimes, they worked. Often, they just got a laugh, which was okay, too. But to be beaten to the punch? Epic indeed.

I leaned closer to her. "I can show you a decent runner-up if you want."

"Show me what you will, Sir Knight."

Her calling me that made me realize we didn't know each other's names. I tucked that away for the moment and went to push open the window above the benches in the front. It was wide and designed for exactly what I was about to do.

I turned to her and held out my hand. She arched her brows but let me guide her up on the bench. "Climb through."

"Are you joking?"

"No. Drop the towel, and I'll help you."

She frowned at me, but she also let the towel fall to the

bench. I knelt down and made a basket with my hands for her to step into, then boosted her up through the window. When her feet disappeared, I grabbed the towel with my teeth and hoisted myself through. She flashed a relieved smile and wrapped herself up again.

We were out on the nose of the boat with a front-row view of the ocean. Leaning our backs against the cabin's wall, the night air whipped around us as the lights from shore blurred past.

"Okay, this is really the best view," she said over the roar of wind and motor.

I lolled my head to look into her whiskey-colored eyes, up at the sky, then back at her. "Top freaking tier."

Her lips parted. I gave myself a mental fist bump before leaning in. But those lips flattened into a line before I could meet her. She pushed my chest gently, shaking her head and looking away.

"Sorry," I said as I retreated.

"No, no. It's... fine. It's just that I..."

"No explanation needed. Not at all."

She flashed me a grateful look. *Come on, love. What kind of prick would think otherwise?*

We finished the ride back in silence. There was no tension in it for me. I enjoyed the view and the way we skimmed over the water. If she didn't want a kiss, she didn't want a kiss. If she wanted to tell me to fuck off, she certainly could.

As we idled to the dock, I helped her through the window again so she could get her stuff. My gear was in its bag already, so I stepped out of the wetsuit, toweled off, and threw on a hoodie.

I did not expect her to wait for me. But there she was on the dock, bag on her shoulder. Her long hair was tied in a messy ponytail. It was too dark to see at the moment, but I'd noticed earlier that it was dark brown with honey-colored streaks.

"Yes, ma'am?" I drawled on approach.

She fluttered her hand. "Just wanted to say thanks for the front-row seats. Felt wrong to leave without a farewell."

"Farewell? Is this where we end?"

"Where's your girlfriend?" she repeated, the same question as this afternoon.

"Where's your husband?"

I was teasing, but she flinched. My smile dropped. "Oh, shit. I'm sorry if I—"

Another flutter with her hand. "Why are you sorry? Not your fault I'm an old maid with no husband. What's the term from Jane Austen? No prospects."

Whatever made her flinch, she did a good job keeping it hidden behind that airy tone. I relaxed my expression and shook my head. "We're a pair of old maids, then. We should get some cats and matching muumuus and buy a condo."

She laughed. "I thought that was next year's vision board."

My god, you are hot. She was beautiful, yes. But her banter drove me absolutely wild.

"So, is this goodbye or not?" I asked.

"Good question. I could say yes and let you go back to the business of rescuing damsels in distress."

"Mm. And I could let you go find restaurant patrons to proposition."

I did not miss the way her lips twitched, but she held the topic. "We could do that. Put this encounter in the history books."

Cue my line. I took a half step toward her and dropped my tone. "Or I could take you to dinner."

She tipped her head up to look at me. "I thought you'd never ask."

"What's your name, gorgeous?" I murmured.

"What's yours?" she purred right back.

That's when my brain regained executive functioning. While my dick was perfectly happy to call the shots all night, reason marched in, waving a red flag. Reminding me of who I was—who I had very recently become. Prepared with a PowerPoint of all the places my name would've showed up in the past two years, plus all the ways disaster could strike if I wasn't careful.

I had no reason to suspect she was a con artist with me as her mark. My face wasn't as high-profile as my name on purpose. But the first things my lawyer had warned me about when I said I was going to Aruba were scams and safety. Only my family knew I was down here. I'd booked the stay under a pseudonym...

So why not just use that?

"Jay. Sir Jay Smith, if you'd like my full title."

She arched a brow. "Jay Smith sounds like a fake name."

Damn. I arched my brows back and didn't reply.

"Fine," she huffed after a moment. "My name is... Jae. With an e. Jae Jones."

I barked a laugh. "Wow. What were the odds?"

She shimmied her shoulders. "Incredible, isn't it?"

What does it matter? No real names, no mess. No bringing the real world to vacation.

I nodded. "Well, Jae with an e, how about you meet me at the hotel restaurant in, say, forty-five minutes?"

We walked up the dock together. She turned for the path to the hotel and glanced back. "See you there."

I watched her go, then jogged for my golf cart and cruised back to my villa.

4

JULIETTE

Jae??? Where the hell did you come up with that? What if Jay Smith is his real name, and you offended him?

"He didn't look offended," I grumbled while I shampooed.

His expression had basically confirmed that at least part of his name was a lie. Did it matter? I stepped out and wrapped a towel around me. While I combed my wet hair, I pondered.

What if he's a spy or something?... He seems too chill to be on a top-secret mission. Maybe he's a criminal... What kind of criminal would be hanging out at a popular resort?

What if he's a movie star? He's hot enough to be.

God, he was hot. Gorgeous, yes. But the way he talked to me made me giddy with pleasure.

I shook my head and went to get dressed. My hair would have to stay wet. Very few hotel blow-dryers had the power to handle my mane. I didn't have time to waste even trying. I stepped into a little romper. All of my clothes for the trip were brand new. This getup was way shorter than I'd realized when I bought it. I turned around in the mirror to confirm that my ass wasn't hanging out. The wrap top plunged pretty low, but at least my bra wasn't visible. I did my makeup and stepped into wedge sandals, then went back to the mirror.

Hi, Miss Jae.

The reflection looked nothing like me. Dark, damp curls hung down my back. My legs looked miles long in this tiny outfit. I'd already gotten a little sun, so my skin glowed. Young, wild, and free.

Jae was a perfect alter-ego name.

Suddenly, I didn't give a shit about worrying or pondering. I blew a kiss to the mirror, grabbed my purse, and hurried out.

He leaned on the deck's rail beside the entrance, staring out at the beach. I indulged in the eye candy before he spotted me. He wore a black and white block print button-down with black linen trousers. His hair was dry and styled. The top was light, but the underside seemed to be a full shade darker.

But oh, that smile. It hit me just then, and my knees went weak. He tipped his fingers to his forehead again. Such a silly move, but this guy could make anything look sexy. I rolled my shoulders and strolled toward him, and we walked together to the host stand.

We were seated overlooking the ocean and ordered cocktails. The smell of entrees from neighboring tables made me salivate. Other than our lunch of fries and pineapple, the last meal I'd eaten was a cup of yogurt on the flight down that morning. I studied the menu and sipped the elaborate fruity drink in front of me, increasingly stressed about whether or not this was awkward. Whether or not this was what dates with strangers usually felt like.

Jae doesn't do awkward. Jae does what she wants.

He broke the silence. "Dare I suggest we start with the conch fritters?"

"Sounds great." After we ordered, I sat back with my drink and said, "What did you see tonight on the dive?"

Those gray eyes lit up. He told me about spotting a sea turtle and a white-tipped reef shark. "It was so much bigger than the nurse sharks that follow me during the day."

"I'm sorry, what?" My eyes were wide. "Sharks? And you dove today, too?"

With a nod, he explained how he'd chosen this resort for its diving. Then he described lionfish hunting and why it was both fun and good for the native environment. Apparently, they were an invasive species that destroyed the coral and had no predators in these waters. Laughing, he told me about the nurse sharks not knowing how to catch lionfish themselves. One shark followed him so much, he'd decided it was his pal.

My breath got shallow the longer he talked. First, because diving fascinated me. His ocean stories made me long to see it for myself. Second, Jay—real name or not—had a way of storytelling that captivated me. His smile was wide, he talked with his hands, and he painted pictures with his words.

He was the opposite of the drunk hookup like I'd planned to have tonight. But I wanted to be nowhere else in the world than sitting across from him.

"I... have so many questions," I said when he reached an endpoint. "How long have you been down here? Is this why you came to Aruba?"

He shrugged. "About a month. Partially yes. I chose Aruba for the diving, but it's vacation, not work."

"A month on vacation? What the heck do you do?"

His smile turned into a smirk. "Rodeo clown."

Definitely a drug dealer. "Wow, coincidence. I'm a trapeze artist. Didn't expect to meet someone else in the circ... circus-ular arts."

A laugh burst from him. "Circus-ular?"

"What do you call it?"

"Ridiculous," he murmured, still smiling.

A really nice drug dealer. "Are you diving nitrox to go out so often?"

His brows walked up his forehead. "Are you sure you're not a diver?"

I waved my hand. "Not yet. Someday."

"Shame."

My drink was empty. The server brought our appetizer, so I got a second round. "Why's it a shame?" I asked as I popped a fritter in my mouth.

"Because I'd love to take you..." He paused, flashed a sly look, and then finished with, "Out on the reef tomorrow."

I breathed a laugh. "I would *love* to be taken... diving. How deep can you go?"

My thighs squeezed together as his pupils dilated. The smile he wore was perfectly wicked, but he barely blinked. "How deep would you like me to go?"

"I just wondered if you had any... advanced or technical skills."

"Plenty, love. I've got plenty. But remember that it's not just about plunging into the deepest depths. There's a lot to enjoy at every stage. Every step requires attention and skill."

Well, there go these panties. I sipped my new drink and let the tension stay wrapped around us. His gaze traveled over my face, studying me in a way I was wholly unused to.

"I appreciate an artisan of their craft," I murmured at last.

"And I appreciate a woman with an affinity for innuendos."

Then you're gonna fall in love with me, buddy. I shook my head as our entrees arrived. Over dinner, I made him tell me more about diving and other places he'd been. Neither of us asked anything related to our real lives. I found I liked that unspoken agreement. No ties to reality meant I was free to be whoever I wanted. Free to flirt with this sexy guy and not worry about my mess of a life back home.

Juliette had responsibilities. *Jae* could sip cocktails and talk about the ocean.

When the waiter set down dessert menus, Jay leaned forward to whisper, "So, I don't know your pleasure, but there's an ice cream store down the road that does a killer key lime flavor. Want to try that instead?"

Jae could also stay out as late as she pleased. I grinned and nodded.

The check arrived, and I frowned. "I was going to ask them to split the tab."

He gave me a look that said he doubted my sanity. "Because when I said let me take you to dinner, you thought I meant let *you* take *me*?"

"Well, but... I'm used to splitting..."

His playful look returned. "In all our time together, when have you ever paid the bill?"

"That time you left your wallet in your rodeo clown pants." *Wow. How did I think of that so fast?*

He laughed and signed the receipt. "Okay, just that once. Glad you had some cash stuffed in your trapeze artist leotard."

The level of rapport we seemed to share was unreal.

"This way." Jay stood up and offered me his hand.

We strolled out of the resort and down the main street.

Bars blared island music for tourists and locals. Souvenir shops were mostly closed, but a few kept later hours. Cars and bikes rolled past on the narrow street.

The walk was about half a mile. I was just starting to regret my sexy shoes when he tugged my hand and turned us down an alley lit with Christmas lights. A doorway in the middle of the wall had a chalkboard with flavors of the day scribbled on it. The kid in the window grinned when he saw us.

"Good evening, friends! What would we like tonight?"

I gazed at the board. "Banana rum with chocolate sauce in a cup, please."

"Key lime and dark chocolate on a cone for me."

Jay again waved off my attempt to pay. He dropped a huge tip in the cup and then handed me my scoop. A little deck with seating was around the shop's corner. We took the swing on the far side, letting it rock gently.

"Key lime and chocolate?" I asked with pursed lips.

"No cone?" He mimicked me and licked his cone.

I would've been perfectly happy watching this guy's tongue work like that for the rest of the evening, but I made myself stare at my dish. The flavor exploded in my mouth, so creamy and yummy that I moaned.

"Told you it was good," he mumbled through a mouthful.

I spoke around my spoon. "You weren't kidding."

We grinned at each other, and bubbles raced up my spine.

Halfway through with my cup, I felt him lean into my shoulder. His breath was cool, but his words tickled my ear. "Remember how you owe me a favor?"

"Okay, but one bite of this makes us even for the fries."

He laughed. "Deal."

I almost handed him the cup but then realized he held the cone. So, I scooped a bite of ice cream and chocolate sauce onto the spoon and held it up for him. Jay opened his mouth and let me feed him the bite. Gray eyes widened.

"Hot damn, that's a good pairing."

"I moonlight as an ice cream sommelier."

"When you're not on the trapeze, stealing my food, or snorkeling." Those eyes crinkled. "A true Renaissance woman."

It was hard not to giggle at nearly everything he said. I nodded slowly and polished off my cup. He watched me with that smile until I set it down and aimed my glance at his hand. "You're melting."

"Oh no," he moaned before attacking the remaining scoops. "Don't just sit there. Help a guy out."

He held the cone between us. I hesitated, unsure about citrus and chocolate right until the moment that it hit my tongue. "Oh, my god, this is amazing," I whispered as I licked again.

"It's my nod to Key West's key lime pie on a stick."

"So good."

"I know. Now hush and eat before it runs down my hand."

We took turns eating and laughing between bites until the ice cream was nearly gone. I was too tired and giddy to care about playing it cool at the moment. I looked up at the sky and sighed.

"This isn't how I'd planned my first night of this trip to go."

"No? This was always my agenda for today."

I breathed another laugh. "Thursday: be accosted by a random chick. Buy her ice cream."

"Exactly. I'll show you my calendar to prove it. But what was your plan?"

"Get drunk and find someone to hook up with."

He coughed out a laugh. "Honest. I like it."

I shrugged. "That's what I wanted from this trip. A wild time."

"As usual."

"Of course." He didn't see me roll my eyes. I shrugged again. "Can I have another bite?" I asked as I was already turning my head.

Which meant I didn't see that he was in the process of licking the cone. Which meant that me turning brought us nose to nose.

"Be my guest," he said softly.

He tilted the cone toward me but didn't back up. I licked at the little mound of ice cream that remained without taking my eyes off him.

"Do it again."

I gripped his wrist and lowered the cone. My pulse was ready to leap out of my throat, but I flicked my tongue out and skimmed his lips.

Those lips parted on an exhale. "Fuck," he breathed. "Again."

I felt him shift to drop the cone into my cup while I obeyed. Then, he held my face with both hands and leaned closer. He dragged his tongue across my lower lip, watching me the whole time. When he did it again, I opened my mouth and leaned forward.

His lips sealed on mine. The swing rocked from how I pulled on him, but his arms wrapped around me and brought me closer. One hand tangled in my hair while his other caressed my cheek.

Holy lord, he can kiss.

Part of me wanted to do a little victory dance. Check making out with a total stranger off my hot girl list. That alone would've been great. But this guy's kiss wasn't just a little tongue in a dark bar. Oh, no. Jay knew exactly what he was doing. He teased me with licks and nips until I was tugging his hair and ready to examine his tonsils.

"I thought you didn't want to kiss me earlier." His voice was like gargled rocks when he pulled away for a deep breath.

"I did. I so did," I panted before bringing him back.

He moaned into my mouth, and the sound lit me up even more. He tasted like sugar and smelled like summer. I gasped when he broke our seal and kissed down my neck. With his arm across my shoulders, he leaned me back so his lips could travel to the hollow of my throat.

"May I continue?"

"Uh-huh."

I bit my tongue at the warm, wet glide of his mouth over my racing heart. He scraped his teeth against my cleavage, and my toes curled.

"You are fucking gorgeous," he said while he worked back up to my neck.

Am I? A vain side of me I didn't know existed preened at his words. But I was too breathless to reply.

Voices floated from around the corner at the ice cream stand, breaking us apart too soon. Jay stared at me in the twinkling light. His hair was a mess from where I'd run my hands through it. I had no doubt my lips looked bee-stung.

Jay cleared his throat. "So, I'm sober. But..."

"But you want to be my wild hookup?"

"Baby, I'd volunteer as tribute any day." He grinned, but he also gave me a little more distance. "Seriously, though. Zero worries if that's not how tonight goes."

"I have a question."

"Hit me."

"Is your name really Jay?"

"No."

"Me neither. So you're okay with an anonymous, absolutely no strings attached situation?"

"Very. I can take the walk of shame as soon as you're done with me. Never contact you again. I've got a hike planned for early tomorrow anyway. Is that what you're looking for?"

Precisely my plan. I nodded. "What happens at the beach stays at the beach. Right?"

Jay nodded back but didn't move.

"So, do you want to go to your room?" I asked at last.

He turned to me slowly. That wicked smirk pulled at his lips. "Nope. Yours."

I stood up and dusted my hands. "Come on then, sailor."

5

JAMES

She fidgeted all the way up to her room. No matter how breezy "Jae" tried to be, it seemed pretty clear that hooking up wasn't her usual MO.

This wasn't my usual MO, either. And I was no stranger to hookups.

No, this one was different because I didn't want it to be a one-off. Not like I wanted a relationship with a woman I met on vacation. But Jae was giving something more. Something *addictive*. I knew even as I stepped into her room that leaving was going to require a lot of discipline.

She dropped her purse on a chair and met me in the center of the room. The terrace doors were open, curtains waving in the night breeze. I felt the tremor in her fingers when she slipped her hands onto my waist. It had nothing to do with the temperature.

"You sure about this?" I asked softly.

Her gaze was lowered, so I watched the top of her head nod. "Very."

My fingers skimmed down her bare shoulders. I grinned to see the goosebumps that broke out in my wake. Jae didn't move. I caressed her again and then did the same to her thighs. A little hum hit my ears, so I walked around behind her. Bending to touch just behind her knees, I took my time gliding up until my fingers played with the curve of her ass, just inside that little getup she wore. Chills sheeted her skin from her neck down. She tipped her head back to lean against my chest and sighed.

Whiskey-colored eyes blinked open. "Very sure."

I bent my head and kissed her again.

Her arm snaked up to wrap around my neck. With a deep inhale, I slid my hand all the way inside her shorts and squeezed her ass. She hummed and pushed back, all the while teasing me with that delicious mouth.

This is going to be good.

I'd been in Aruba for a month. Not once had I looked to get laid. Might've been a record. All the cautionary messages from my lawyer had put the fear of god in me. I didn't want to be scammed, kidnapped, or worse just because I needed a break from reality. So I'd stuck to myself, focused on hobbies and relaxing, and had the time of my life.

But then she sat on my chair and ruined my streak.

As I slid my other palm down the front of her body, I acknowledged that this wasn't careful or safe. And I gave not one damn.

Gliding my hand over her fantastic cleavage made my mouth go dry. I was torn between rushing to tear her clothes off and wanting to take as much time as possible. If this was all we got, I should savor it.

Jae sighed again. "Mmm... Ughh—ohmygod-whatisthat?" Her sounds of pleasure dissolved into a panicked hiss.

I opened my eyes. "My hand?"

But Jae shook her head. Her eyes were screaming. "There... there is something... on my foot."

I leaned over her and looked at the floor. A large iguana had come to rest right on top of her toes. I bit my lips into a line to keep from laughing. Jae didn't seem amused at all.

"Looks like you had a friend sneak in the open terrace door."

She slowly stood up straight and looked down. A little scream stayed inside her mouth. "What do I do? Do these things bite? What if it pees on me?"

I couldn't hold back my laugh as I walked to face her and nudged the fella off with my toe. "Nothing to worry about, love. I'll save you."

"It's not funny." She squealed when it darted to behind the terrace curtain. "It's still here!"

She hugged herself tightly while I went to call maintenance. I'd just picked up the phone when a second iguana darted out of the bathroom—followed immediately by a third.

Jae shrieked and jumped onto the chair, gripping the back for stability. "Oh, my god, I'm infested! How did this happen?"

I doubled over in laughter. "You left your terrace doors open. It's nighttime, so it's warmer in here. Not a huge mystery."

"This is not funny! This is a horror movie!"

I punched the speed dial, spoke to the front desk, and hung up. Jae still stood on the chair. Her dark hair whipped side to side as she tracked the invaders, who were slowly lumbering across the floor. I walked over to her and titled my head up to meet her eyes.

"I promise they won't bite—any harder than I was about to."

Her gaze snapped to me. Confusion and panic turned to that sparkling humor I enjoyed so much. She managed a little smile. "That doesn't assuage me. I was hoping you'd bite hard."

I flashed my teeth, and she laughed.

Maintenance was there in minutes. They herded all three into a humane trap and whisked them away, promising they'd be set free in the trees on the property. They even ran a mop over the floor before I tipped them on their way out.

When they were gone, Jae sank down to sit in the chair. We traded a look that said what we were both thinking.

"Cock blocked by a reptile is usually a figure of speech. Not sure I've had it happen literally before," I said with a shrug.

She quirked a brow. "I have a hard time believing you get cocked blocked often."

"Ooh, she thinks I'm a player."

"I know you're a flirt."

I laughed. "Glass houses, love. You're the one who hit on me."

She pouted, and I crossed the room to her. "It's late. I'm gonna go, okay?"

"I don't want you to. But okay."

"And I'm gonna say this for what it's worth. I'm around all weekend. Do with that what you will. And by do with that, I mean do with *me*."

Her lips twitched again. Every time that happened, I wanted to high-five myself.

"How am I supposed to find you? I don't even know your room number."

"Bat signal. Obviously."

She nodded. Her eyes narrowed in a mock-serious look.

"I see. Except instead of a bat, it's just the eggplant emoji, right?"

I bent in half laughing. "Jesus Christ, woman."

She giggled. "Fine, fine. Leave me alone to nightmares of a lizard invasion. If I see you again, I see you again."

"I'd like a better guarantee than that," I admitted as I stepped closer and held her waist.

"No can do, buddy. The plan is to be wild and free, not commit to dates."

"That's the plan, hmm?"

She nodded.

"Then I guess I can't fight it. But *my* plan is to kiss you one more time before I go."

I raised one eyebrow, and she grinned and nodded.

One kiss probably didn't define the exchange between us. Finally, after a few minutes, I tore myself away and backed out of her room, eyes on that beautiful girl until the door shut.

Sunrise hiking and views of the island suddenly seemed very mundane. It was only when I reached the summit and took in the 360 view of glittering blue ocean that I managed to appreciate the experience. For most of the trek, my mind flipped between thoughts of work and thoughts of her. I sat down on a rock, ate a protein bar, and tried to find my island chill again.

My month in Aruba wasn't a breakdown or anything. Far from it. In fact, this trip had initially been planned as a romantic getaway with the woman I'd been dating for a few months. With my track record, a few months was a serious streak. She was a lawyer. We'd met on a dating app. It was clear she knew who I was and appreciated the perks of my new status.

The day we took the company public, I'd gone to her apartment with a Birkin bag as a celebration. The details of our vacation were printed and peeking out of the top.

Imagine my surprise when her fucking boss answered the door, dressed in her pink silk robe. She was in the shower. Apparently, the guy she constantly talked shit about had an intimate knowledge of her underwear drawer.

He'd actually asked me if I wanted to wait.

I laughed in his face and walked away, leaving the itinerary in shreds on her doorstep. The Birkin bag became a gift to my mother, and the trip became my own retreat from reality.

But what had started as a two-week getaway had already become a month. I knew my people at home were worried I'd had a mental crisis—a fact I worked to disprove with the LLC's biweekly meetings. It wasn't a breakdown. It was a fucking *break*.

For years, I'd been testing ideas and brainstorming, dreaming of designing a product that the world would want. That would make me rich. One night, when I was sitting around with all of my friends, it occurred to me that our strongest bond wasn't music or going out. It was talking. And talking was becoming a lost art. Society had reduced conversation to taps on posts and "'sup" as a way to match on dating sites.

Chat Me Up! was born as a social connection app built on talking to your matches instead of swapping pics. With a brilliant, beautiful platform and a top-tier marketing campaign, my dream of hitting it big came true.

And then we took the company public back in December.

I never imagined success like this. Dreaming of making money and actually making it were wildly different. It was quite a thing to go from a middle-class upbringing to suddenly having more cash than I could ever spend. Awesome? Absolutely. Overwhelming, complicated, and life-changing? Hell yeah.

With the app going strong and money literally rolling in, there was no reason I couldn't take this time to chill out. But now Celeste had gone and brought up Liv's idea for...

Not now. Just be here now. You've got thoughts on it. There's no rush.

... But maybe it's time to go home. One more week here. A few more days of diving, then a day just sitting on the beach. It's Friday. I'll go home in exactly one week.

I drew in a deep breath and started the hike back to my car.

But maybe I'll hit the bar tonight. Just for fun.

I hadn't hit the resort bar since my first weekend. I rolled my eyes at my own bullshit. "Admit you want to see her again, jackass."

I definitely wanted to see her again.

I wanted to see her so bad that I made my way to the pool deck before returning to my suite. No sign of a gorgeous brunette with a wicked sense of humor there or on the beach. I shook my head and hurried to my golf cart, irritated at myself for being a damn stalker.

Back at my bungalow and inexplicably restless, I dialed my brother. He answered on the third ring.

"Hey. I think I'm coming home next week."

He hummed. "Is this about what Celeste said in the meeting yesterday?"

Ben and his wife were my business partners. Every lawyer and accountant I'd ever met said I was crazy to mix family and business, but I didn't care. Those two were the creative geniuses I'd always known would be perfect to help me build my vision. We'd signed a tight operating agreement when the LLC was formed that kept everyone's cut and role crystal clear. That had been modified to bring on our CMO, Luke. The team was incredible. As I expected, the few disagreements we'd had only served to better the company.

I shoved a hand through my shaggy hair, mentally scheduling a haircut as soon as I was stateside again. "Yeah, and no. I've got thoughts, sure. But it's time to get back. How's Max?"

"He's good. I have to run him pretty much daily, or else he's ready to reupholster my sofa."

I laughed. "He's used to a yard to patrol these days. Sorry."

"Nah, it's fine. I've called a fencing company about doing part of the backyard for future visits."

"Nice to have a house, isn't it?"

He laughed. We'd both bought about a year ago. His apartment was the standard meetup spot for our group. Saying goodbye to that place had been emotional for everyone, but it was time. I'd built a place in the country, and he and Celeste had renovated a house on the river, not far from the old apartment.

We bullshitted for several minutes more. They were going out that night to our favorite haunt, Bar 40. Memories of nights with friends punched me in the chest—even more evidence that vacation was nearly over. I told him to tell our friends hi and ended the call, falling back on my bed for a long nap.

By the time I woke and showered, I was famished. I dressed nicer than I would've if I was going to dinner at a local dive bar, then headed back to the resort's restaurant for the second night in a row. The restaurant was divided into fine dining and a lounge/club. Being Friday night, the bar was already filling up. I grabbed a high-top, ordered a steak, and forced myself to stare out at the beach while I ate. Only after my plate was cleared and I'd ordered a beer did I peruse the crowd.

Of course, I spotted her immediately. Talking to another guy.

6

JULIETTE

Basically the second that he left my room, I fell facedown into the pillow. I think I had time to let out a frustrated groan before I drifted off, but maybe not. Maybe it was just a snore.

Honestly, I'd been lucky not to pass out on him. Even in those moments where his hands had been on me, hot as they were, my brain was screaming that we were way, *way* past our bedtime. An early morning flight, an afternoon in the sun, sunset on the water, and then a leisurely date that kept my brain and body humming—I'd lived more in that one day than I had in ages.

And, since this was my vacation to do just as I pleased, I slept late the next morning. I couldn't remember the last time I got to sleep so late. I rolled around in the sheets and let the ocean breeze blow in through the *screen* doors, which maintenance had kindly noted for me. Safe from all the iguanas of the island, I drifted in and out of consciousness until my rumbling stomach pulled me out of bed. I slipped on a sundress and looked at my phone.

Ten o'clock? Holy crap. I had planned to go for a morning run, but it would be far too hot by now to do that. Instead, I grabbed brunch at the café and hit the pool until my afternoon massage.

Sitting solo didn't feel as weird today. There were a lot of perks to being alone. I pondered that as I sat under the umbrella. Holding my left hand out, I stared at my pretty blue polish. There was the faintest band of pale skin around my ring finger that made me scowl. I scooted down my chair so my hand could catch some rays.

No one to tell me to wait up, that we could "go in a sec" after some stupid game level was done. No one to comment on my clothes.

No one asking me for a snack.

That one made me smile. Being alone was nice, but I loved home, too. I pictured our house. Mom and Ivy talking in the kitchen.

My heart swelled, and I sighed. *You can be happy here and still miss them. Both are true.*

I rolled off the chair and went to the spa. Yet another indulgent splurge thanks to traveling solo, thanks to a budget for two being spent on just one. I nearly cried with joy while the masseuse worked on my shoulders. The hour was over far too soon, which was to say ever. I drifted back to the bar, boneless and blissed, and climbed into a chair for lunch.

My fish tacos were in front of me when the seat beside me was occupied. "How are they?"

I glanced over at a guy in a backward cap and swim trunks. He sipped a beer and flashed a smile.

"Not sure yet." I bit one and flashed a thumbs-up.

"Saw you at the pool earlier. You by yourself?"

"Yeah. You?"

"With my friends. We're a semi-pro volleyball team at the tournament this weekend."

"That's awesome."

We chatted while I ate and he drank. He was perfectly nice. Maybe a little young, but what did I care? He'd have been an excellent prospect for a random encounter.

Except I kept thinking of Jay.

To be fair, he'd been in the back of my mind the whole damn day. But talking to this guy didn't draw out that airy, playful side of me in the same way. I definitely flirted with him. I just didn't have that helium-in-my-head sensation like yesterday.

And then I saw Jay out on the pool deck.

He strolled around the edge in track pants and a black tee, hands in pockets, shades on. He seemed to be looking for something.

Or someone. My heart leapt to my throat, but my mental boss held up a stern pointer finger. *Juliette Reid, are you seriously flattering yourself that much? He said he was hiking this morning. He's probably looking for a waiter to bring him lunch. Get over it.*

"... later?"

"Hmm?" I jerked my head back to the guy.

"I asked if you'd be here later. I hear this bar is pretty hot on weekends. Would love to talk to you more, maybe dance a little?" He grinned.

I nodded slowly. "Yeah, sounds good. I'll be around."

"Sweet. What's your name?"

"Jae." I sipped my seltzer quickly, but the lie was easier the more I told it.

"Cool name. I'm Clint. Later, Jae."

When I looked back at the pool deck, Jay was gone. I pushed my plate away and wandered out to find a free chair, failing totally to stop myself from looking for him. But no. He wasn't in the area at all anymore.

For the best. Yesterday was incredible. That doesn't mean you need to try and recreate it.

Eventually, I left the pool and went back to my room to nap and shower. At dinnertime, I put on another skimpy outfit. This one was a one-shoulder pink floral dress with cutouts at the waist. Thankfully, my hair was dry that night. I made two braids to keep it off my face and tied them at the back of my head. My fingers itched to pull out the phone and call home. I had it in my hands when the screen lit up.

Mom: Pizza night!

A photo of her and Ivy came through, and my grin stretched wide. I sent a string of hearts to tell her how much I appreciated the check-in. Then, I left my phone in the room and hit the bar.

The volleyball guy, Clint, found me right away. I said hello but declined an offer to eat with his teammates. My plate had just been cleared when he was back, asking me to dance. For nearly an hour, I was out on the dance floor, spinning between him and his teammates. By the time the band took a break, I was sweaty and grinning.

Clint walked me back to the bar. "Hey, so... my friends think you're hot. *I* think you're hot, too."

I flashed a little smile. "Thanks."

"Yeah, so, are you, you know. Interested?"

"Interested in wh-ohh." I cut myself off as I realized what he was asking. My gaze slid to the table of six guys, and my stomach twisted in a knot.

Not even Jae was that brave.

I wrinkled my nose. "Oh, gosh. That's so... flattering? But this isn't that kind of adventure."

His brow wrinkled.

"I mean, I'm not that adventurous. Sorry."

He shrugged. "Don't have to be sorry. It was worth a shot. So, uh, what if it were just you and me?"

All my warning bells blared. *Yeah, sure. You and me... oh, and hey! Your friends just happened to have a room key!* I looked away, hoping he'd get the message.

My gaze collided with Jay's.

He was watching me from a table across the lounge. I had to bite my tongue to keep from grinning, but Jay didn't smile. Clearly, he'd noticed I wasn't alone.

I faced Clint again and slid off my stool. "Sorry, I need to go talk to someone. But good luck in your tournament."

Clint grabbed my wrist before I'd taken two steps. "Whoa, whoa. Where are you running off to, sweetheart?"

I tugged my hand. "I'm leaving. Let me go."

"You're not trying to be a fucking tease, are you?"

Another tug. "Let. Me. Go."

He opened his mouth to speak, but just then, we both heard, "Hands off the lady."

A bouncer roughly the size of a brick wall loomed over us, shooting death rays out of his eyes at Clint. He didn't have to speak again. Clint flung my wrist free, straightened his collar, and stalked back to his teammates' table. The bouncer nodded at me and made his way back to his post. I blew out a breath, shook my head, and turned back around.

Only to walk straight into a broad chest.

"Sorry!" I jumped back.

"Shh. Hey. It's me." Jay's voice was quiet, but there was a hard edge to it.

I blinked up at him and tried for a coy smile. "Oh, hey you. We've met before, right?"

His lips twitched. "Pretty sure you're familiar, yeah. Didn't we meet at roller derby back home a few years ago?"

"Your memory is incredible."

That got me a wink, but his mouth was set in a grim line. "We can reminisce in a few minutes. First, I need to go talk to your friend."

I sank my nails into his bicep. "Oh, no, sailor. No way."

He glanced down at my hand and then my face. "Are you telling me no?"

"I am absolutely telling you no."

"I don't get told what to do much anymore."

"Does it turn you on?"

Another little smile. "You turn me on. But that asshole needs to know—"

I squeezed again. "I'm fine. Really. A little shook, yes. But no worse for wear. Please. Don't start trouble and bring the bouncer into it again."

Something sparked in his expression. "Excellent idea. You stay right here. I'll be back in one second."

Since he didn't head toward Clint—who was still glaring at me—I didn't argue. Instead, I watched Jay skirt the bar and find the bouncer on a stool in the corner. He gestured a few times and then shook the guy's hand and smiled. Then, he was back by my side.

He shrugged at my pursed lips. "Outsourcing. I just made friends with security and requested he keep a sharp eye out for your friend."

Sure enough, the bouncer relocated to a chair just a few feet away from the team table. I tried to glare at Jay. "You..."

"So, about that roller derby competition." He sat on the empty stool and gave me a teasing wink.

I huffed and put my fists on my hips. He stuck out his lower lip and tried for a puppy dog look. I stamped my foot. He slapped his knees as if inviting me to approach.

I totally took that invitation.

He spread his knees wider to let me stand between them, and I rested my palms on his biceps. This close, his summery scent hit my nose again, bringing back tingly memories from last night that felt too damn far away.

"We were on opposite teams. Bitter rivals, remember?"

Jay's gaze combed my face again, similar to last night at dinner. Again, the way he studied me kicked off a pretty flutter in my stomach.

"What the hell are we talking about?" he chuckled softly. "Because all I'm thinking about is kissing you."

Heat licked up my neck and into my cheeks. "Then do it."

When his mouth met mine, all the noise and music around me went silent. I threaded my fingers into his shaggy hair and fought the urge to make this obscene. Jay's kiss was restrained, but his thumb swished on my pelvis in a way that drove me wild. I tugged his hair and forced myself to pull back. Those gray eyes opened slowly, shining with wicked delight.

"Now I remember you," he murmured.

I couldn't hold in my laugh.

Jay trailed a light touch down from my shoulder to my elbow. I shivered as chills broke out everywhere. His fingers melted me, even with my clothes on.

He watched his hand glide along my skin and said, "I wasn't going to interrupt you. I'm sorry if—"

I grabbed his shirt and leaned in again. Gazing up at him through lowered eyelids, I purred, "I was coming to see you, actually."

His hand stopped moving. I fought to hide a triumphant grin while his gaze slid to my face. "You were... do what now?" he drawled.

A corner of my brain registered that he had to be from the South. His voice was like smooth bourbon: rich and indulgent, with a subtle drawl like a drop of water to enhance the pleasure. I'd noticed it before, but a phrase like *do what now* made me certain.

"I was coming to see you. To say hi." I angled my chin so that my lips brushed over his. "So... hi."

"Fuck," he breathed, tickling my lips right back.

"Say that again."

"Fuck." He drew out the word, so slow and teasing. So hot.

Check making out with a guy in a bar off my list. There was definitely some tongue in this exchange. And there were definitely people seated on either side of us.

"What do you want to do?" Jay growled in my ear when he finally broke us apart.

"Dance. Drink. Dive."

He nodded slowly. "What do you want to do right now?"

I leaned to his ear and mimicked him. "Fuck."

7

JAMES

Her flirty whisper rolled straight from my ear to my semi-erect cock. I was on my feet in a flash, lacing our fingers together to walk her out of the bar. Good thing that table of jerkoffs wasn't in our path, or I'd have struggled to keep my mouth shut. I'd been ready to put his teeth down his throat for grabbing her like that.

But fuck that guy. Because Jae was in step with me all the way to the elevator. She punched her floor and spun to me, so I threaded my hands in her hair and backed her against the wall. She wrapped one leg around me. I was ready to pick her up, but five floors weren't really far enough to get something going. The elevator dinged, and she raced me down the hall.

She paused at the door and crossed her arms. "Safety talk. I've got condoms."

"Right. Good. We stop the moment you say. No questions asked. Oh, but my bloodwork is all clear."

She nodded. "Me too."

"Good. Because I definitely want to go down on you." I grinned, and her pupils dilated. When she'd stared at me for a long moment, I gestured at the knob. "Maybe open the door so we can begin?"

She rolled her eyes and reached into her purse. "Silly me."

"Very silly you." I fingered the hem of her little dress while she fussed with the room key.

"I'm trying to concentrate," she huffed as it beeped red again.

"I am concentrating," I murmured into her hair, inching my fingers higher. "This ass. Goddamn."

"Jay!" She squealed when I pinched her. "Hold on!"

I grunted and withdrew. Her fingers shook as she swiped at the door, and I grinned again. "Are you nervous, love?"

"Oh, please. When am I ever nervous?"

"Cool hand Jae. Your pool hall name. But if you'd like some help, allow me." Grasping her wrist gently, I waved her hand and the card over the scanner.

Green light: go.

The door jumped open as we fell into the room kissing. Jae stepped back and stared at me with hooded eyes. "I'm not nervous. I have anonymous, wild flings on sexy vacations all the time. I think *you're* nervous."

"Baby, I'm sweating bullets. This is my first time."

Her lips twitched. "You're a king of bullshit."

"Hmm, long live the queen." Even in this moment, it was too easy to trade lines with her. Too easy and too hot.

I reached out and lifted her hand to my face. "But these fingers are trembling. So either you're lying about being nervous, or you're very, *very* thirsty."

Her gaze dragged up to watch me nip the pads of each of her fingers. "I... um."

All of it hit me just then. The heady elixir of an anonymous hookup with this fascinating woman. Paradise as the backdrop for an incredible, meaningless connection. My blood surged. We were free. Free to be and do whatever we wanted.

"Which is it?" My voice was thick. Raw.

"I'm thirsty." She was hoarse, but she swallowed hard and flipped her hair.

"For me."

Whiskey-colored eyes blinked. She sucked on her upper lip—but she also nodded. "For you."

Fuck. I slid to my knees and palmed her ass to bring her closer. Jae stumbled on her heels, but I wasn't about to let her fall. Instead, I buried my face into her dress between her legs. That thin fabric did nothing to hide her heat, and I groaned. My hands kneaded her cheeks until her thighs clenched and she gripped my hair. I rubbed my nose up and down her pubic bone, inhaling her scent.

"Jay," she whispered with a tug on my hair.

"Hmm?"

"I can't touch you if you're down there."

I looked up at her and quirked my brows. "You want me to stop what I'm doing so you can touch me?"

"I... I... yes? No. Yes. But also no."

"Be quiet, M'lady. And by be quiet, I mean tell me exactly what you like." I laughed and hitched her skirt over her hips, revealing a tiny black thong that made me hiss in a breath. "Pretty. But we don't need this."

"It's soaked anyway," she muttered.

I yanked it down her hips and then dragged my knuckle between her legs. "So fucking wet."

Another glance up at her made me smirk. Her face was bright red. My mouth watered for her, but I stood and walked her to the bed, slipping off her dress in the process.

"Take the bra off for me?" I asked as I stepped back.

She reached behind her and unclasped the hooks, and I swear the room spun. Jae was a fucking *indulgence*. Her legs were toned as hell, but she had an ass I wanted to bite and tits I wanted to bury my face in. That dark hair curled over her shoulders and made her look like a damn painting of a goddess.

I rubbed my jaw, unable to stop staring. She fidgeted, and I shook my head.

"Don't be nervous, love."

"Not easy when someone is staring at your naked body."

"Not staring. *Admiring*. You are..." I breathed a laugh. "So fucking hot."

Her brows ticked together, lips parting as if she was going to say something. But I didn't need her answer. I needed her moan.

So I lay her back on the bed and climbed on top of her.

I spent a long time kissing and touching her. She eventually grunted and demanded my shirt come off, so I obliged as fast as I could to get back to her mouth. Finally, I let myself kiss down that body and get lost in her breasts. She arched up off the bed while I licked and played with her, but she was patient. I kept expecting her to demand I get on with it. Lucky me, she seemed to enjoy this extended foreplay as much as I did.

Finally, *finally*, I slid off the bed to kneel between her legs.

"Oh, god," she moaned as my tongue slipped between her lips.

"The name's Bond, love. James Bond."

Her eyes fluttered open. "Oh, Mr. Bond? Is that better?"

I winked. "You can just call me James. All my friends do."

Two fingers plunged inside her as my tongue swirled around her clit.

"Oh, fuck... *James*...please," she half-moaned, half-laughed.

But I wasn't laughing. I closed my eyes and let the sound of my name reverberate in my head while her taste soaked my senses.

Paradise. Pure fucking paradise.

It took nothing to get her over. We'd been going for so long already that I wasn't surprised. Feeling her walls throb against my fingers while I teased her clit made me moan, finally acknowledging how long I'd been rock-hard in my pants.

Jae went limp on the bed, and I sat back to wipe my mouth.

"Oh, you're good," she panted. Then, she lifted her head and waved me forward. "But you're also half-dressed, and that's a problem."

"Didn't seem to be a problem for you."

She smiled. "Come here, Jay."

Part of me wanted to hear her say James again. Part of me was relieved that she'd not put those details together.

But most of me just wanted to be buried inside of her. So I stopped thinking and got my ass on that bed.

8

JULIETTE

He lay down beside me, and I wasted no time opening his trousers and helping him out of them. His cock's outline in those black boxer-briefs was... obvious.

It's pretty rude of you to be this flawless, you know.

He'd made me feel like a goddess with the way he stared at me. And the way he'd literally worshipped my body with his mouth for the past hour. *And* the way he'd pushed me to a body-quaking orgasm. But I was no goddess. I was a girl.

A girl currently having a fling with the hottest guy she'd ever met. And—I skimmed my hand over his underwear— yep. Confirmed. He wasn't just hot. He was the literal total package.

I lifted his waistband and pretended to peek. Jay's eyes crinkled with a little laugh. "Don't be shy, love. I'm yours. Use me for all the filthy sex you need."

"Well, when you put it that way." I rolled his underwear off, and he sprang free. "Fuck," I muttered.

Jay gripped his cock and stroked slowly. "Yeah, you can do that if you want."

I wanted. So, I did.

I threw one leg over his hips and sat on the top of his thighs, just for the fun of stroking him a little. He flexed to my touch, but his gaze stayed on my face.

"Oh. Condom." I blinked hard because I'd been seconds away from forgetting that part. He blinked and nodded, so I hurried to go get one from my drawer. Jay rolled it on and then lay down again. With a deep breath, I climbed back on top of him.

And sat down hard on his cock.

My head tipped back with a moan as fiery pleasure ripped me in half. And I hadn't even started moving. "Oh fuck, Jay," I strangled.

"Mm-fucking-hmm," he rumbled.

I forced my eyes open to look at him again, and he nodded slowly. "Ride me, Jae. I'm fucking yours right now."

There was some kind of magic in the room at that moment. Some cocktail of pheromones, island vibes, and the rush of wanting someone I didn't even know. It all collected and let me forget how careful I liked to live my life. How unlike all the sex I'd ever known this was. How not me this whole moment felt.

It felt very much like me.

Me, about to drive myself wild all over him.

I took a deep breath—and then proceeded to ride him hard.

Jay's jaw clenched at first, but he gave that up and groaned. Those gray eyes rolled back in his head as his fingers gripped my thighs. "Fuck yes," he moaned again and again. "Bounce that pussy all over my cock. Make it filthy, you wicked little tease."

"I'm not a tease," I hiccupped.

"You know you are. You've been teasing me since

yesterday at lunch. You've been trying to make me hard for you since that first moment."

"Did it work?"

He reached back and slapped my ass. "Damn right it did. *Tease*," he finished with another slap.

"Tell me more about how awful I am."

"Fucking terrible. Filthy girl. Sucking on that fry and making me think about that mouth on my dick. And I'd just met you. Wearing that little dress last night, licking my ice cream, leaning in with those tits pressed into my arm. I want to fuck your tits, Jae. I want to come all over your chest."

"Oh," I strangled. My tongue caught in my throat. Every word he said made the lights go dim in my vision. Terrible, guilty pleasure pooled low in my belly.

"Mm-hm. Harder, love. Go harder."

Sweat slicked my forehead while I rode him. He stared up at me, finally reaching to flick his fingers over my nipples.

I was done for then.

Another orgasm crashed over me, different than the first but still mind-blowing. Jay rocked my body as I started to go slack. Just before I collapsed, he thrust up, groaning between clenched teeth.

I fell forward onto his chest.

And he wrapped his arms around me. Kissed my head. Made me forget for a long moment that this was anonymous, dirty sex.

A long, perfect moment.

Finally, he stirred, and I slid off and reached for my robe at the foot of the bed. Jay cast a distasteful glance while he discarded the condom.

"You should be naked all the time," he said as he stepped into his boxers.

"I lived six years in a nudist colony."

His laugh made me grin. The fact that he sat down on the bed beside me made my heart flutter.

"Nudist colony, trapeze artist, roller derby champ... damn, woman. You've lived a lot of lives. How old are you, anyway?"

"Forty-two. You?"

"Nineteen."

We tried to glare at each other's obvious lies. We wound up kissing instead.

What started as a smiley kiss devolved into a little tongue. And then a little more. I sucked in my breath, Jay reached for my hair, and the next thing I knew, I was on my back. He flexed against me, already half-hard again. Propping himself up with one hand, Jay yanked my robe open and skimmed his touch down my body. I moaned, and he growled against my lips.

"Did you want me to leave?" he said between kisses.

"Uh-uh."

"Good. Turn over. Lose the damn robe."

I couldn't believe how meticulous he was. That was the best way to describe the way he explored my body. Lips traveled over every inch of my skin. Hands explored at a delightfully torturous pace, inciting chills from my scalp to my toes. Since he worked on my back this time, I didn't get to watch like before. Instead, I closed my eyes and tried not to fidget while he found erogenous zones I never knew I had. Fidget or no, it was clear Jay knew each time he hit a new one. He'd either growl or laugh softly. Either response just intensified the pleasure.

My eyes opened when his hands planted by my head, and his cock pressed between my ass cheeks. "Have you ever?" he asked in my ear as he flexed his hips.

I clenched and shook my head.

"Do you want to?"

"N-now?"

Another soft laugh. "No, love. You should work up to that. Besides, we don't have lube."

I did not have lube. And I didn't even know what *you should work up to that* meant.

Jay kissed my temple. "I'd *love* to be the man who took you there. But really, I was just curious how you felt about it."

I felt like it had always been an obvious no. But with him grinding against me, I felt like I'd have been open to exploration at least.

Suddenly, he was gone, jolting me out of my thoughts. I twisted to look behind me as he slid down my body. Gripping my ass, he pushed my hips in the air. I buried my face in the pillow and moaned as his tongue ran between my lips —and dragged backward way farther than I'd expected. Not all the way. Not quite.

But close.

And, oh, was that lovely.

I lifted higher in the air as he teased me, sliding a finger into my pussy and drawing a slow circle. Just when I wondered if I'd actually come like this, without so much as a nudge on my clit, Jay disappeared again. I collapsed, but seconds later, strong hands clamped down on my thighs.

"I'm going to fuck you like this, okay?"

"Please," I groaned into the pillow—and then groaned again as he plunged into me.

"Fuck," he gritted between his teeth. "You are so fucking hot, I can't take it."

I got myself onto my elbows so I could breathe. My head hung low, forehead bumping the mattress. Jay thrust against my front wall again and again. Light exploded behind my eyes. He grumbled out a stream of obscene compliments about my body, more of what he'd said the first time but dirtier.

And all of it was wonderful. But what really made me glow was the idea of how I must look in that moment. That *this isn't me/this is so very me* sensation hit again, seemingly contradictory, and yet so very reasonable in my heart. This wasn't me. And this was suddenly, totally, *delightfully* me.

I'd lost the thread of what he was saying, but the phrase, "Bad girl," hit my ears. "Such a bad, filthy girl."

"I'm not bad," I muttered.

He gathered my hair in one hand and reached for my clit with the other. "Mm-mm. You are fucking filthy, you little flirt. Teasing that poor boy tonight when you knew you needed this cock to satisfy you. Bad, bad girl. Shameful... little... tease."

And that's what sent me over the edge again.

Again too, he was close behind. I was still quivering with aftershocks when I heard him groan and felt his deep thrust. After a moment, we stilled. He collapsed backward on the bed. I struggled to push up after so long in that position. I let myself fall so that my head was beside his shoulder.

He lolled to gaze at me. "Hi."

"Hi."

"Have we met?"

"You seem familiar."

We both huffed dusty laughs.

Jay rubbed his eyes. "Christ. That was..."

That vain side of me preened more than ever to know he felt it, too. Clearly, this guy knew what he was doing in bed. Hearing him voice my thoughts made me want to punch the air in triumph.

Eventually, he discarded the condom and stepped into his boxers. This time, I didn't bother to fuss with the robe.

He sat on the edge of the bed, stroked my hair, and said, "I'm going to leave."

I refused to flinch.

Those wicked fingers skimmed my scalp, bringing chills even as I prepared to see him out. But Jay twisted his lips and looked into my eyes. "I have a plan."

9

JAMES

I'd built an empire on plans and schemes. Most of the time, I marveled at how the hell I'd actually pulled it off. But in that moment, I knew this might be my most reckless idea ever.

She blinked and sat up slowly. "Tell me more."

I helped her get her arm through her robe's sleeve. "It seems an inefficient use of your trip to try and find drunk hookups. How long are you here, anyway?"

"Until Monday morning."

"Two days. You might as well use me for whatever you please." I winked, but I wasn't joking. This woman had a spell on me that I wanted to stay under.

Her eyes sparkled. "And is that limited to the bedroom, or are you a multipurpose Jay?"

"I told you last night that I have plenty of specialty skills. I don't want to interrupt your trip, though. So you tell me what we do."

"I told you at the bar. Three Ds. I want to dive, dance, and drink."

"And fuck."

Her cheeks colored. "And that."

"So four Ds."

A giggle slipped out of her. Every time I got her to laugh, I felt like I'd hit a jackpot. She clearly worked hard to keep a straight face during most of our bullshit.

"I can do all of those things. I'm diving in the morning. Do you want to come?"

She sighed. "That one's a dream. I'm not certified."

"You can snorkel."

"Hmm. So are we making plans fueled entirely by orgasmic hormones or what?"

"We definitely are."

She nodded. "Then I think the right answer is, I should decide in the morning."

I took the hint and got off the bed. With an exaggerated bow, I said, "Miss Jae, that's the most sensible thing I've heard you say. I hate it."

She threw my shirt at me.

At the door, I turned around and braced one palm into the frame to lean toward her. She turned sleepy eyes up to me. "My plan is to see you tomorrow. But you do what's right for you, yeah?"

Those pretty lips pressed into a line as she nodded.

I blew her a kiss and headed back to my suite.

~

The next morning, I geared up on the boat and chatted with the captain. I was tired as hell but wide awake. Four hours of sleep never felt so good as after a marathon fuckfest like we'd had.

Just before we left the dock, I heard: "I have a new plan."

I spun around and tried to keep my goofy grin in check.

She stood on the planks, clutching her gear bag and wearing a simple one-piece suit. I held out my hand to help her onto the boat. She stepped onboard and looked around with a frown.

"Where are the others?"

"Others?" I busied myself rechecking the air tank.

"Is this not a group dive?"

"Oh. No. Just me this morning. Well, and you, it seems." *I totally didn't buy out the excursion on the chance you'd join me. Nope. Definitely not.* "What's your plan?"

She set her gear down as the captain got us going. I met her in the middle of the boat and crossed my arms to keep from hugging her.

"I don't want anything complicated."

"Me neither."

"When I go home, this will all just be a fairytale. A memory of an awesome trip."

"Cool."

"You included."

I ignored the little jolt that gave my heart. "Obviously. You don't even know where I live."

"I'm betting you're a southern boy, but never mind that. My point is, that's the plan."

"You'd bet right, but back to that in a second. Good plan. What's the problem?"

She squinted at me. "Is that really something you're into? Not just a one-night stand, but, like, time together? And then—nothing?"

"Seems to be working for us so far."

Of course I was into it. Why the hell would I try and start a relationship with a stranger I met on vacation from god-knows-where? I didn't know her name, her zip code, or what she did for a living. And I didn't need to. She gave me the best high with zero complications.

What more could a guy like me ask for?

"So... okay. You're glad I'm here."

I grabbed her waist and guided her to sit between my legs on the bench. With my arms around her, I said in her ear, "I'm very glad you're here, Miss Jae. Your fine ass can be wherever it wants as far as I'm concerned."

She squirmed, bumping that very fine ass against my growing cock, and I bit her lobe. "Careful, ma'am. You're gonna start trouble if you keep squirming like that. Unless you'd like the captain to watch you get finger-fucked, of course."

That earned me a slap on the wrist, but her stomach vibrated with a laugh. "You are so bad," she said as she snuggled against me.

I held her tighter. "Should've been the first thing you learned about me. How'd you know I was from the South?"

"The way you said, 'Do what now?'"

I laughed. "Guilty as charged. From a little town you've probably never heard of." *If you've been living under a rock for the past 15 years.* "How about you?"

"North Dakota."

"No one is from North Dakota."

She pursed her lips as if to say, *exactly*. I kissed that pretty pout.

We spent the morning out on the water in a good spot for snorkeling. Back on land, she only stopped talking about all the things she'd seen to ask me questions about diving. We went to lunch still discussing everything. She'd discovered an excursion for the next day, so I promised to book it. The smile she flashed, fuck me. So lovely.

Once we'd eaten, I eyed her. "You got a little more in you?"

"I could."

"Or—" I put my elbows on the table and motioned her to lean forward. "Do you want to have a *lot* more in you?"

Her pupils dilated even while she laughed. Never in my life had a line like that earned better than an eye roll. Certainly not a reply like—

"Hell yes, boy. Let's go."

Jae pushed back from her chair and grabbed my hand. I barely had time to toss my napkin down before we were out of the café and on the elevator again.

We spent the afternoon in her bed. The ocean breeze cooled our sweaty bodies as we caught our breaths and bullshitted lines back and forth about utter nonsense. I teased her about being so loud for an afternoon tryst. She hit back with something about being a mime. Her impersonation had me in stitches.

But that was between rounds. The sun was way past peak by the time I left her room with a promise to take her to dinner in a few hours. She was so spent, she waved at me from the bed.

Exactly like I wanted her to be.

My grin wouldn't quit on the drive to my suite. This was the best weekend ever. I had never felt this free.

10

JULIETTE

The next morning, I finally got up early enough to go for a run. We'd gone to dinner the night before at an amazing local spot. Unfortunately, when we got back to the hotel bar, we discovered a guitarist for the night instead of a dance floor. It had been hard to not drag him into my room when he walked me to my door, but we'd both laughed and agreed to save our strength for our last day together.

Which was today.

I tried not to think about it on my run. Instead, I soaked in the pristine grounds at this beautiful resort. The tropical flowers burst color among lush green grass and trees. The ocean twinkled in the morning sun. I took it all in while I looped around the resort and pool deck. On my third loop, I noticed the path pointing to the villas and took it.

A solid half-mile road without much view opened up into a small village. Six bungalows faced the ocean in a semi-circle, basically screaming exclusive and elegant. The grounds over here were just as pristine, if not more some-how. I hesitated for a moment as if I wasn't allowed in this area. Two signs stressed that the pool and beach were for villa guests only. This area had a private entrance just down the road, but I clearly was still on my resort. Nothing indicated I'd be tased on site for stepping my non-designer sneakers onto the paths here. So, I took a quick breath and ran on.

The security guard near the entrance waved at me as I covered the back road first. I returned the wave and rounded the corner toward the beach. Deciding to work my way in and then out toward the water, I followed the path that cut closest to the villas. *It's just after 7am on a weekend in the islands. Everyone's asleep. This is fine.*

Except they weren't. The first house I passed had a man on a laptop on the shaded terrace. He seemed to be on a call, but he lifted a hand in a wave when I ran by. The second had a couple outside, both on their laptops. They didn't look up.

Is this like a convention or something? I looked ahead. People were outside at villas three and five as well. Four and six seemed to be quiet. I shook my head and tried to mind my own business.

The terrace door slid open on the last villas as I ran past. The movement caught my eye, but when I glanced over, the door slammed shut again. *Weird.*

I finished looping the village and ran back to my room. All in, I'd logged five miles. Decent jog for vacation. As soon as I went home, I'd start marathon training again.

So, tomorrow.

Shut up.

My bossy brain had a point. No sense in wasting time lamenting the dwindling hours when I could be living them. I hurried to shower and get ready for our adventure day.

Jay met me in the hotel lobby. My breath caught at the smile that lit his face upon seeing me. *A girl could get used to that... or not.* I doubted a smile like his would ever get old.

And I had no reason to ponder it. We had the day. This fairytale we'd created. I got to be Miss Jae for a little while longer, and I was going to live every second of it.

So I greeted him with a kiss.

He pulled back and purred in my ear, making me giggle. *This is going to be the best day.*

"How was your run?"

I jolted as we walked to the bus. "How did you know I went running?"

"Saw you." He made circles with his hands and held them to his eyes, and I laughed again.

"Creep."

"Oh, totally. Totally stared at your ass the whole time, too." He pinched me for emphasis.

"So rude."

"You're right. Your cleavage deserves more respect."

I put my fist on my hip and huffed. "I don't appreciate this objectification. Now, get on that bus first so I can stare at *your* ass for a second. While you're at it, carry my bag like a big, strong man should."

He took my little backpack and curled it like a dumbbell, then boarded the bus, swishing his hips. I had tears of laughter in my eyes by the time I slid in next to him.

Jay kissed my temple. "You can objectify me any day, Miss Jae."

Or just today.

Shut up.

Right. New topic.

"My run was good, thanks. I snuck over to the villas." Jay hummed, so I went on. "I was surprised to see so many people up and working over there. I figured if you could afford a private bungalow, you'd probably sleep in until your butler woke you with breakfast in bed."

He laughed. "Most people who stay in villas like that work their asses off all the time, vacation included. But the other ones, no. Totally right. Grapes in bed and all that."

I puckered my lips. I hadn't thought of that, but what did I know about wealthy vacationers? The fact that he had that insight made me more suspicious about what he did for a living. Good thing I had no reason to ponder it, as it had nothing to do with an island excursion day.

The bus collected several other travelers from different resorts and then dropped us at a parking lot full of two-person ATVs. Our little group slathered on sunscreen while the tour guide gave directions. The vehicles had roofs on them, but our guide handed out complimentary bandanas that we were to wear over our faces to protect from dust on the road.

Jay tied his and pulled a plain black ball cap low on his head. His gray eyes glinted down at me. "Who's driving?"

I cinched my bandana and raised my hand.

Driving the beast was both terrifying and fun. Once I got the hang of it, I bounced us down the road at a good clip, whooping anytime we hit a bump. He was a total sport and didn't once try to tell me what to do. When I thought back on that day, that was a big thing that stood out to me. No critique. No "pointers." Just a lot of laughing and cheering me on.

Our tour had many stops, including a wildlife sanctuary and several natural wonders. The beaches were wild and gorgeous. It felt like a different world than the calm waters at the resort. Our final stop of the day was the natural pool. This was what had drawn me to this adventure. We parked and hiked along a rock formation. The ocean crashed off to one side, hitting us with a refreshing spray at intervals. Jay was behind me the whole time, and with the wind in my ears, there was no point trying to chat.

We filed along to an opening in the rocks. About ten feet down was a crystal-blue pool. Other members of our group whooped and hurried to leap off. I dropped my bag and turned to him with an excited grin.

Jay, however, was not smiling. For the first time, I saw his jaw clench and his lips set in a line. "Are you going to jump?" he asked.

"Of course. Aren't you?"

He blew out a breath and shook his head. "Think I'm good here, thanks."

"So a rodeo clown, secret agent, spy, drug dealer—"

"Drug dealer?"

"Who dives with sharks can't jump off a high dive?" I finished with a smirk.

"I don't love heights." He eyed the ledge again and sighed. "But I obviously can't let you leap to your death by yourself."

"You did promise I could use you however I pleased."

"That was under the heavy influence of pheromones."

"Should've brought some of your drug stash then."

He cut his eyes to me. "What the hell? You think I'm like an underworld kingpin or something?"

"Yeah, pretty much." I shrugged. "Who else can afford to stay in this hotel for a month straight?"

He opened and closed his mouth. "Fair point. You caught me. Let's get this over with."

"Thank you!" I jumped up and down with a little squeal while he tugged his t-shirt off.

"When you jump around like that, you could get me to say yes to anything."

"And when you tug off your shirt like that, you could get me to do the same." I blew him a kiss.

His perfect grin creased his face. "You're the worst, Miss Jae."

"You love it."

I squealed again as he swooped down and kissed my neck. "I really do, though," he said into my ear.

We caught hands and walked to the edge. The rest of the group had already had their fill of jumping and were lazily swimming in the pool below. Some lounged in the sun.

Jay looked at me. "Ladies first."

"Hell yeah." I dropped his hand and leapt out, plunged down in the cool water, and surfaced with a whoop. "Come on, sailor!"

He shook his head once and then jumped. I swam toward him as soon as he popped out of the water.

"Fuck. Fuck, fuck, fuck," he spluttered, shaking water from his hair. Jay swam for the rocks while I followed. When he hauled up to sit on the side, he blinked at me through wet lashes. "I am terrified of heights. Holy fucking shit."

I scrambled up and squeezed his arm. "Oh, no. I'm so sorry! I didn't realize it was that serious. You shouldn't have jumped, silly."

"Do I seem like the kind of man who makes sensible choices when it comes to gorgeous women?" He hung his head and laughed. "You've had me eating out of your hand since we met. Literally. Of course I was going to follow you."

I didn't know how to answer that. His words gave me a weird mixture of affection, jealousy, and pain. Affection because he was right. He *had* been literally eating out my hand since we met. Who was I to get a guy like this to follow me on crazy adventures? Jealousy because I wasn't the only woman he'd done crazy shit for. Pain because after today, there would be no more wild moments or epic stories and adventures. And as right as that was, as necessary and true as it had to be—it still fucking hurt.

His wet shoulder nudged me, and I realized I was staring at my hands. "Is that your favorite color?" he asked, nodding at my nails.

"Yeah."

"Why are you sad?"

"I'm not."

"You little liar."

I crooked a smile. "Not at all. Everything I've ever told you is true."

He glared playfully but didn't push further. "We've got like twenty minutes here. If you're going to take your life into your hands again, do it soon. I'll still have time to cancel our dinner reservation if you wind up getting air-lifted out of—*mmph!*"

I clapped my hand on his mouth. "Shh, don't even joke about that kind of thing. What is wrong with you?"

He grabbed my ribs, and I dissolved into helpless giggles. Our tour guide walked up while we were laughing together. He smiled and waved his phone. "Let me take your picture. I will share them to your phones when we get back."

Jay hugged me close. I put my arms around his neck and leaned into his chest, grinning while the phone stayed aimed at us. Just before the final photo, Jay twisted his head and pressed his lips to my cheek. My eyes went wide as I laughed, and the guide lowered the camera.

"You are models. Such a beautiful couple. I have your numbers from the signup form and will send them today," he said with a smile.

We looked at each other, seeming to silently agree not to overthink the idea of having photos of each other. Time later to worry about that because Jay scooped me up and stood like I weighed nothing at all. He tossed me into the pool. I landed with a yelp and a laugh, and just like that, we were back in the fairytale.

I let him drive us back to the meeting point. I'd had my fill of it by then, and watching him drive wasn't the worst view to end an adventure. His biceps flexed as he turned the wheel. Each time, I squeezed my thighs together and said a little prayer of thanks for ever meeting someone this hot and hilarious.

We boarded the bus and had just slid into our seat when we heard, "Is this y'alls honeymoon, too?"

A man and woman sat across from us, grinning in our direction. Jay and I traded a glance, and then he smiled and said, "How'd you guess?"

Their grins got wider. The woman said, "You two looked so cute together. We figured it was probably another pair of newlyweds. Where are y'all from?"

"Nashville."

We said it at the same time and traded another look. Jay gave me a tiny squint but then nodded.

She squealed. "Us too! Hendersonville. Are you in Nashville proper, or a suburb like us?"

Neither of us answered for a long beat. Finally, I said, "Nashville proper. We're transplants, I'm afraid. Just moved there in January. Still getting our bearings."

The guy chuckled. "Oh, lord. Where from? Brooklyn?"

"Naw," Jay drawled. "I'm from Tuscaloosa. The missus is from North Dakota."

Their smiles dropped. "Tuscaloosa?"

"Go Vols," Jay said quickly, a hand to his heart. "Don't you worry about that."

Damn, he really is Southern... Is he really *from Nashville? Is that possible?* My heart skipped despite myself. Tuscaloosa was the home of the University of Alabama. In the South, college football was practically a religion. Jay had just assured them that he cheered for the University of Tennessee, aka the "Vols." And he'd known what to say simply by their expressions.

And I knew all that because I'd attended UT before moving back home to my mother's house. In Nashville.

So the possibility that Jay also lived there...

"Tiny town no one's ever heard of." If he does live in Tennessee, it's not Nashville. Unless he was lying. Unless he...

"Honey?" Jay's nudge shook me from my thoughts.

I shook my head and smiled. "Sorry, what?"

"I asked how you met," the woman said.

"At a *Star Wars* con. We were both dressed as Princess Leia in *A New Hope*."

Jay coughed and sank his fingers into my thigh. I had to bite back helpless laughter.

"Oh, that is too sweet! You must really be fans."

"It was our wedding theme," Jay said with a nod. He coughed again.

"Well, congrats to you both."

"And to you," we returned with bright smiles.

"Maybe we'll run into each other in Nashville sometime!"

The man laughed. "Honey, that's a needle in a haystack."

"Well, still." She gave us another smile and turned back to her husband.

I twisted to look at Jay. His eyes were round, lips bitten tight. "*Star Wars?*" he murmured.

I smirked. "Felt right."

He finally let out a quiet laugh. "Hell yeah, it did."

"Nashville?" I couldn't not ask.

But Jay just shrugged. "Everyone's from there these days. Figured it was a good story."

"Exactly what I was thinking."

He ran his hand up and down my thigh, inching higher each time until his fingers slipped under my shorts. I squirmed while he teased along my hip. "What I'm thinking, dearest wife, is that it's been too long since I had my hands on you."

I caught his hand and slid it toward my inner thigh. "Come to my room with me?"

"Thought you'd never ask."

"Okay, but I have to have time to get ready for dinner."

He hummed. "Well, bossypants, in that case, I think I'll make you wait."

I pouted, lip practically on the ground. "Meanie. But probably smart. After the run and adventure, I might just pass out for a while."

"How far did you run?"

"A few miles."

He squeezed my thigh. "These legs seem like they could do more than a few miles."

"I've done some races in my time." *Four marathons and counting, baby.*

Jay kept tickling me as we rode back to the resort. He kissed my cheek at the elevator. I yawned in reply and stepped in.

It didn't occur to me to wonder which floor he was staying on or why he didn't ride up with me.

11

JAMES

I returned to my villa with one thing on my mind. If Jae had put a spell on me after a few encounters, by now, I was well and truly enchanted.

The memory of this morning made me laugh. Coffee in hand, I was about to go read on my terrace when I saw a very familiar ponytail run by. I'd slammed the door and pressed myself against the wall so she wouldn't see me. She'd made enough little comments in our time together about affording things. While I'd have loved to have her all over this bungalow—and loved to spoil her with the outdoor hot tub, too—I knew it was too revealing. Too obvious that what I did for a living warranted questions. Possibly Google searches.

And I'd dropped that Nashville comment like a total fool.

Strange that she'd said Nashville, too.

Everyone lives there now. It makes sense as a good lie.

Except I'd noticed that her accent, while fairly neutral, tended to twang on certain words. And that had made me wonder if North Dakota was accurate at all.

And *that* brought me back to shutting the fuck up. Anonymous worked both ways. She was no one from nowhere as far as I was concerned.

As far as I was concerned, she was also fucking perfect.

We had one more night together. I wanted it to be as perfect as she was. So, I took a short nap, ran an errand, and got ready to give my no-strings-attached girl a memory she'd keep forever.

She stepped off the elevator, and my mouth went dry. Jae wore a sexy-as-hell little blue dress that cinched at her waist and hit her high on the thigh. Her hair spilled around her shoulders. As she walked to me, I stared without blinking. Trying to memorize her.

As if I could ever forget.

"I'm a lucky bastard," I said when she approached.

"Not bad yourself." She nodded at my button-down and linen pants.

"This old thing?"

She laughed, and I kissed her knuckles and guided her toward the beach. The restaurant was up the main drag. I figured beach walking was more serene than strolling along the strip. Jae kept my hand but didn't say much for a while.

"What are you thinking?" I asked at last.

She gazed at the orange sun heading toward the horizon. "How I don't want this fairytale to end."

I stopped walking and pulled her close. "Hey. Me too."

She tipped her gaze up to me. "Tell me who you are without telling me who you are."

"Details that don't add up to anything?"

"Exactly."

We walked on. I thought and came up with nothing. "Give me an example."

"When did you lose your virginity?"

That made me laugh. "Great example. Uh, seventeen. My sister's friend."

"Creep."

"*Older* sister's friend. She hit on me."

Her brows went up. "Damn, then. You've been a ladies' man forever, huh?"

I scratched my chin. "Not sure if that's a fair term."

She laughed. "I am."

"I enjoy women. I very much enjoy the game of flirting."

"I had no idea."

"Listen, just because you have your PhD in flirting..."

She swatted my arm with a yelp. "Me?"

"Hell yes, you. You're the worst tease I've ever met."

Her lips parted, then snagged in a little smile. "Well. At least I'm memorable."

I lolled my gaze to her in a come-on look. "Unforgettable, love. Don't get it confused." A long beat passed between us before I shook my head and broke the stare. "This is it. Follow me."

We walked up the ramp to the restaurant. The hostess sat us at a private table overlooking the ocean. Jae's brows went up as she looked around.

"It was the only thing they had left," I said with a shrug.

"None of the other tables have flowers." She gestured to the hibiscus in the vase.

Another shrug. "Weird. So, your turn. Tell me about, hmm, your first kiss."

She sipped her water and laughed. "Oh, god. Is that ever a hot story? I was fourteen. It was a guy I liked who had come over to 'study.'"

"Study you, you mean."

"I guess so. It was awkward as hell. I remember he put his tongue in my mouth and just kind of left it there." She shuddered, still grinning. "The French foreign exchange student I met the year after, though. Now *he* knew how to kiss."

"I hate him."

Whiskey-colored eyes sparkled at me, and my chest tightened. The little hourglass in the back of my mind wouldn't totally disappear, and I was not prepared to think beyond this night. So, I kicked the feeling aside and read the menu. We ordered drinks, appetizers, and entrees before she sat back and put those eyes on me again.

"So, you have a sister."

I nodded. "Older sister, younger brother. My sister just moved back to—ahh, home. She was living... elsewhere. Christ, this is hard," I finished with a laugh.

"Right. Tiny town in The South, USA. Sister moved home. Brother is young. What a dossier."

"Not young. Just two years younger."

She gave me a playful glare. "But you said you were nineteen, right?"

I just laughed. I'd totally forgotten that bit of bullshit among all the other silly stories we'd shared.

Jae tapped her finger on the table. "Let's see, other questions. Got any kids?"

"Yeah, like... seven? Maybe eight by now." I rolled my eyes. "Nope, no kids. Just a niece and nephew, thanks to the sister. You?"

She rolled her eyes right back and waved her hand. "Yep, just the one."

But something about the way she said it made me think that wasn't a lie. I arched my brows in a silent question.

She blew me a kiss. "Next."

"Do you really think I'm a drug dealer?"

"Exhibit A: this private table. B: the top-shelf drinks. C: the tips you throw around. D: the month-long island vacay. E: the beach bum vibe. I rest my case."

I cheersed her cocktail. "Hell yeah, then."

Those long lashes blinked slowly. Her voice was soft. Serious. "Are you a dangerous person? For real."

I leaned over to put my lips to her ear. Drawing in a deep breath of her fruity, coconut scent, I said, "I am not, Miss Jae. I promise. Just dangerously close to putting my hand up your dress right here and now."

Her knee pressed against mine. "Dare you."

But I hummed and sat back. "Not yet, love. Not yet."

Dinner went on like that. We didn't run out of things to talk about despite keeping pretty much all personal details hidden. And neither of us pushed the other to give away more than they wanted to. Like all our other moments together over these past few days, it was sublime.

I just really needed that little hourglass to go away.

Once I'd paid the bill and laughed off her attempt to split it, we continued down the beach to a club with a hot dance floor. Even on a Sunday, the place was already filling up.

Jae squealed and gripped my hand. "Dancing! Yes!" She tugged me to follow her to the open-air bar. "I'll warn you now, I'm not a good dancer. But I love it."

I laughed and spun her around in my arms. We moved to the beat as a song closed out. She clapped and grinned up at me. "Thank you. I only got to dance a little with the volleyball douche on Friday. This is great."

My eyes narrowed. "Mm, yeah, when you were trying to

execute an obviously flawed plan. Any plan that didn't feature us together should've never been considered."

That coy smile appeared. "But I thought you were unavailable. What was a girl to do?"

We started dancing again. I held her waist and gave her a tsk. "Press a little harder, obviously."

Her arms circled my neck so those fantastic curves could *press* against me from my chest to my crotch. "Like that?"

I held her close, letting my hips sway against hers. "A lot harder, actually."

"So very hard?"

My lips dusted hers. "So very hard. Press me all you want, Miss Jae. Swear I can take it."

She tilted her pelvis into me, and I laughed. "Let's go, you little tease."

"Where are we going?"

"You and I are going down to the beach. I'm going to make you come while you dance for me."

I stepped back and held out one hand to her. She slipped her palm into mine. "Cruise" by Florida Georgia Line started—not sexy, but perfect for the dancing we were about to do.

There were plenty of patrons out on the sand. Jae gripped my fingers tight, but I grooved her over to the shadows just under the porch. My palms held her waist to pull her closer until her legs were on either side of one of my thighs. Her hips rolled, bumping her body against me just like I wanted. Jae's head dropped to watch us move. I felt her hesitate, but I gave her a quick squeeze.

"Toes" started next, slowing things down. Perfect.

We found the rhythm, but I wasted no time in spinning her around so that she danced with her back to my front. My hand slid from her hip to her thigh.

"Dance for me, baby. I'm going to touch you while you do, got it?"

She nodded. I felt the tremor run through her body, but she kept swaying while I stood still and caressed her hips and thighs. My heart raced already. I didn't give a damn that I'd have to wait to come. I was dying to make her explode.

"Now remember," I said into her hair, "you can't let anyone guess what I'm doing to you. If someone looks over, they see you dancing."

She twisted her head to look at me. Her little smirk appeared. "Duh. I do this all the time."

I smirked back. "Yeah? I haven't done this in years, so forgive me if I'm a little rusty."

"What, when you were, like, twelve?" She pursed her lips, a clear reference to our age discussion earlier.

"Yeah. Middle school was wild," I said without dropping a beat. In truth, I'd only done this once, at a club in college. But I was itching to make my girl shake with pleasure. This seemed like the right kind of reckless for her weekend.

I wrapped one arm around her waist and slid my right hand between us to squeeze her ass. At the same time, I flicked my left index finger over her nipples. It was quick and subtle, but she jolted.

"Mm-mm. Don't lose the beat."

She didn't look at me when she nodded that time. She found the rhythm again, obeying when I nudged her feet a little wider apart.

A couple strolled past us just as I slid my fingers between her legs. They paid us no mind at all. Good thing. I bit down to stifle a moan at the way she instantly soaked my hand. I flicked her nipples again, just to feel her tense while I teased her lips.

"Now, dance this pussy all over my hand." I nipped her ear with my teeth.

She sucked in a deep breath and hesitantly swished her hips.

"Just like that. Don't stop," I said through clenched teeth.

She didn't. She kept up that sway as "Kokomo" came on. Good song for island sex. I let her swivel and play against me. At the chorus, just when she seemed to be getting comfortable, I plunged two fingers into her and let my thumb find her clit.

Drawing a lazy circle, I encouraged her to keep dancing. Kept whispering to her, alternating between praise and shame for being so filthy. Everything I said made her wetter until she was well and truly fucking my hand.

She started to tense up as that song faded out. I tapped on her clit and pulsed my fingers, and she forgot to dance. "Filthy little tease. Such a fucking flirt," I said into her ear.

That was all she needed.

I felt a moan vibrate her diaphragm, but she kept it in as her walls contracted against me. My cock got harder just thinking about being buried inside her later.

When she stilled, I held her up. Her hands gripped my arm around her waist while she panted. Finally, she locked her knees, and I released her.

She turned to stare up at me. Her tongue skimmed her lips before she cleared her throat and said, "Well. That was... amazing."

"I thought your plan was wild, reckless fun all weekend. Didn't that fit?"

She grabbed my shirt and hauled me in for a kiss. "Hell yes, it did," she gasped when we broke apart.

"Good. Let's go get a drink."

A couple of hours blurred by while we danced ourselves

sweaty in that bar. The music was perfect—classic beach music like Jimmy Buffett and Kenny Chesney mixed with hip-hop and pop. "Cake By the Ocean" had us both singing and somewhere between laughing and making out at the innuendo. The song that followed it was one I'd never heard, but Jae beamed and shimmied her shoulders. I cocked my head at the unfamiliar lyrics.

"It's BTS," she said over the speaker. "Don't tell me you're not a fanboy."

"I loved them before they got big." This was a total lie, although I had at least heard of them. I made a note to search some of their music soon.

We danced on. When the ukulele version of "Somewhere Over the Rainbow" came on, I pulled her close and let her rest her head on my chest.

For just a moment, I drew in a deep breath and closed my eyes. I wanted to save this moment. No matter what else my life might hold, good or bad, I wanted this night—this woman—imprinted on my mind forever.

We stepped apart and stared at each other.

"It's getting late," I said.

She nodded.

"So I better get you back to your room."

Another nod. But the way she wet her lips made me grab her hand and head out the front for a taxi.

12

JULIETTE

We made it to the elevator before he picked me up, and I wrapped my legs around his back. He raced me down the hall, hands all over me, only to fall into my room tangled up in each other.

"Remember the time you had an iguana infestation, and we almost didn't do this?" he mumbled between kisses.

While he spoke, I opened his pants. Then, I nodded. "What a nightmare. Imagine my horror... if I'd never gotten to do this."

I dropped to my knees, yanked his boxer-briefs down, and slid him into my mouth. Jay groaned and gripped his hair.

"Goddamn. That's—*fuck*. I—oh, fuck, Jae. You're incredible."

His eyes were like polished silver when he dropped his head to gaze down at me. I swirled my tongue and pushed him deeper in. Jay groaned again, so I sucked harder.

While I teased him, I imagined this moment like I was looking at it from the ceiling. Me on my knees, loving every second of it. Loving how he tasted. How he felt. Such a far cry from my usual self. So unrestrained and reckless. So fucking *free*. Free to be sexy. To enjoy this man. To wear this skimpy dress and feel like it suited me.

What a fairytale.

Princess Jae gets wined and dined by the handsome, proba-bly-not-a-criminal prince. Princess Jae is a filthy little tease. God, this has been the trip that I needed. An entire pause from real life.

My thoughts scattered when Jay flexed his hips and gasped. Salty come filled my mouth. I gripped him tight and flicked my tongue against his head. That made him shout and flex again with a final shudder.

Slowly, he pulled back. I swallowed the last taste of him and wiped my lips.

"Fuck," he rasped. "Your mouth. Holy shit."

He helped me to my feet. My knees wobbled, so I held onto those strong arms and smiled up at him.

With a long, deep breath, Jay said, "I hope you weren't intending to sleep tonight, Miss Jae."

"I wasn't."

"Good." He grunted and hoisted me over his shoulder. I yelped, but he marched me to the bed and laid me on my back. His tongue met mine while one finger hooked my panties and slid them off. When he began to kiss down my neck and over my chest, my thighs clenched because I knew where this was going.

"Oh, please, yes, please," I whined when he pushed my legs open and teased his tongue against my clit.

"Uh-huh. Gotta give me a minute to recharge," he mumbled, tongue out.

"Take your time." I ran my fingers through his hair.

He brought me nearly to the edge of climax, and I was still wearing my dress. Just as I started to really wind up, though, Jay backed off and hauled me up to sit. He yanked the dress over my head, so I stood and clawed at his shirt with shaking fingers to undo the buttons. I skimmed his cock and grinned to find him hard again.

"Yes ma'am," he said while I stroked. "It's yours. Is that what you want to hear?"

"Uh-huh. I want you hard for me. I want your balls to ache because of how bad you want me." *Whoa. Did I just say that?*

That silver gaze glinted in the low lamplight. "You knew the moment you sat on my chair that that's exactly what you wanted."

"No."

"No?"

I smirked. "No. I knew the moment *before* I sat on your chair that I wanted your cock."

He smirked right back. "Good fucking girl."

"I'd rather be a bad girl getting fucked right now."

His look was absolutely feral. "Go sit that fine ass on the dresser. Now."

I hopped up, and he pulled my hips forward. The height was perfect—I tipped off the dresser and sank onto his waiting cock. My nails dug into his shoulders as I wailed. Jay gripped my ass and began to thrust, keeping me just barely braced on the dresser. He fucked hard and deep. Each slam into me made me moan from the ecstatic bliss. Sweat slicked my forehead and stood on his shoulders.

"Don't stop, don't ever stop, I need this so much, please don't let up..." I mumbled, absolutely out of my mind with pleasure.

His voice was dark and choppy against the rhythm of his hips. It was 180-proof whiskey over tumbled stones. "No fucking way am I letting up on you. God, you take my cock so good. It's un-fucking-real how good you feel. You need it?

I'll give it to you, baby. This is yours. Whatever you need, as long as you need. I will make it happen."

In the fairytale, I knew he would.

"I want it, Jay. I want... I want... oh, please, please..."

His left hand released my ass to sneak between us. Two fingers found my clit, and I exploded. The potent cocktail of physical pleasure and all this filthy talk had me shaking with wave upon wave of pleasure for what seemed like forever. Jay rode it out, praising me for coming so well, telling me how beautiful I looked while I did.

He paused while I caught my breath. As soon as I could open my eyes, I gave him a daring look. He quirked his brows.

I lay down with my back on the dresser and lifted my legs from around his back to rest on his shoulders. Jay's eyes rolled at the initial change of angle, so I crooked my finger.

"Fuck me like this. Finish for me like this."

His teeth flashed with a quick grin. "Oh, yes *ma'am*," he said with a laugh.

My fingers latched onto the sides of the dresser to keep from sliding up. Jay took a moment to find the right position, and then he resumed our rhythm—and the talking. This time, I just listened to the stream of beautiful obscenities pour from him.

"Look at you. So gorgeous. So fucked. I'm not gonna last long like this, love, but god, your tits. I want to fuck them so bad."

I raised my brows. "Why?"

He huffed a laugh. "Because they're spectacular. I would paint you in my come if you let me."

My face heated. I knew I would totally let him. I also knew it wasn't going to happen. So, I grabbed my breasts and pressed them together. "You're so filthy."

"You're damn right I am. Should've guessed that from day one."

I grinned and tossed him a wink. "I did."

That took him over. He sank his teeth into my ankle and groaned out, "Yes, yes, hell yes, you are incredible."

When he finally stumbled back to discard the condom, I slowly slithered off the dresser. My shaky legs barely got me to the bed before I collapsed again.

Jay lay down beside me and wrapped me in his arms. He kissed the top of my head and said tenderly, "You have five minutes to recharge. Then we're going again."

I huffed a laugh, but my eyelids were already heavy.

13

JAMES

I woke with a jolt. The lamp was still on, but Jae was nowhere to be seen. I rolled off the bed, stepped into my underwear, and looked around. Finally, my gaze landed on the terrace curtains billowing softly with the breeze.

She sat on a loveseat, staring out at the moon over the ocean. Her knees were bent on the cushion, arms wrapped tight to make herself a little ball. I yawned, and she stirred.

Without turning her head, she said, "Do you know that John Lennon lyric, 'life is what happens while you're busy making other plans'?"

I shuffled to sit beside her. "Yeah."

"That's me. I make plans, and they go to shit. And life happens in between. Why do I even bother trying to plan things out anymore?" Her voice was soft. Distant.

I thought about this. "Guess you haven't learned your lesson yet."

She huffed a little laugh. "Guess you're right about that." Her gaze slid to me. Those lips flattened into a hard line before she said, "This was my honeymoon."

"Talk about telling me something without telling me

something," I murmured because I had no clue what else to say. My stomach clenched at that news, even though I had no right to a reaction.

"Yeah, no kidding."

"Was he... military?"

"Oh, god no. He was a dickhead. We called off the wedding three months ahead of the event. I'd paid for the honeymoon already, so... I kept it for myself."

If the mood hadn't been so dreamy and somber, I'd have high-fived her for that. Instead, I looked her over appreciatively. "Hell yeah. Great decision."

"I'd planned a wedding. Life happened instead. Then, I regrouped and planned a hot girl weekend. I was going to flirt with strangers. Have a random hookup. Drink all day."

Her gaze landed on me again. "And instead, I met you."

Her lips twisted. So did my heart.

Before I could speak, she went on. "And since this whole fairytale ends in a few hours, I don't care about filtering what I say. I met you, and this has been... so special. So much more than I ever imagined. You will never, ever understand how much this has meant to me."

"I will," I muttered.

If she heard, she didn't show it. "But it wasn't what I planned. I wanted to make blurry memories that would make me laugh to think about later. I made these memories. And I'll laugh, and cry, and swoon when I think on them. So much so that it's better if I don't." She wet her lips. "I'll miss you, Mr. Smith."

"I told you, love. The name's Bond." I smirked.

She laughed at that. "Right, sorry. I'll miss you, James."

I nearly crumbled. I couldn't talk for a long moment. When my breath finally evened, I said, "I'm going to miss you too, Miss Jae. This has been... unreal. So much more than just a weekend fling. You're fantastic. I hope you know that. I hope you've felt that in our time together."

"I really have."

Don't say it. Don't say it. Don't— "I'm going home on Friday. Are you sure you don't want to give me your number?"

As soon as the words left my mouth, I rolled my eyes and shook my head to tell her I knew it was a silly question. "What happens at the beach, stays at the beach. Right?"

She nodded quickly. "You just said I'd not learned my lesson yet about making plans. To try and keep this going, even in a loose way, sounds like trying to plan. And that definitely is a plan I would screw up. I don't want this spoiled by real life."

"But even that sounds like planning. You're *planning* not to see me again. What if the story's not over?"

Suddenly, Jae sat up on her knees. Next thing I knew, she straddled me and held my face in her hands. "It's not over yet. My flight leaves in six hours, which gives us about four together. After this, back to reality. Hold on to this fairytale with me as long as we can."

She dipped her head and kissed me. Dark hair tickled my shoulders as her body arched to mine. I held her close and kissed her back with everything I had. I hated the thought of letting her go. None of the women I'd dated compared to her. No one compared to her. I knew part of that was the magic of the setting. Perfect weather, no work, cocktails, and minimal clothing.

But part of me knew beyond a doubt that the real magic was *her*.

I stood up and carried her back to the bed. For the next hour, I kissed her body and touched her everywhere. I'd already memorized her, but I made damn sure I couldn't forget. At last, she pushed me to sit against the headboard and sank onto my lap. I closed my eyes and imprinted her sound on me, too. Her little moans and whimpers. Her raspy voice, telling me how she liked it. The gasp she made when her climax hit.

The fucking sexy way she coaxed me to follow suit.

In the quiet that followed, she reached out and skimmed her fingers over my chest. "Tell me more nothing about you."

I yawned and stood up. "I will. I'll tell you about how this was supposed to be a trip with a girlfriend and why that went to shit. I'll tell you about my friends. But first, I have to pee. Be right back."

She yawned, too. "Okay."

Taking a piss and washing up couldn't have taken three minutes. But when I stepped back out, Jae lay with her head on the pillow, the sheet pulled around her. Her eyes were closed, and her breathing was even.

I stared at her for a long moment, trying to ignore the unfamiliar ache in my chest. Fighting the urge to wake her up—to keep her with me for the week at least. I could easily fly her home on Friday...

After that long moment, I found my clothes and dropped the box in my pocket with a note beside her phone. Then, I dusted my lips against hers and let myself out.

The sky was beginning to lighten as I cruised back to my villa. And the only thing on my mind was the growing certainty that I'd never meet a woman like her again.

14

JULIETTE

My alarm blared at 6am. I jolted awake, disoriented as hell. *What is going on? Where is Jay?*

"Ugh," I groaned, crashing back to the pillows. "You fell asleep, you loser."

I couldn't have slept more than an hour. My body made that painfully clear when I rolled out of bed. Muscles and joints complained loudly, but no time for that. I stumbled around, shoving the remaining items in my suitcase. I could've soaked in a shower for hours, but all I had time for was a quick rinse. Then, I stepped into jeans and a top, grabbed my jacket, and was ready to go.

I'll never be ready to go.

I pushed that thought aside and reached for my phone. The little box and folded paper beside it nearly got missed completely. I noticed "JAE" written on the folded paper at the last minute. *Dammit, my heart doesn't have time for this.*

Sucking in a deep breath, I dropped it into my purse and grabbed my suitcase.

That little box burned a hole in my tired mind on the cab ride, through security, and all the way onto the plane. It whispered to me through takeoff, but I refused to indulge until we were airborne. Until I could breathe and deal with this.

When a cup of coffee sat in front of me, I finally sighed and reached into my purse. It was a small, flat box. The note was written on hotel stationery. My fingers trembled as I flipped the paper open to read:

Jae,

Thank you for stealing my lunch. Thank you for whatever in the world possessed you to flirt with me. How I got to be your wild weekend hookup, I'll never know. But, my lady, it was my honor indeed to be your knight—and share your nights. (See what I did there?)

I'm struggling not to give you my number in case you ever need anything. But I respect your wishes, and so I won't. But if you ever need. Bat signal, baby.

Good luck on the trapeze. If we ever meet at another Star Wars con, I promise to show you my lightsaber.

Ps. I'm kissing you one more time.

xoxo

"Jay"

Two drops blurred his name—tears, leaking from my eyes. I lifted a shaking hand to my lips. I could still taste him. Smell him on me. I knew part of that was my imagination, but part of it wasn't.

And a lot of me wanted to never forget.

With a shaky breath, I opened the box. A silver chain with the most beautiful blue, heart-shaped stone sat inside. The blue was a rich turquoise, unlike anything I'd ever seen.

More tears slipped out. My fingers still shook as I clasped it around my neck. I reread his note a hundred times, knowing I should throw it away. Totally unable to do so.

Back to reality. This story is over. You have to put it on the shelf.

In the end, I folded the note and stuck it in a tiny pocket in my wallet. Good luck. Good energy, but out of sight. Seemed right. Then, I heaved another shaky sigh and let myself sleep for the rest of the flight.

I was still yawning as I rode the escalator down to baggage claim at the Nashville airport. My foggy brain cleared fast when a tiny blur flew toward me and latched onto my leg.

"Mommy!"

My heart swelled. I dropped my carry-on and lifted her into my arms. "Ivy! Momma missed you!"

"I missed you too, Mommy."

"Hey, wait a second. Aren't you supposed to be at daycare?" I narrowed my eyes playfully, but my gaze was on my mother, who had walked up to join us.

Mom just smiled. "We decided a day at home was okay in honor of your arrival."

"Has Nana been spoiling you?" I asked Ivy.

"Yeah," she replied with a grin.

I set my daughter down to hug Mom. She eyed my denim jacket and tank top. "You'll need more than that. We're having Dogwood winter right now. Typical March. Good thing I've got the seats warmed in the car and potato soup in the crock pot at home."

Tears stung my eyes, and Mom gave me a sharp look. I shook my head. "Just tired. That sounds amazing."

"Good to have you back, honey."

It was good to be home. Painful and wonderful all at once.

The March weather was dreary and cold, but we spent the day warm and cozy in our home. I played with Ivy and helped around the house. She "helped" me unpack and stuff all my skimpy beach clothes into a vacuum bag for storage. This took forever because each dress had to be oohed and ahhed over. Two of them became dress-up clothes, with Ivy prancing around in front of my bedroom mirror until I laughed and gave her some heels, too.

A typical day with a four-year-old.

After her bath that evening, Ivy and I walked to her bedroom for story time. "Did you see the Rainbow Fish at the beach?" she asked when I closed the book.

"I sure did. You know what she said?"

Her eyes, the same color as mine, widened as she shook her head.

I hollowed out my cheeks, waved my hands by my jaw in a classic fish face, and used a silly, bubbly voice. "Tell Ivy I say helloooo." I swooped down and blew a raspberry on her neck, making her shriek with delight.

"That's silly, Mommy!"

"It is silly. And you're a silly girl. But now it's time to be a sleepy girl, okay?"

But Ivy was wound up, thanks to my homecoming. She squirmed around and put her head on my arm. Those eyes turned up to me in a diabolically cute move. Her little hand lifted to touch my throat. "So pretty," she said, sitting up higher to examine the necklace. "Can I see?"

"It was a present," I found myself saying. "I brought you presents. This one was for me. From a friend."

"You should wear it all the time."

"Yes ma'am." I couldn't help the jolt that ran through me at the memory of Jay growling that phrase.

I took the necklace off so she could look at it. While she

turned it over in her hand, she mumbled out of nowhere, "Mommy? Why don't I have a daddy?"

Nausea rolled my stomach. "Honey, you know that Brad is your father."

"Mm, but he went away. Is he coming back?"

Brad and I had gotten back together a year ago. Before that, he had not been in Ivy's life beyond intermittent checks in the mail. I'd gotten pregnant in college. He was from Knoxville, over two hours away from Nashville. By the time I paused school and moved home to live with my mother, our relationship was in shambles. He wasn't ready to be a dad. As if motherhood was in my plans for college. He sent money when he could over those three years.

Then, he'd showed up in Nashville, saying he was ready to be a family. Asking me to marry him and move to Arizona within a year for a job he had lined up.

Then, just before Christmas, that job suddenly needed him to go right away. And that press, that demand of now or never, put the spotlight on how absolutely wrong he was for me. He'd shown up with a plan that sounded right. Family. Responsibility. But nothing about it worked because we were never meant to work.

I wasn't wrong in what I'd told Jay. Brad was a dickhead. He was arrogant and irresponsible. In college, I'd been attracted to his "intelligence" which was really just a lot of opinions. I guess becoming a mom had given me some wisdom because the past year with him had made me acutely aware of that. He had plans of becoming this bigshot finance guy, but the job he moved for was a sales position with an accounting firm. On top of all that, he never lifted a finger with Ivy. Never spent time with her when I wasn't there, never played with her, never really worked to make her understand who he was.

Her neutrality about him made sense.

I swallowed hard and pulled off my reading glasses. "No. Brad isn't coming back. Does that make you feel sad?"

She looked up and passed the necklace back to me. "No."

"Do you wish you had a daddy?"

Shrug. "Kelsey at daycare said she didn't have a daddy either. She has two mommies. I said I have a mom and a nana. Right?"

I kissed her forehead. "That's right, baby. That's your family."

"Do you have a daddy?"

Jesus, honey. Go to sleep. You're killing me. I forced a gentle smile. "I did. He was a good man. He died a year before you were born."

"Do you miss him?"

"Yes, I do. But I have you and Nana."

"Kelsey has a dog. Can I have a dog?"

"Not at this time, missy."

She yawned at freaking last. "Okay. Will you sing now?"

"Will you go to sleep now?"

"Yes, Mommy."

"Then, yes, Ivy Juliette Reid, I will sing."

She beamed when I said her full name. She didn't understand yet how special it was to me that she shared my name. Brad had been irritated as hell when he found out, but why would I give her his name? He hadn't even known when she was born.

I sang "Octopus's Garden" until her eyes closed. Then, I crept out of her room and blew out a breath.

Mom looked up when I staggered down the hall into the living room. I shook my head. "God, having a kid is rough."

She laughed. "No shit, Sherlock."

I giggled and plopped on the sofa beside her with a bottle of nail polish remover and some cotton. As I wiped off the pretty blue polish, I summed up my little chat with Ivy.

Mom hummed and smiled. "You're such a good mom."

"Yeah, right."

"Seriously, Jules. Home run response. And, for the umpteenth time, I'll just say that I'm so glad y'all didn't move to Arizona."

I twisted my lips. "I am, too. It seemed like a good plan, but it definitely wasn't."

"So. Tell me all about vacation."

Suddenly, the cotton balls were extremely interesting. "I, uh, you know. Got a tan. Went dancing. Ate seafood."

"Were you lonely?"

I shook my head.

Mom's head turned to me. "Juliette Reid! You are blushing!"

I jumped up to trash the aqua-streaked cotton. "I am not," I hissed. "And don't wake Ivy!"

Mom crossed her arms and waited for me to sit back down. She pursed her lips, clearly waiting. "I meant were you lonely to be on your own. But you're blushing like you met someone. Spill it."

"You are too saucy to be a mother."

"Hello pot, this is the kettle."

We laughed.

I collapsed against the sofa and fingered the necklace. "Fine. *Fine.* Kind of, yes. I guess you could say I met someone."

She gasped. "He gave you that, didn't he? Oh, young lady! You better tell me everything."

I laughed again. "Tall. Handsome. A scuba diver. Funniest man I've ever met. He, uh, well. It was pretty magical." I gave her some basic details about a few of our adventures.

Mom practically vibrated with excitement. "And what's his name? Are you going to stay in touch?"

I bit my lip. "Um, I... I don't know what his name is. I don't actually know anything about who he is or where he lives. We were both kind of into the anonymous vacation fling thing. After this year, the last thing I want is to try and get to know someone."

She frowned. "But you've hardly dated anyone since college. Why... sorry. I'm meddling. Okay, no name, no details. I'll try not to have a conniption over the danger of such a thing..."

"Yeah, yeah, but I'm home safe, and he has no idea where that even is. It was just a vacation thing, Mom. But... wanna see a picture?"

"This instant. I have to live vicariously through you, you know."

I scrolled on my phone to the photos the tour guide had sent. Mom got quiet, then glanced at me. "Good lord, Jules. What a beautiful photo."

"A beautiful man," I agreed.

"No. Both of you look so stinking happy. Ooh, honey, I'm so happy for you!" She hugged me tight.

I hugged her back and darkened the phone. "Thanks, Mom. It was really great. But now I've got to go to bed to start this awesome new job in the morning." I rolled my eyes.

"It's only temporary," she reminded me.

At the doorway to the hall, I turned back to her. "Don't live vicariously through me. That's super depressing to even think about. Dad wouldn't want you to do that. He'd want you to be thriving and happy."

Her brows ticked up, but her smile was sweet. "That's a very good point. I'll consider it. Maybe you can help me find a hobby or something."

"Done."

I wandered down the hall to my bedroom and stretched out. I was exhausted, and the job that started tomorrow gave me absolutely no joy. Real life was back with a vengeance.

But as I closed my eyes, my mind went straight to where I knew it shouldn't. Where I knew I could get lost if I wasn't careful.

Straight back to my fairytale.

15

JAMES

My shark and I caught several lionfish together during the first half of the week. After I spent Monday sleeping, moping, and thinking about Jae, I got my ass back out on the water for two days. I swear that shark missed me, but obviously that was ridiculous.

As planned, I packed up Thursday night and chartered a morning flight to Nashville on Friday. My first errand after unpacking was to visit my stylist and get a damn haircut. From there, I went to my brother's house.

Max bolted out of the door and ran straight for me. I knelt down and opened my arms, and he nearly bowled me over. His paws landed on my chest while I was treated to a full face wash with his tongue.

"Okay, boy, okay," I laughed, scratching his ears. "I missed you too. Who's my good boy? Who's the best boy?"

"Hey, stranger." My sister-in-law, Celeste, hugged her jacket around her and smiled from the doorway.

Max and I walked forward so I could sweep her into a hug. My brother appeared. I tossed him an exaggerated wink as I hugged his wife. He rolled his eyes, and I laughed.

"If you touch my ass, I'll castrate you," Celeste said into my chest.

I released her and laughed again. "It's good to see you guys."

"Most of the crew are coming over in about an hour," Ben said, clapping a hug on me.

"Fucking great. I brought beer."

My first night home was full of music, laughter, and talk. I buzzed to be back among my people after so many solo weeks. It was late when I finally loaded Max into the car and made the drive to my house. I used to live just a few minutes away from Ben and Celeste, but I'd built this place outside of the city last year and only moved in in December. It really didn't feel like home yet, given that I'd been gone one of the four months since move-in day. But, like my car, it did feel like fucking *mine*, and I loved it.

And it had all started at Ben and Celeste's place, hanging out with our friends.

My original dream had been to make an app everyone would use. What that was, I had no idea for a long time. And then, one night, we were all hanging out and bullshitting in our regular way. I had started using a dating app and was showing them my match deck.

And it hit me. Why not a social app based on conversation instead of photos?

Chat Me Up! was born. From the first planning sessions, I had a good feeling about where it was going. We built a pitch deck. Celeste mocked up some designs. We did a first round of investment pitches and secured enough funds to do a small launch. One afternoon, our buddy Will said he knew a marketing guy we should talk to. Enter Luke Paris, our CMO. He created an aggressive debut campaign that was fucking brilliant. And *then* we got our windfall investor.

We wouldn't learn that it was actually one of our best friends, Megan, for several months. But Megs gave us all the capital we needed to expand. Our first summer was a wild-fire of growth and expansion.

And it just got better from there.

My parents now lived in a new home and drove new cars. My sister's kids would go to any school they wanted, and she'd never have a mortgage again. Ben and I had made sure of all of that before we started upgrading ourselves. We were considering starting a charity, too. For the time being, a percentage of my money went to organizations I supported. Ben and Celeste also had their causes. But even with all of that, the new lifestyle was... *choice*.

Back at my new, custom-built home, I parked in the garage and let Max go have a sniff to reacquaint himself to the grounds. The perimeter had a healthy security system. It also had an electric fence that meant my pup was free to roam as he pleased.

While he did, I unpacked my suitcase and stored my dive gear in the basement. When Max was smiling at me through the deck's glass door, I let him in, gave him some water, and went to crash after such a full day.

My last thought, as it had been every night that week, was of her. Of that fairytale weekend and the most beautiful girl I'd ever met.

I strode into our offices on Monday in a dress shirt, slacks, and dress shoes. It felt weird to not be in linen and t-shirts anymore, but I knew I'd get used to it fast. It also felt a little weird to have an office with our logo on the wall. We didn't get this space until December, either—when we took the IPO public.

Now, here we were. Sitting on a company with an obscene valuation. Capital-R Rich beyond our wildest dreams. *Holy shit, this is real.* I still felt it every day. It hadn't been on my mind in Aruba. Here in Nashville, the thought was back in bold neon lights, as bright as any bar on Honky Tonk Highway.

Celeste, Ben, and Luke all sat in the conference room when I arrived. An assistant poured me a cup of coffee. I took a sip and sat down with my brilliant think tank.

"On last week's call, Celeste mentioned Liv's idea for a new app. Some kind of platform to connect parents based on their children's age so they could share ideas and make friends. Right?"

Celeste nodded. "That's the gist. Now that Liv's teaching kindergarten, she's noticed how hard it is for parents to feel like they can ask questions of each other. This would be like a spinoff to *Chat Me Up!*."

"Mm, right. Which means making an entirely new product, going through investments again, etc. We created the product already. Do we want to go through all of that a second time for such a similar concept?"

"Absolutely not," Luke said with a headshake. "Inefficient. Poor use of funds."

"Right. The better idea is to..." I paused for effect. "Expand *Chat Me Up!*"

All three of them sat forward, ready to hear more. I grinned and took a quick breath before going into my idea.

Damn, it was good to be home.

16

JULIETTE

"What's this one say?" Ivy pointed to the next item on the checklist. Her little legs swung through the holes in the red Target cart while I pushed her around the store.

"Crayons. We better go this way." I turned the cart on a hard angle and made screeching noises just to make her laugh.

If someone told me ten years ago that a month before my 27th birthday, I'd be shopping for school supplies for my kindergartener, I'd have punched them and walked over their moaning body. And yet, there I was. The plan had been a career in medicine. Fabulous travel. A Maserati in the driveway. A new handbag every quarter and new shoes whenever I pleased.

Life had happened.

So I shuffled my off-brand flip-flops through Target with a perfectly good, if a little old, purse on my shoulder. But I was smiling. My daughter was bubbling with excitement for school. What else did I really need?

School started in August, five months into my job at the coffee shop. Retail hell is what I usually called it. The company was fine. The literal company, aka my coworkers, were a mixed bag. Most of them were kids, which made sense. But my manager, Steve, was a creep. He wore his hair in a greasy ponytail and liked to touch my arm when showing me, aka mansplaining, how to make a drink correctly. When I started the job, he "joked" repeatedly about us going out for coffee—"to check out the competition," he'd say with a wink.

He stopped joking when I said I had to get home to my daughter. Still liked to sneak in the leering and the occasional touch if I wasn't sharp enough to keep six feet of distance at all times.

At least I managed to be off for Ivy's first day of school. Good thing, too—I cried like I was shipping her off to the Marines. But I also did another round of job searches and found something interesting in my email. An old colleague of mine knew of a part-time receptionist position in a cardiac health office. The word was that they would be looking for a full-time exercise physiologist in the new year. My colleague had recommended me in the hopes that I could fill the role when it came open. Three days a week there plus three at the coffee shop was a grueling schedule. But this job had the potential to get me out of retail hell. I called and scheduled an interview.

A few days later, I was back at Ivy's school for an open house night. Someone handed me a welcome newsletter on the joys of kindergarten. I read it, then folded it into a tiny square while hovering by the wall in the gym. Ivy was busy playing, but I felt every inch out of place. No one came up to talk to me. It seemed like all the other parents knew each other already.

While I stood and fidgeted, a silver-haired lady approached with a smile. She introduced herself as Mary

Mason, Ivy's teacher, and invited me to help chaperon a field trip in a few weeks. I said I would and got myself out of there as soon as possible.

Back home with Ivy in bed, I unpacked all this with Mom. "There were other moms there who seemed pretty young. But I just felt so out of place and awkward."

She laughed. "Your father used to fake allergy attacks to get out of PTA meetings. Try not to fret too much. Remember it's all for your daughter."

"But I wish I could, I don't know. Ask questions. Check I'm doing it right. See if Ivy's routines are normal compared to her peers."

Mom shrugged. "It would be nice, but we never had any of that. Funny how there's this code like you're supposed to know what you're doing, right?"

"In a lot of ways, yeah. I read all the books about development and stuff, but still. Practical application is always good to see. So, how's dance?"

We signed Mom up for dance lessons in the spring after that chat about not living vicariously through me. It was just what she needed. She had already made friends and started going twice a week, sometimes more. I was thrilled to see her so vibrant and never tired of hearing her gossip or tell me new steps she'd learned.

Mom glowed at my question, which made me raise my brows. "It's good. I, uh, have a date for Friday night. Martin asked me to dinner."

I clapped a hand over my mouth and squealed. "Mom! Look at you!"

She waved me off, but I wouldn't stop gushing over it. I made her promise to tell me everything and laughed when she said it "wasn't like that."

Life went on. I got the receptionist job, which made Steve
frown when I said my schedule needed to change. He grumbled about "missing me" on Mondays for a week, but I said a
flat no when he offered to put me on the pm shift. I needed
money, but I wasn't broke enough to go through all that.
Mom confirmed this with a "Hell yeah" when I told her
about it.

The new schedule sucked, especially with changing
gears every other day from office environment to pre-dawn
barista. Thank god for Mom. She helped me find a routine
with Ivy that even allowed a few hours each week for my
marathon training. That usually meant running after Ivy's
bedtime with reflector gear on, but it was worth it to have
that time to myself.

I told Steve there was no way I would work on my birthday, which happened to be the same day as Ivy's field trip. So I
celebrated turning 27 with a trip to the science museum and
takeout with my two best gals that night. Ivy was over the
moon to have the day with me. I met her "best friend Maddie,"
and all in it was pretty fun. That night, we ate in front of the
TV and stayed up past all our bedtimes watching movies.

When the credits rolled, Mom clicked the remote and
turned to me. Ivy was curled up fast asleep between us.
"Does this movie remind you of your vacation?"

I whipped my head to her. "*Before Sunrise*? It's my
favorite movie. What do you mean?"

"You and that handsome guy. Leaving things to fate."

"Oh. No. We didn't leave things to fate. We just... left. Not
the same."

She hummed. "Show me his picture again."

"Mom, come on." I tried to ignore her pleading stare but finally huffed and scrolled through my phone. My heart twisted to look at those pics again. I didn't let myself scroll to vacation photos often.

She leaned over my shoulder and sighed. "You were silly not to give him your number. Look how much he cares about you."

"What does that even mean?"

She gestured to his face. "That smile is a man infatuated. Silly girl."

I pocketed the phone and hopped up. "You're just swoony because of Martin." I blew her kisses, and she laughed and shooed me off to bed.

In my bedroom, I pulled out my pink silk nightie—the one I'd bought for Aruba—and slipped it over my head. Memories rushed back of long nights and the shushing ocean. Of lazy mornings sleeping in. *God, when did I last sleep in?*

Of gray eyes glinting at me from between my legs.

I tumbled to my bed and reached in the nightstand for my vibrator. I couldn't remember the last time I'd come. The last time I'd had the energy for this. But for freaking once, I let go of duty and routine and surrendered to the moment.

As I shuddered and gasped with my climax, I wondered if any fantasy ever would replace the memories of that trip.

Summer wouldn't let go. It was the first week of October, and still hitting 85 degrees. Everyone was over it, me especially because it made long runs such a sweatfest. But the calendar said *hello, fall,* and so Ivy and I were back at her school for a chili supper night.

I met a few moms on the field trip, so I didn't feel as terribly out of place as the first gathering. Ivy and I made our way through the line to fill our Styrofoam bowls and grab cornbread. It was pretty clear no one was keen on a warming stew with the air conditioners blasting, but we sat at a long table and did our best. Ivy stirred her chili. Suddenly, her head whipped around. I heard someone call her just as her spoon hit the table, and she was off like a shot.

I followed to find her with Maddie. The two were chattering with a woman who wore a wide smile. She had knelt down to their level, and as I walked up, I heard the girls telling her about something that happened at recess. I braced for the awkward introductions and obligatory chitchat. But when I reached the trio, the woman's eyes cut up to me and went wide.

"Ivy, is this your mommy?"

"Yeah!"

"You look just like her. Hey, girls. Let's go get some food."

"We have food," Ivy said seriously.

"Then save us a seat, and we'll be right there." She stood up. At full height, this woman was tall and striking. Even with a low ponytail and minimal makeup, her black-brown hair and olive complexion gave her a beauty that would turn heads. But the light in her eyes and the smile on her face negated any sense of insecurity or intimidation I might've had to stand next to this bombshell.

"Hey, I'm so glad you're here tonight. I've been trying to get in touch with you."

I looked behind me, as if someone else must be there. Then I pointed to myself. "Me? I'm—"

"Mrs. Reid, right? You're Ivy's—oh, crap. Maddie's almost at the chili. I'll talk to you in a second."

She ran across the gym to help Maddie, so I returned to Ivy, who had stopped pretending she wanted the food. I fetched her another cup of juice and sat down just as Maddie climbed into the chair by my daughter at the round table. Her mom sat beside me.

"It's not Mrs.," I said in greeting. "It's Juliette."

"Juliette, got it. Sorry. You really get into the habit of formal monikers when you're a teacher." She laughed and rolled her eyes.

"Oh, wait. You're a teacher? I thought you were Maddie's mom."

"Mm, no, no. Maddie's my niece, but I'm also the other kindergarten teacher."

This woman looked nothing like my mental definition of a kindergarten teacher. Runway model? Scary litigator? Either worked.

Stop stereotyping her. That's not fair.

Besides, the way she passed Maddie an extra napkin and kept eye contact with me seemed like a pro move. She lifted the red Solo cup to her lips and sighed. "These events are so draining. I wish this was whiskey."

I laughed. "You and me both."

That made her grin return. "Oh, good. I was hoping you'd feel me on this."

I clinked my cup to hers. "Absolutely, I do. But, um, you said you tried to contact me?"

"Yes! I've sent you like five emails in the last couple weeks. You're a hard one to nail down."

"Oh, shoot. Sorry. I'm really bad with emails, and I've been busier than usual lately. Is everything okay?"

"Totally. I have a proposal for you."

I took a sip of iced tea and decided to just be myself with her. "Indecent or otherwise?"

My stomach unknotted when she threw her head back and laughed. "Oh, my god. You are so my people. Bravo, lady. Bravo. But no, this one is purely on the up and up. Do you use *Chat Me Up!*?"

"That dating app?"

She held up her index finger. "The *social* app."

"No. Why?"

"Okay, so hear me out. *Chat Me Up!* is piloting some new features and creating a website. It started as a conversation thing, yes largely for meeting potential dates. But it's expanding into social circles. Groups where you can connect with people around a niche—such as, ahem, being the parent of a kindergartener. Still all focused on conversations, of course. Just for a different purpose."

I tilted my head. "That sounds cool. I have tons of questions I would love to ask other parents, but I feel like that's kind of forbidden."

She beamed. "Precisely my point!" My confused stare made her shake her head and refocus. "Anyway, exactly. This is a space where you can do just that. I've pulled about ten families in for this pilot program so far, all from my class. But I really wanted to get you in since Maddie talks about Ivy all the time."

"Wait. How are you connected to this?"

"Oh. Hmm, well, I'm not supposed to say much because I don't want to bias you, but whatever. I know the app creators. I had, ha, kind of suggested they do something for parents, and this is what they dreamed up. So, I got the job of helping beta test it."

"That's... awesome. I didn't know it was a Nashville company. To be fair I don't really know much about it at all."

"Well, if you say yes, you'll have the opportunity to learn and tell me what you think. Can I count you in?"

"Sure, why not? Sounds like a potentially good resource."

"Awesome. And then, you know, maybe we can grab a beer and discuss it while *Ivy comes over to play with Maddie on Sunday.*"

Her voice rose on the girls' names, causing two little brown ponytails to whip to us. Maddie and Ivy's eyes grew round. "Can we, Livi? Can Ivy come play Barbies?" Maddie gasped.

"Sure, sweetie. Your dad won't mind."

The girls looked at each other and let out a collective squeal. I stared slack-jawed at the woman's smirk.

"See what I just did there?" she murmured.

"You're evil. I respect it," I said with a laugh.

"Doesn't have to be Sunday. Whenever's good for you, but I thought it might be fun. If you want. If not, no big deal. Just break two adorable children's hearts."

I laughed again. "Sunday works. Let's do it."

"Cool. Give me your number, and I'll text you the address. And I'll email you the invite link *again* if you promise to check your email."

"Yes ma'am, Mrs.—" I broke off, realizing I hadn't gotten her name.

She seemed to realize it, too, and smacked her forehead. "Gah. Put me in front of a group of children, and I seem like a reasonable adult. Get me one-on-one for a business deal, and I go back to bumbling geek with no manners. Sorry."

"It's totally fine." She had me smiling like I hadn't done in ages.

"Thanks. Anyway, I'm Olivia Milani-Langer. Miss Langer at school, but you should call me Liv."

17

JULIETTE

Liv emailed me the invite link that night, so I went ahead and downloaded the purple and yellow icon to my phone and created a login as "Jules27." Not the most original, but whatever. Jules had always been my nickname—except for those few brilliant days of being Miss Jae—and it seemed more casual and simpler than Juliette.

I explained all this to Liv on Sunday when I took Ivy to the address she'd texted. It was a cute two-story about ten minutes from home. There were several cars in the drive, so I parked on the curb and rang the bell.

Liv and another woman answered the door. Behind them we could hear a TV and male voices. "Hi, I'm Erin. Maddie's stepmom," the unfamiliar woman said. She knelt down to greet Ivy while Liv grinned at me.

Inside, we bypassed the living room and went upstairs to Maddie's room. Immediately, Maddie dragged Ivy to her toybox, and the girls were in the play zone. Erin gestured to the stairs. "You all go talk. I've got some work to do anyway, so I'll stay up here and keep an eye out."

Liv led me back downstairs and took a right turn into the

kitchen, where she went to the fridge for two beers. "This is my brother's house, but I used to live here."

"Was he pissed you invited us over?" I asked with a laugh.

"Not at all. Tom's awesome, and Erin is the sweetest. So, business first. Tell me about the app. Oh, and I noticed you joined as Jules. Do you prefer that to Juliette?"

"Whichever is fine. Figured Jules was less of a mouthful."

"Jules. Okay, cool, I can handle that."

I told her what little I'd learned thus far, which was good. The focus on conversation meant no one was posting memes or quizzes or anything like that. Somehow, that led to more productive discussions. Instead of side notes about politics or pop culture, the circle I was in was entirely focused on parenting discussions. I'd gotten some good feedback already about Ivy's reading routine and been able to offer an idea to a mom with a picky eater.

"One thing that really helps is how small the group is," I added. "And the fact that we're all in the same school means we have a common experience of what the kids are learning. I'm wondering how that works if the circles are bigger. What would give us a common experience then? Besides the general demographic of kindergarten parents, I mean."

Liv's eyes narrowed. She whipped out her phone. "Say that again."

I repeated myself.

She typed it and then set her phone down. "That's a great point. I'm going to pass it to the creators."

"How do you know them? Tell me about it."

"We're old friends. I've known those guys for years, way before they launched the company. You'd never know they were drowning in money and in charge of the hottest app around."

"Nice. That's awesome."

"You should meet them sometime. Hey, what if—"

Liv broke off, her gaze cutting behind me. Her smile turned softer. Eyebrows ticked up. "Oh, hey you."

I turned around and tried not to let my jaw hit the floor. If Liv was tall and striking, this man was the male version. He had broad shoulders and dark, angular features. He'd have been scary as hell in some circumstances, but, like Liv, the smile on his face undid his imposing air.

"Well, hey yourself. Excuse me, I just lost a bet to Tom over the Predators' score and need to fetch some beer." He went to the fridge while I stood up from the seat at the table.

Liv gestured him over to us. "Will, meet Jules. Jules is in my pilot program."

"Ah, I see. Pleasure. I'm Will Langer."

There was zero doubt this was Liv's husband by the way they looked at each other. I shook his hand. "Sorry if I'm intruding," I said to both of them. "It feels like I'm interrupting family time."

He shook his head. "Liv doesn't have enough patience to let someone intrude on her family time. If you're here, then you are most welcome to be."

"Hey," Liv whined, but then she grinned at me. "He's not wrong. I'm glad you wanted to hang out. Our chat the other day made me think we'd get along."

My cheeks warmed. "Me too, actually." I wished my voice wasn't so shy. I wished I had more practice with meeting people and making friends.

Will nodded at both of us and retreated to the living room. Liv cocked her head at me. "Is everything okay? You kind of look like you want to cry."

I plopped into the chair and stared at the kitchen table in front of me. "Sorry."

She sat down and sipped her beer. I glanced up, and she shrugged. "Spill it if you want. I'm not one to judge."

So, for god knows what reason, I dumped my purse to this woman. "I just feel kind of awkward because I don't spend a lot of time around adults my age. Becoming a parent before I could graduate college interrupted a lot of my plans. It killed my ties to the small friend group I'd formed at school.

"The last five years have been all about Ivy. I'd figured I'd be studying to become a physical therapist. Instead, I finished my degree in exercise physiology while breast-feeding my daughter. Between work and parenting, my social life had gone out the window. So I guess it's, uh, really nice to just... hang out."

I clamped my lips together and wanted to crawl under the table. But Liv stared at me, her eyes narrowed thoughtfully. "God, I literally cannot imagine. I mean, I saw what my brother, Tom, went through when his wife died, but that was so different. You're an exercise physi-ologist?"

"Yeah. Well. Not at the moment. Currently I'm working two jobs to pay bills, but E.P. is the idea."

"Boss. I used to CrossFit. I had to stop, though."

"Why?"

She smirked. "I'll tell you next time we hang out. It's a long story—with a happy ending, but still."

Between her comment about her brother and that mysterious promise, I understood that Olivia Milani-Langer was a woman who knew about tough choices.

She sat back and broke the tension. "Well, whatever the last five years have brought you, Ivy and Maddie are the cutest duo. They became fast friends and are always together on the playground."

I laughed. "I'm glad to hear that. Do they play with anyone else?"

"Oh, yeah. It's a whole group, but they're definitely besties. Guess that makes us lucky enough to have an excuse to hang out now and then, right?"

I clinked my beer to her. "Sounds good to me."

We spent a good hour chitchatting and laughing in that kitchen. I met her brother and only needed one, "Pllllease, Mommy?" from Ivy to say yes when they invited us to stay for dinner. We ate pizza with the four adults plus Maddie. At some point, I mentioned running and then had to wave off Liv and Erin's exclamations over me being in the marathon next weekend.

Ivy turned to her friend. "My mommy is fast," she said seriously.

"Aunt Livi can sing," Maddie replied calmly. "And Erin can turn a cartwheel."

We all laughed at their discussion, but I flat refused Liv's offer to come cheer me on at the race. She pouted but then grinned. "Fine. We'll go out after."

"Maybe," I said. "I don't know if I'll have the energy with work the next morning."

"We'll see," she said.

Work blurred past that week. Mom had dance plus another date with Martin, who she described as "nice." Ivy seemed to be loving school. I dropped in on the chat app once a day, liking it more and more as I developed connections with the parents. I mentioned my thoughts about the common bond of a shared school to them. Many agreed that some kind of unifying experience would be cool.

The following Sunday, I was up before dawn to make the starting line. The weather had finally broken just a few days ago, so I got a crisp fall morning to start my fifth marathon. My playlist was on fire, and the shoes I'd chosen for this year's run kept my legs fresh. I crossed the finish line two minutes faster than the year before.

What really mattered were Mom and Ivy standing there, cheering like I'd just won Olympic gold. We celebrated with brunch at The Pancake Pantry before I went home and crashed into a deep sleep.

My phone jolted me from my slumber. "Hmm?" I mumbled as I swiped at the screen.

"Bar Forty, seven pm. I'm buying you a beer, and you can tell me how it went."

I blinked at the caller ID. "Liv?"

"Damn right, girlie. Put on some sexy pants and be there. Ever heard of the group You & I? They're playing tonight in your honor. Not really, but still. It's a good excuse."

My head swam. "You and I? I love them."

"They're gonna love you, too. See you tonight!"

Once I showered, I spent forever in my closet. I'd Googled Bar 40 to learn it was a lounge downtown known for live music. Sure enough, You & I, the hot local music duo, was playing tonight. But what did someone wear to a bar on a Sunday night? Finally, I picked black jeans and a black tank top with a denim jacket. I walked out to the living room to find Mom and Ivy on the sofa.

"Do I look alright?" I asked Mom.

"Pretty, Mommy!"

We laughed at Ivy's vote. Mom nodded. "You look like a young woman going out with friends."

"I feel like an old woman who never leaves the house."

She rolled her eyes. "Time to change that, then. You're taking a taxi?"

"Yes, ma'am."

"Good. Be safe, and text on your way home."

I kissed them both and went out to the waiting car.

There was a line outside of the venue, but Liv had instructed me to go straight to the bouncer and give my name. Sure enough, the rope lifted, and a hostess walked me right inside. I followed her to a private table toward the back with another velvet rope around it. As we approached, Liv stood and let out a wolf whistle that made me laugh. She was seated beside Will. The table was full except for three empty seats. I took the one between Liv and another woman who seemed to be there solo.

Liv spoke up after I put in a drink order. "Okay, so. Aaron, Mel, Nick, and Celeste." She pointed in turn. "Friends, this is Juliette—uh, Jules."

"Either is fine," I said with a wave.

But Celeste's eyes widened. "Oh, Jules Twenty-Seven! Right! You're in the beta group for the app. Sorry, Liv, I know you said that. But it's cool to put a face to a handle. Thanks for doing this for us."

Liv leaned over while I shook Celeste's hand. "Celeste is the CPO for the app," she said in my ear. "She's an artist, and a phenomenal coder."

"Oh, wow. Okay. Thanks for working to create a product for parents."

If Liv didn't look like a kindergarten teacher, Celeste would have never struck me as a wealthy chief product officer of a company. I looked around at the other three at the table. *What do they do? Music megastars? Astronauts?*

But Nick spoke up with a smirk. "Hang on. You're a mom? You don't look like a mom."

Funny. Y'all don't match who you are, either. It was easy to think it about them, but his comment jolted me. "I don't?"

"Nah, you look way too cool to be a mom." He laughed.

Mel rolled her eyes. "Stop stereotyping her. Moms come in all shapes and sizes. You've met *my* mom." Another eye roll.

Nick made a purring sound. "I have indeed. Although if I remember right, the one who *really* met your mom was—"

"La la la," Mel cut him off suddenly, hands over her ears. The rest of the table died laughing.

I looked to Liv, totally lost. She shook her head. "Guys, we're confusing our new friend. Try to stop talking in inside stories for a minute, please?"

They all flashed me regretful smiles. I waved it off. "No worries, and you totally don't have to. But forgive me if I just sit here smiling politely."

"Not at all, Jules," Celeste insisted. "Tell us about you."

"Not a lot to tell, I'm afraid. Outside of being a mom, I'm pretty nondescript."

"False." Liv's voice was loud and flat. "How can you say that when you're an exercise physiologist who just ran a freaking marathon?"

That got the table buzzing. They asked me about my job but focused mostly on today's race. When I motioned it was my fifth marathon, they looked at me like I'd walked on the moon.

"Fifth?" Liv echoed. "You didn't tell me that part!"

"That's fantastic," Will said. "How do you fuel for it?"

"I use block chews. They're better for you than gel. And chocolate milk as my recovery treat."

Aaron spoke up. "Tell me, Miss Jules. Is it true what they say about chafing nipples and lost toenails?"

I shuddered, and they all laughed. "Unfortunately, it can be. I've got a toenail that's on its way out right now. Want to see?"

Aaron shrieked, which was exactly what I wanted. "Lord, no child! I like my feet callus-free and ready for sexy times. How does your baby's daddy feel about ragged toenails to suck on?"

The whole table turned to stare at him. Aaron looked around. "What? Am I the only one into that?"

"Yes," came the general response.

He rolled his eyes. "Amateurs. You don't know what you're missing. A pair of pantyhose and feet wrapped around my—"

"Aaron! Stop!" Liv wheezed, she was giggling so hard. "We have a new friend. You're going to scare her away."

The whole table was red with laughter. I was red, too. Half from giggling, the other half because holy shit, did people really talk like this? These guys were funnier than a scripted show and more relaxed with each other than a family reunion. Plus, they were all so attractive. Not just physically, although they were. They were good people, and it radiated out of them without having to be announced.

Do I fit in here? Can I fit in here? They were so lovely that it was worth my best shot. So, I channeled a little "Miss Jae" energy and flipped my hair.

"Aaron, my dear. You can be into all the foot play you want. But if you insinuate that an arrogant flake sperm donor shares my bed again, I'll be forced to question your judgment."

His eyes went wide before his jaw dropped dramatically. Finally, Aaron began to applaud. "Oh, my god. That was amazing! Olivia, you have found us a keeper." He feigned bowing down to me, then Liv.

Liv threw her arm around me and raised her glass. "Hell yes!"

We quieted down soon after because You & I took the stage. I loved their music but—of course—had never heard them live. They were even more incredible than I'd imagined. When their show ended, our table was on its feet, shouting louder than the rest of the room. We sat back down, and Aaron nodded toward the stage.

"We're going into the studio in the new year. Get ready for another album, friends."

And that's how I learned that Aaron was their manager. When You & I themselves sat down in the two empty chairs at our table, I nearly passed out.

But David and Kira were just as wonderful as the rest of the group, and we spent a long time talking and drinking together. I found out that Nick and Mel were a music producer and author respectively. When Liv asked how work was going, though, they both set their mouths into a line.

"What?" Liv asked, and I was glad I wasn't the only one who lost the plot.

"No, it's good. Just... a certain someone has had a come-to-Jesus moment. I'm worried about him. Sorry, can't say more." Mel shrugged.

Liv's fingers moved under the table while she nodded at this. A moment later, my phone vibrated.

Liv: She's talking about Jesse Storms. You looked lost. Thought it would help. ;)

I worked to keep my brows from flying over my hairline.

Jesse Storms, the singer? The freaking superstar? What does he have to do with these people?

... Are you really surprised? They seem to know literally everyone.

I shook my head and typed back a "thx" before trying to follow the conversation again.

It was quite late when we finally rose from that table. Most of the bar had cleared out. I fumbled for my phone, more than a little tipsy and most definitely exhausted. But Liv linked our arms and insisted Will would take me home. I tried to protest but wound up tucked in the back seat of a sleek Audi.

"This is a nice car. Sorry, I'm a little out of it," I mumbled.

Liv and Will chuckled. "Don't worry, girl. You earned it after running about a hundred miles today. I could never have done that," Liv said.

"You don't run? I figured you would with CrossFit."

I sensed a pause in the conversation even though my eyelids were heavy. "We've gotten into cycling," Will said. "Even did a bike tour of California as part of our honeymoon last year."

"Oh, gosh, you're newlyweds? Congratulations. Liv, everyone was so nice. *So* nice. This was *so, so nice.*" I knew I was gushing.

She laughed again. "They're great. You've got to meet the rest of the crew, though. Megan and Luke are traveling right now, and Ben and James were busy tonight. Oh, and then we'll have to go see Cellar Door play sometime soon, too, of course."

"God, you know literally everyone. Who are all these people? I can't keep them straight. I need a visual."

"It'll make sense over time. You'll just have to keep

hanging out with us to get the whole picture." She blew me a kiss over her shoulder.

My eyes watered. "You are so nice. This meant a lot, that you'd want me to come out with your friends."

"Hush, silly. You deserved to celebrate!"

We rolled up to my house, and Liv hopped out to give me a hug. "Schedules these days are kind of hectic, but I'm serious, Jules. I'll text you soon, and we'll do something."

"I work six days a week. I might not be able to," I warned.

"When you can. No stress. And we'll get Ivy and Maddie together again soon, yeah?"

"Sounds great."

Mom was on the sofa when I stumbled inside. She grinned at my tipsy ass. "Fun?"

My tears leaked out. "It was so nice, Mom. I felt so..." I put my face in my hands and cried. "So young and fun."

Her arms were around me, guiding me to sit. "I know things didn't turn out the way you'd planned, honey, but you're allowed to be both of those things."

My fuzzy brain flashed back with sharp clarity to that day in Knoxville. Sitting in a shitty apartment, seven months pregnant and more alone than I'd felt in my life. I'd called Mom the day before to tell her I was quitting school and going to find a job up there. Brad and I were still pretending to tolerate each other, and it seemed like a plan.

A knock on the door had shaken me out of my thoughts. Mom had marched in, grabbed my shoulders, and squeezed till I gasped. She informed me in no uncertain terms that I would be moving home *that day* to live with her. I would finish school online. Mom had been retired from her nursing job for years. She worked part-time as a consultant for an insurance company, which mostly meant phone conferences. She didn't blink as she explained that *we* would raise my child and that I wasn't going to compromise my future on some "foolish plan based on hormones or pride."

So if Annette Reid said I was allowed to be something, I tended to listen.

Mom patted my back, bringing me out of my memories. "Ivy is doing great in school. I'm having a blast with dance, and I have no problem babysitting anytime you need. You're working like a dog right now. If you can steal an evening here or there to go let loose, don't hesitate to do it. You hear?"

"Yes, ma'am." I sniffled again and staggered down the hall to the bathroom.

"There's water and aspirin on the counter," she called after me with a little cackle.

"You're a saint, Dorothy Mantooth," I answered, pulling a line from *Anchorman*. I grinned when she laughed again.

At least the room didn't spin when I laid down in bed. I had a shift that started in five hours, but my mind wouldn't sleep. I pictured that table at Bar 40. The way they laughed at my jokes and made me laugh, too. I pictured sliding into the seat like I owned it. Like of course there was a place for me with such lovely people.

And then I pictured what I shouldn't. The dream I only let myself have on my longest days. My hand drifted to my throat and closed around the pendant I still wore every day. I pictured that table in Aruba that overlooked the ocean. His hand on my leg. His eyes lit with amusement at my silly stories. The way he smelled. The unreal pleasure of his fingers running over my skin.

Just before I drifted off, the fantasies merged. On the precipice of sleep, my hand still clutching that necklace, I dreamed of the table at Bar 40 with Liv on my right and Jay on my left. His arm around my shoulders, both of us laughing at Aaron's latest story.

What a dream.

18

JAMES

"What have you got for me?"

Liv waited. Her brows knitted together.

"Liv?" I asked at last.

"Oh, sorry. I just... I figured with a question like that, you'd pin an innuendo joke to the end of it. Something like, 'I hope it's black and lace and tucked in your purse.'"

I barked a laugh. Ben and Celeste followed, and Liv cracked a smile.

Liv was a sport at bullshit and gave as good as she got. But this wasn't a party at Ben's old apartment or a hangout at Bar 40. This afternoon, Liv was seated in our conference room downtown. She'd just come from work, so all of us were in professional mode.

"Damn, you're right. I should've been all over that. I guess this whole running a company thing has me off my game. Next time, don't you worry. I'll have something special saved for you, Liv, baby."

"There's the James I know and love," she said with a smirk. "Okay, okay, for real though. I have something for you to chew on."

I snorted. "Now you're just daring me to lose focus."

They all laughed again.

Liv tossed her dark hair and pulled out her phone. "The parents are really liking the app. Most of my class has asked to join by now, so I've given them access. They give me feedback every week or so. But I've also got a couple of parents from the other class on board, and they're into it, too."

I nodded. My idea to expand the app into a website with niche circles wouldn't just encompass Liv's suggestion for an app for parents. It would open up tons of pockets where people could connect for a purpose.

It seemed fucking perfect. The team was on board. Liv's focus group was one of several niches in beta already, but I was leaning on her to really make this part right.

Hearing that it was "good" and people liked it didn't give me much to work with.

But then Liv gestured to her phone. "Luckily, my new pal is insightful AF. Ahem. 'What would give us a common experience beyond our kids being in the same class?'"

I cocked my head. "What? They're parents. Isn't that the point?"

Liv put her phone down and cut her eyes up, thinking. "No, it makes sense... Jules is saying that they bond over the fact that their kids are having a similar experience at school. Otherwise, it would be more generic. Why chat on this platform when other sites have groups, too? If they aren't in the same class, what does *Chat Me Up!* give them to connect over?"

I stared at the table as she spoke. Silence fell in the room. I knew everyone was looking to me, but I pushed back from my chair and went for the door. "I have to think about this. Later, guys."

Since founding *Chat Me Up!*, I'd earned the right to be a

bit eccentric. The truth was, I had always brainstormed like this. Just in the past, I was conscious of social conventions. Vanishing to get lost in my head had looked more like declining invitations. Now, I could do whatever I needed in order to think things through. Storm out of a meeting to go for a six-mile run with Max. Put a *Go Away!* sign on my office door.

Disappear to the islands for a month.

This time, it was the run with Max.

I got home as fast as I could and changed into running clothes. Max leapt around when I grabbed my sneakers. Australian Shepherds had damn near boundless energy. Max had a treadmill in my gym just for him, but I still wanted to give him as much of my time as I could. It wasn't uncommon to find him in the offices with me. The only reason I didn't take him to Aruba was because I figured he would freak out to fly.

I rescued this red merle beauty when he wasn't even a year old. Aussies are one of the most rehomed dogs because people want lap dogs, and Aussies want to work. I admired that personality and thought it was shitty to give up on a dog just because he did what he was born to do. Max and I had gone through obedience training until we had an amazing rapport. The other thing about these dogs was their unyielding attachment to their people. My 60-pound boy slept at the foot of my bed—only because I wouldn't let him sleep on a pillow. Ben laughed about that after he kept him while I was away. He warned me it would kill my dating life.

Joke was on him. I didn't bother with one of those anymore.

Every single time I went running, I spent the first mile or so picturing my island dream girl running past my villa that morning. Picturing her beside me on the trails near my house.

Aw, hell. Just picturing her.

It was partially the running and mostly the fact that this activity gave me time to think. And anytime I had that chance, odds were I'd spend at least a little time wondering where she called home. Kicking myself for not getting any fucking details that would let me find her. Replaying those perfect days and nights with the most amazing woman I'd ever met.

Who could fuck around with dating? I'd already had the best.

What did Liv say? Focus, man. Focus.

Max darted off the trail after a squirrel. I whistled, knowing he'd be at my side in moments. *Why chat on this platform... why us... what do we give people...*

By the time we were back at the house, I had it. I called Liv, still breathless.

"Your buddy. Ask her what she thinks about brain games. A learning product that parents could buy."

Liv sucked in her breath. "I'll ask her, but *I* think it's fucking genius."

"Aw, Liv. I know I am." I blew her a kiss and hung up with her laugh in my ears.

By the first of November, Luke had done his homework as our marketing mastermind. He confirmed that we had an audience for a physical product. Which led me to dream up a *Chat Me Up!* game for adults. Which led us to scout a game company that could make anything we wanted.

We were on fucking fire. Even more than before.

Celeste schemed up designs for my ideas. Ben worked on the interface for an online game while we figured out the physical product. That put Luke on an aggressive travel schedule to market-test the prototypes.

It was beautiful.

It was also exhausting. None of us were the type to sit on an idea, and so we found ourselves working long hours and turning down invitations to hang out. Finally, the Friday before Thanksgiving, Celeste came into the office waving her phone.

"Nick says if we don't come to Friendsgiving next Friday night, we're fired from the group. Told me to pass the word."

I laughed. "Fair enough. Tell him we'll be there."

I spent the holiday running with Max and eating with my parents and sister's family. Ben and Celeste spent Thanksgiving with her parents. Friday, I worked all morning and kind of got lost in it. By the time Max whined to go out, I realized it was dark. I jumped up, let him out, and hurried to shower. The party started an hour ago. Now that I lived out in the country, it would be another hour easily before I got there.

I texted the group.

> Me: omw, guys. Sorry, running late. ETA 1hr

My phone chimed as I hopped into my jeans.

> Liv: PUNK! I wanted you here with bells on an hour ago!

> Me: Patience. A little anticipation never hurt anyone. ;)

She sent me the middle finger emoji.

It was 7:30 by the time I parked and knocked on Nick and Mel's apartment door. The whole crew was there, sipping drinks and nibbling delicious-smelling food. We'd started this tradition last year and agreed to rotate who hosted going forward. It was pretty awesome, and I finally felt the laser focus I'd had on work begin to loosen.

I made the rounds, kissing cheeks and saying hello. Liv was in the kitchen, glaring at me with Celeste by her side.

"You were supposed to be here like three hours ago," she greeted.

"Is Will neglecting you? I'll go have a talk with him if you—"

She groaned, and I flashed a wicked grin.

"No, jackass. I wanted you to meet Jules. She literally just left a few minutes ago."

I cocked my head. "Jules? Who's that?"

"Ugh, I *told you*. Jules is the one in my focus group who said the thing about the shared experience. The one who's put you in a total rabbit hole for like two months? Sound familiar?"

"Oh. Why was she here?"

Celeste shook her head. "You know, when I met you, I didn't think you knew how to do anything but flirt. I thought *I* got in the zone with a project. But you literally shut out all noise when you're working, don't you?"

"Basically, yeah." I shrugged. Apologizing wasn't even an idea. Why would I apologize for something that put me on top of the freaking world?

"Dammit, I hate it when you impress me," Celeste teased.

I blew her a kiss.

Liv waved. "Ahem. Jules was here because she's my new friend. She's hung out with us several times lately. I keep hoping you'll be free so you can meet her. She's awesome. Super funny. I think you'd like her. Although why in god's name I'd try to set someone up with your hopelessly flirty ass, I really don't know."

Her cheeky grin made me laugh even as I shook my head. "Setting me up? Really, Liv? Surprised you can stand the thought of sharing me with someone else. Unless you're suggesting..."

Both women pushed me for that one. Ben walked up while I pretended to collapse into the wall. "Telling him about Jules?" he asked with a wry glance at me. "She seemed cool. A little quiet, but hey."

Liv shook her head. "She was exhausted. She works two jobs and had a long shift today. Plus, she had to leave because her mom couldn't babysit tonight, and... and I'm not making her sound like the awesome, funny person she is, am I?"

"Sounds responsible, I'll say that." Who was I to judge someone for working hard and taking care of a kid?

"So does that mean I can get you to make an appearance sometime soon and finally meet her? If nothing else, I figured you'd want to ask about her thoughts on the platform."

I blew out a breath and ran a hand through my hair. "Yeah, I'll talk to her about the product as soon as I can make a hangout. Sounds good."

They all three stared as if I'd just spoken a different language. Fair enough. It wasn't like me to dismiss the idea of getting to know a new girl.

Well. It wasn't like me before that damn weekend in March, at least.

"I'm too busy for much these days," I said with a shrug. "But anyway, where are those ham biscuits?"

The party flowed on with music, food, and good conversation, just like all of our parties did. We'd grown and changed a lot over the years. This group had started with Ben, Nick, and me. We'd met Jack Spencer thanks to Ben and Nick's work in music. Jack's band was Cellar Door, but he was good friends with David Underhill, who brought us Kira Ireland—You & I. They were just a local open-mic duo when we met. Now, they were out on tours every other year and had hundreds of thousands of followers all over the world. Cellar Door, on the other hand, had a strong local following, but their real work was running their own studio in town.

Then Ben had started dating Liv right after he finished college. She was still in school. They didn't last too long, but Liv and her best friend Megan remained in our crew. She and Ben decided they were better off as friends.

Then, Ben met Celeste. And from there, my friends had fallen like dominos when it came to settling down. Nick and Mel got together next, followed by Liv and Will. We brought Luke Paris on as our CMO, and now Megan Riley was soon to be Megan Paris. Somewhere in all of that, David and Kira went from strictly professional to seriously in love, too.

I'd been to more weddings in the past several years than I could hardly count.

I never envied them. Never wondered if it would be my turn sooner or later. Jack and I were the only bachelors left standing, and we both seemed good with it—not that we ever discussed relationship status or anything. It never made sense to me why you'd want to change your life for someone.

It still didn't. But it sure as hell made sense now how you could find someone who hit different than anyone else. How one person could change the way you thought about connections.

And I'd only had a few days with her.

Celeste sat down beside me while Nick and Jack strummed their guitars. She caught my eye and nodded toward the kitchen, so I followed.

"What's up, sis?"

"I just wanted to ask. Are you okay, James?"

I winked. "I'll back myself as above average, thank you very much."

That got me the eye roll I wanted. "Seriously, goofball. I've noticed for a few months that you seem... different. Sad? No, not sad. Like... I don't know. Like you're looking for someone out of the corner of your eye."

My stomach clenched, but I held a neutral expression. "That's pretty poetic."

She wrinkled her nose. "Yeah, a bit. Sorry. Hard to put my finger on—don't say it. Don't you dare."

"What?" I asked innocently.

"'I've got something you can put your fingers on.' I know you well enough to know that's exactly what you were thinking."

I laughed at that. "You're not wrong. How can you say I'm sad? I'm still on my game if you can read my mind that well."

"Yeah, but it's not the same. I don't know. Am I hallucinating?"

My smile dimmed. "I'm good, sis. But thank you for worrying about me. Promise I'm always ready to make your eyes roll—however you'd like to interpret that statement."

"Jesus Christ, you're the worst." A giggle burst out of her.

I held up my hand for a high-five. "You love me."

"I do. And I'm here if you ever want to talk."

I forced my breathing to stay neutral. Dammit, why hadn't I moved on yet? Why did all of my fantasies feature that honey-streaked hair and those whiskey-colored eyes? Why couldn't I find the energy or interest to even talk to women these days?

You're busy with work. You'll get this project off the ground and find time again.

But as I lay down in my bed and let my mind fill with memories of ocean air and the sweetest moans I'd ever heard, I wondered if that were true.

19

JULIETTE

I stumbled over the doorway and into the kitchen. Mom frowned and pressed her hand to my cheek. "That's it. I'm staying in. Martin can just—"

"Take you dancing, is what he can do," I mumbled.

"You're working too hard, honey. Ten hours today, five yesterday, five more tomorrow? It's too much. We don't need the money."

"I made the choice. I quit my job when I thought I was moving to Arizona. I'm not freeloading, Mom. It's fine."

Okay, so I had burst into exhausted tears when I saw my Thanksgiving weekend schedule. Steve had taken advantage of my days off at the receptionist job. Opening shifts three days in a row with Friday being a double. Why, why, why had I given up my job at the downtown fitness center when I knew I didn't love Brad? When I got a queasy feeling every time I thought of moving to Arizona?

It had been part of the plan.

And so, working twenty hours in three days was how I spent my Thanksgiving weekend.

I shooed Mom out the door and trudged to greet Ivy in

her bedroom. She had been missing me more lately. This afternoon, she'd had a meltdown when I left to go to Liv's Friendsgiving party. I'd been half an hour late and frazzled by the time I soothed her into a nap with the promise of special bath time when I got home.

She had not forgotten. Her bath toys were all lined up on the sink. So, I ran her a bubble bath and let her play until she was pruny and smiling. Then, I piggybacked her to bed for two stories. "Okay, sleepyhead?" I asked when her brown curls were tickling my arm.

Ivy pulled my glasses off. I only wore them for reading, so they stayed in her room most of the time. She put them on and said, "Mm-hm. Can we have pancakes tomorrow morning?"

I sighed. "Nana will make them for you. Mommy has to work."

My god. The devastation in her eyes. My heart cracked as her chin wobbled. "Mommy, no." Two alligator tears slipped out.

"Shh." I kissed her forehead. "I'll be home at lunchtime. How about we make a pizza together tomorrow night? And then... what if we asked Maddie to come to the park with us on Sunday? I'll be home all day. Would that be good?"

The tears still shimmered, but Ivy paused her crying. "Mm-hm," she sniffled.

I got her to sleep with extra cuddles. By then, it was after eight, and I was about to pass out cold. But instead of dragging to the bed, I ran another bubble bath—this one for me —and eased into the hot water.

Liv had so many friends, it was hard to keep track. I think I'd met most of them that day, but it seemed like there was always a new face and name to remember. *Who did I meet today? Oh, right. Jack. Jack and... ugh, I don't know.*

Celeste's husband. Ben, I think? Damn, he was handsome, even though I saw him about two seconds before Liv whisked me away.

And then there was the absent guy. The big brain behind the company. Who's brother? Celeste's?... No. Nick is Celeste's cousin. Ben's? Maybe. So who was Jake... James?... Jay?...

Oh, Jay.

I let out a huge sigh as tears pooled in my eyes. I knew it was exhaustion, but that didn't stop the ache in my chest. The yearning for fairytale moments instead of the cold, grueling reality of this autumn.

Tears leaked out, and I squeezed my eyes tight and shook my head. *Make it to January. Then, things will change. The full-time position is all but guaranteed. That means you'll give your notice at Christmas and finally be back to the life you were building. It won't be massages and orgasms on the beach, but it'll be a good plan again.*

One more month. I could make it.

Six a.m. shift be damned. I lay in my bed and reached into my nightstand. The couples energy at Nick's apartment had left me feeling lonelier than ever. Since I was, in fact, alone, the only person to touch me was me.

So, I did.

I skimmed my fingers over my face and down my neck. It felt awkward at first, but the longer I did it, the better it felt. I toyed with the necklace chain and tried to recall how his voice had sounded when he whispered to me.

Such a filthy little tease...

"That's it." I sighed and let my fingers trail lower, teasing my nipples until I throbbed between my legs. Imagining the sexiest gray eyes I'd ever seen, lust-drunk and pinned on me. Watching me turn myself on. Imagining him murmuring encouragements, telling me to play with myself.

Telling me I'd never feel lonely after all the things he'd do to me.

And then imagining the way it felt when he did all those things to me.

Left me spent and craving more. Blanked my mind with unending pleasure before, during, and after each round. That cock in my mouth. In me. Those hands in my mouth. In me. On me.

"Oh, god," I mumbled and finally switched on my vibe.

I barely touched the toy to my clit before I went off. Waves of pleasure hit me, arched my spine, and made me gasp his name. The name I knew for him, at least. It didn't matter what I called him. He would always, *always* be my dream guy. My fairytale.

When the last of my pleasure subsided, I dropped the vibe into the drawer again. Within seconds, I fell fast asleep. My alarm would blare far too early, but that little session of me-time gave me the boost I'd need to get through this weekend.

By the time we had our tree up, the full-time position was a guarantee. I could quit my retail gig on Christmas Eve, take a freaking break for a week, and then get into a regular 9-5 groove with benefits and paid vacation time in the new year.

Thank. God.

Mom wanted me to quit the coffee shop as soon as the guarantee came through, but I was nervous. What if it disappeared suddenly, and I was back at zero? No. Better to tough it out and keep saving. Stick to the plan.

And, of course, there were presents to buy. Ivy had been so good all year with my comings and goings, with her sperm donor father hitting the bricks and never calling again, and with starting school and adjusting to it like a champ. I wanted to buy her a pony, I was so grateful for her sweet, adaptable nature. Not to mention feeling like I owed Mom a kidney for being so supportive and helping with Ivy like she did.

Nope. A few more weeks of retail it would be.

But that meant that my tiny social life had to wilt again. The holidays were very special to our family. I didn't want to disappoint Ivy by bailing on traditions if I could help it.

Liv all but insisted I meet up with her the first week of December, though. I resisted but finally agreed to drinks on Tuesday night, when Mom didn't have plans and not much was going on.

I walked into Bar East, not far from my house, and spotted Liv in a booth. Across from her was another woman. I slid in beside Liv, who gestured grandly.

"Okay, so I know I've introduced you to a lot of people, but you must meet the queen of all queens, Megan Riley-soon-to-be-Paris. Megs, this is my new best friend, Jules."

I startled at that label. Megan glared at me as she shook my hand. "So, I've been usurped, hmm?"

"Oh, gosh no. Liv talks about you like you hung the moon. She's *way* over-inflating my position."

Of course I'd heard of Megan Riley. Liv talked about Megan like they were sisters. I knew the reason I'd not met her yet was because she and her fiancé had been traveling a lot thanks to the *Chat Me Up!* expansion.

I ordered a cocktail and settled in. It was nice to realize I no longer felt like such an intruder among her friends. I even had Celeste and Mel's numbers despite being too busy to hang out for now. It was definitely part of my new year plan to budget more time for social events. With a consistent work schedule and actual weekends, I could be with Ivy plenty and still take Mom up on offers to babysit.

"How's Luke? Where have y'all been this time?" Liv asked Megan.

"Chicago, California, and Idaho—strong usership in Boise. Things are great. I mean, damn woman. They're cutting you in on this, right?"

She wrinkled her nose. "We haven't discussed it."

"Olivia. Ugh, fine. I'll have my lawyer call you, and—"

"Whoa, Scrooge McDuck. These are my friends. I just had an idea I thought they could use."

Both Megan and I frowned at her.

"I don't know the details," I said at last, "but if you helped them create this expansion, then yeah. It would be decent of them to credit you somehow. Wouldn't it?"

"Jules is right, babe. Tell those Addisons that you want shares of the company."

"Okay."

Megan whipped out her phone. "Matter of fact, I'm calling him now."

Liv tried to snatch her phone, but Megan jerked away. After a moment, she smiled. "Well, hey yourself... Piss off. The wedding is definitely still on, and I don't need a getaway car." She giggled and rolled her eyes at Liv, who seemed to understand. "This is about money, so listen up. My best gal fed you some brilliant ideas, and you need to—yep. You read my mind. So... okay. Right. That sounds right. Now, apologize for not bringing it up yourself."

She held out her phone but didn't put it on speaker. The voice was nearly drowned out by the bar's ambient noise, but we heard a man faintly shouting, "Sorry, Liv! You can have a piece of me anytime you want!"

I clapped a hand over my mouth as a giggle burst from

me. *Who is that? What corporate exec makes a joke like that?* Knowing Liv, it made sense that he'd have a sense of humor.

Liv groaned and shouted toward the phone. "This time, babydoll, I'll take you up on it."

Megan put the phone back to her ear. "Her people will be in touch. Laters. Muah." She set the phone down. "Now that that's done, I'll tell you—holy shit, girl. This whole games idea is huge."

"Games?" I asked. "Also—Scrooge McDuck?" I also wanted to ask about this innuendo-cracking person, but I didn't want to push too hard at once.

"Oh, never mind Liv and her silly nicknames," Megan said, and Liv snorted. "Games. Wait—you don't know?"

Liv nodded at me. "Your comment about bonding over an experience was gold. *Chat Me Up!* is creating products to go with their forums. They're starting with educational games for kids but also doing, like, conversation games for adults to keep the social element going."

"Wow. That's... because of what I said about a shared experience?"

Liv nodded and arched a shapely dark eyebrow at me. "I'll have to get you a cut, too."

I waved that off. "I certainly didn't expect something like a product to come out of that conversation! It was just a thought."

"Mm-hm, but that's what he does. He takes an idea and runs with it."

"And makes innuendo jokes. That was—Ben's brother, right?"

"Yep. And yes. He's the *worst* with innuendo jokes. But I still really want you to meet him." She grinned wickedly.

"Ugh, seriously? I've got enough on my hands with my

skeevy manager leering at me. Plus, some of the cardiac patients at the clinic are chronic old flirts."

Megan laughed. "Chronic flirt is accurate. If you're not into that, you're not into him."

I can be into it, actually. And I can dish it out pretty good, too. I sipped my drink and kept the thought in my head. But suddenly, I was curious to meet this mysterious man, if for no other reason than to put a face to the stories.

No, ma'am. You are not fooling yourself that the head of a huge company is anywhere near your league. Leave it alone. Let life happen on this one.

Megan spoke again, pulling me from my thoughts. "So mark your calendars and get out your best dresses, gals. Can confirm *Chat Me Up!* is hosting a big bash for New Year's Eve to announce the product launch. Black tie."

"Is the black tie bit their idea or yours?" Liv asked.

Megan smirked. "I mean, I do love a reason to put a bunch of guys in tuxes. Besides, it's New Year's Eve. Why not snazz it up?"

"Always thankful for your commitment to top-shelf eye candy." Liv laughed and high-fived her friend.

"Wait. Sorry, I'm lost. You're... how are you connected to this whole thing?" I rubbed my forehead.

Megan hesitated. "My fiancé is the CMO. I... well. I'm an investor. It's complicated."

"Y'alls whole group is complicated." I breathed a laugh to lighten my tone. "I can't keep it all straight."

"You'll come to the party and finally meet everyone at once. Right?" Liv bumped my shoulder.

"I'll try. We usually go away on New Year's, but maybe."

She frowned. "Shoot. I don't want to ruin a vacation for you."

I shook my head. "Nah, it's a family cabin with Mom's

sisters and their kids and grandkids. I just need to see if Mom will take Ivy on her own. If not, maybe I could find someone else to watch her."

"Oh, you can totally bring Ivy with you. It would be fine, right Megs?"

Megan nodded. "Sure. We can work with that."

I laughed out loud. "Spoken by non-parents. The idea of a child in the middle of a black-tie event, up at midnight... no way."

Megan rolled her eyes, but her smile was kind. "We'll have a babysitter staffed in that case. There are ways to handle this."

I shut my mouth. That hadn't occurred to me. But then, I wasn't in the habit of orchestrating ritzy parties—or funding them. I took another sip and nodded. "I'll come. One way or another, yeah. I'll come."

Liv squealed and hugged me. "What a great way to celebrate leaving that shitty coffee shop job!"

"Trading an apron and cap for champagne and a gown?" I grinned. "Count me in."

I told Mom about the party as soon as I got home, including the option to take Ivy.

She laughed in my face.

"Hey," I said with a smile. "I'm being responsible here! Don't laugh at me. I don't want to assume anything."

She pursed her lips. "I had my twenties. Jules, you have spent years working yourself to exhaustion—none more than this year. My family didn't up and move to Arizona. My daughter parents her child and works two jobs. I'm gifted with a beautiful granddaughter who is pure joy. Seeing you go out and live life is a delight. You will go with your friends. Ivy and I will ring in the new year with her cousins. She's going to have a blast—just like her mom will."

I threw my arms around her. "You really are the best. You know it?"

"Enough about that. The real question is, what will you wear?"

We plopped down on the sofa and opened Rent the Runway on my phone. An hour blurred past while we scrolled through endless options and finally wound up with a set of five options to order.

A black-tie New Year's Eve to end this wild and wacky year. Why not?

The next three weeks blurred past. I got more duties at the medical office and started meeting potential clients. My head swam with new names to learn half the time and coffee orders the other half. I tried to keep up with texting Liv about the gala, but after sending her my dress options, I really didn't reply much. Every time I thought of her, I promised myself that I'd get together with her the week between Christmas and New Year's. Maybe she knew where I could get my hair cut before the party. My hair had gotten super long lately. No time to think about a salon with my work schedule. I didn't have the time or energy to think about much until my last shift.

My auto-pilot life probably didn't help the morning I got into a wreck.

A week before my last shift at the coffee shop, someone ran a red light, smashed my front right side, and spun me around. It wasn't my fault, although I'm sure my reflexes weren't the sharpest. At least I wasn't hurt, but my poor little Mazda took a beating. I was two hours late for work and had to get a car home. The auto-body shop confirmed almost immediately that my baby was totaled. Insurance would, of course, take time to process the claim.

Since Mom was taking Ivy to school each day, my 5:30am departure became 4:30 so I could take the bus.

Even with all that, before I knew it, I was waking up for my last shift. My last two trips on the bus. My last day wearing that apron. Last hours with Steve and his wandering hands and eyes. Last time counting the hours before I could escape. After today, I would have over a week off. Then, I'd be doing what I loved for a living. And, making it even better, the insurance money came through. I would have a car before starting my job. I already had it picked out —another midnight blue Mazda 3, just like my last one. Tomorrow was Christmas and my first Saturday off in forever.

Liv had texted that her friends were doing a casual get-together that night at Celeste's place. I'd told her I was a maybe. At that moment, a few hours of being social sounded fun.

I pulled my uniform black cap on my head and nodded at the mirror. "It's going to be a good day."

20

JAMES

I went for a run Christmas Eve morning. It was supposed to snow a little later, and I wanted to get Max a good workout.

Ben and I had a meeting with our lawyer that day. Production was on schedule for the games. We'd found a company in New Jersey that made everything in the USA. Luke and I were flying up Monday to tour the facility in person and attend a shareholder's meeting in New York.

The meeting with our lawyer was simply a sign-off on a few agreements in the long paper trail that was running a company. Since it was Friday and Christmas Eve, we scheduled it for noon with the idea of taking the afternoon off. Ben and Celeste were hosting a get-together later. No need to push hard at the moment.

The day was cold and dreary, but I still loved the woods around my house. Max and I did our usual five-mile loop, and then I showered and dressed for work in a button-down and trousers. Because it was so cold, I pulled on my wool driving coat and flat cap before giving Max a good pet.

"Be good, boy. I'll see you later."

He licked my face.

My car purred to life as I eased out of the driveway, and I grinned. I loved this baby so damn much. Living this far from the city was a bit of a pain, but driving was pure fun in a machine like this.

I was zipping along the interstate when Ben called. "Glenn says there's some heinous traffic inside the four-forty loop around the city. He's asking if we can meet at a Starbucks in Brentwood to avoid downtown. I'm at home, so it works for me. Cool?"

"Yeah, sure. Just text me which Starbucks, and I'll meet you there."

Ben's Mercedes was parked outside the free-standing Starbucks that shared a parking lot with a Kroger grocery store just off a main road. He exited his car as I got out of mine. We both glanced up at the sky. Gray clouds hung low, making the day gloomy and all-around unpleasant. The kind of day where you really just wanted to be in front of a fire.

"We should go skiing next month," I said out of nowhere.

"Yeah, that could be good. Get this product rolling and take a break. We need it."

"Hell yeah."

He glanced at his phone. "Glenn is two minutes out. Let's go get coffee."

The place was spacious, with booths that would be good for a quiet meeting. But as we shuffled along the queue, I noticed the tables were filling up. Ben and I traded a glance, and I nodded.

"I'll hold our table. You get the drinks."

I staked the back corner booth. It was the most private one in the place, so perfect. From this vantage point, I saw Glenn walk in, but I couldn't see the counter. Ben appeared from around the corner, holding one cup and sipping from it.

"Where's mine?"

"They said it'd be a minute. I gave them your name."

"What'd you get me?"

"White chocolate peppermint mocha with sprinkles and whipped cream, of course."

All it took was me opening my mouth for him to laugh.

"Kidding. Venti Americano with oat milk and an extra shot. As if I don't know you."

"That's better," I grumbled.

Glenn walked up and handed us each a copy of the agreement with several flags in it to discuss. We got through the first four before I looked up, realizing my name had never been called.

"I'll be back. Y'all keep talking." I slid out of the booth and went back to the line. When I got to the cash register, I nodded at the man with the little ponytail and felt tie. "Hey, uh, I had an order for a Venti Americano a while ago and never got it."

"Oh, my gosh. I'm so sorry. *I need that Venti Americano on the fly!*" He shouted the last line down the counter toward the espresso machine, then gave me a saccharine smile. "That'll be right out, sir."

It felt a little aggressive, but I shrugged and wandered over to peer at the mugs while I waited. The espresso machine whirred and burbled. In just a few moments, Ponytail Guy said my drink was up. I walked to the end of the row just as the barista called out.

"Venti Americano on the fly for—"

My hand was outstretched before her voice completely died.

I think I died, too.

Whiskey-colored eyes widened under the brim of her black ball cap. Her face turned the color of the cup in her hand. We stared at each other for an eternal moment that was probably only a couple seconds.

Finally, I cleared my throat and croaked, "James. My name is James, love."

The cup fell from her trembling fingers. It crashed to the floor and made her jump back. She muffled a cry, and I leaned over to make sure the coffee hadn't burned her. There were only a few splatters on her shoe and pants—nothing too alarming, I didn't think.

Ponytail Guy marched over, hands on hips. "What the hell, Juliette? How hard is it to make an Americano, sweetheart? This gentleman is tired of waiting."

She looked at him, her lips moving over silent words. Finally, she shook her head.

I leaned into my palms on the counter, just to have something to anchor me to the world in that weird moment. I bit my tongue, ready to burst into maniacal laughter. "It's fine, really. I—"

But he barreled on, his tone growing angrier. "Get the mop and clean this mess up. Then, go ahead and clock out. You're done. Just go home."

She limped away toward the back, and I glared at the dude. "That wasn't necessary." My voice had gone cold, but he just gave me that saccharine smile again.

"I'll get that drink for you now, sir. One moment."

"You know what? Forget it." I turned around and strode back to my table. Halfway across the café, I stopped moving as the reality of what just happened hit me.

It's her. It's her. Is it her?

It was definitely her. My girl. I... what am I going to do?

I stumbled the rest of the way to the booth and slumped

down. Ben did a double-take when he saw me. "What's wrong? Did you see a ghost or something?" he asked.

"Kind of," I mumbled. I tried to refocus on the agreement, but it was all a blur of words and highlighting by then. My brain was doing nothing productive. Glenn paused to take a call, and I turned back to Ben. My eyes pleaded with him for something I couldn't name.

His brows drew together. "What the hell, dude?"

"I... It's..." I glanced back toward the front. I couldn't bear the thought of her mopping, not that I would've seen from this vantage point. But as I looked up, I saw her standing in front of the counter, pushing her hat and apron toward Ponytail Guy. She nodded once, her gaze cast down, and then shuffled to the exit.

I jumped to my feet so fast, my knee banged the table. I didn't even register the bruise.

"I have to go. Can you take care of this? I'm sorry, man. I just—I have to go. Now. Right now." I grabbed my coat with shaking hands.

"Sure, but—"

I didn't wait for the end of my brother's thought. I just booked it the hell out of there.

She was already across the street, sitting at the bus stop with her elbows on her knees. I noticed the taillights of a bus disappearing over the hill as I jogged to her. My pace slowed when I stepped onto the sidewalk, but I had no idea what to say. Her hair curled around her shoulders, flattened against her scalp from the cap. Even in the fresh air, I could smell coffee on her.

"Go away, please," she whimpered at last, not looking up. "I know it's you, but can you please just leave? This is too embarrassing for words."

I blew out a breath. "Uh, no. Afraid I can't do that."

She was silent another long moment, then covered her face with her hands. Her shoulders trembled. A sob escaped her at the exact moment icy rain started falling on us. She held a palm out to feel it and sobbed again, curling into a ball so tight that she looked like a turtle.

I dropped to my knees in front of her. No way would I touch her in this moment, but I was desperate to stop her crying. "Shh, please, love. Don't cry."

Dammit. That made her sob harder. "This was supposed to be a good day. The start of something new, not a coffee-soaked clusterfuck. Oh, Christ, *go away.* You're not supposed to be here. You're not supposed to see me like this. This cannot be happening."

She hugged herself tighter while I sat back on my heels, stunned. "Jae," I started, but she shuddered and sobbed again. "Jae, please."

"Jae," she echoed, finally looking up. Her red-rimmed eyes glittered with fresh tears, but at last, she managed a watery smile. "Miss Jae."

Before I could smile or speak, those eyes shut tight again with another shudder. Her mouth curved down. "No. That's not me. You have the wrong person."

I cleared my throat and stood up. The rain had soaked my knees on the pavement by then. "Be that as it may, it's raining, the bus just left, and there's no cover on this bench. So let me take you home."

I held out my hand, and she stared at me like I was speaking Mandarin. I twisted my lips. "Don't look at me like that. Just come get in the car," I said softly.

She sniffled hard. "Really? I mean, no. No, I couldn't. The next bus will be here in..."

"In?"

"Thirty minutes," she mumbled, gaze back on the pavement. Another shudder racked her.

"Right. So I guess you'll either sit out here in the freezing rain or go back inside and chat with that asshole with the cheap tie. *Or*, you can come get in my car and let me drive you home. I know which one I'd choose. What will it be?"

I realized then that I'd been holding my hand out like a putz for too long, so I jammed it into my overcoat. After another long moment, she sighed and stood. Her face tilted up to stare at me. Rain droplets shimmered on her hair and mixed with tears on her cheeks. Her complexion was pale and splotchy all at once from crying.

And she was still the most beautiful girl in the world.

I wanted so damn bad to hold her. To pull her close and feel her hold me. Give me some bit of evidence that this was real and not all a strange dream.

She looked away again. But she nodded as she did. "If you don't mind, then yes. A ride would be lovely."

She followed me to the curb, her gaze still lowered to the point that I had to hold out my arm to stop her from walking right into traffic. She jumped, and I glanced over to give her a look that didn't need words with it. A tight, grateful smile flashed in return just before she pulled her hood up to keep the sleet off her. It was coming down harder by the minute, so I popped my collar and touched her shoulder. "Let's go."

A sideways glance as we walked up to my car let me catch the way her jaw went slack. I half cringed, half smirked at that. In Aruba, I'd deliberately kept the fact that I stayed in a luxury villa, over twice as expensive as the regular room, a secret. Now, I couldn't pretend even if I wanted to. So I just went with it and opened the passenger door for her. She looked the car over twice, cut a quick glance up at me, and then shook her head and slid inside.

Oh, my fucking god. Twenty minutes ago, I was in a meeting about operating agreements. Now, I'm sitting beside... what the hell did that prick call her?

I dropped into the driver's seat and took a long, slow breath. Too many questions mingled with too many comments. Add in the vague screaming in the back of my head chanting *holy shit, holy shit, holy shit* over and over again, and my brain was a noisy place to be at the moment. I took another steadying breath as we listened to the sleet on the roof.

She stirred, and I snapped to life. "Sorry, let me just send a quick text."

"I can go ins—"

I waved my hand to cut that off and tapped my phone.

Me: Let me know if there's a problem. Otherwise, I'll be over later.

Ben: It's good. Are you okay?

I darkened my screen and turned on the engine. "So, where to?"

She gave me an address in East Nashville that GPS said would take thirty minutes with traffic. I couldn't decide if that was a painful eternity or far too brief a commute. But with the sleet coming down and Nashville drivers unaccustomed to such conditions, I had enough to focus on.

The silence in the car quickly became unbearable. She still had her hood up and was burrowed in her seat, arms crossed. I cleared my throat. "Did the coffee burn you?"

Headshake.

"Good. Did I get you in trouble?"

"No." Her voice was barely a whisper. "That was my last shift."

"Oh."

Silence fell again for a good fifteen minutes. Finally, I blurted, "Are you going to talk to me at all?"

Her head turned toward the window. "No. There's no point."

"Excuse me?" I barked the words harsher than I'd meant to, but *dammit*.

"What's the point in talking? This isn't real. This has to be a crazy nightmare. When I wake up, I'll work my last shift, go home, have a bath, and look forward to a normal weekend for once. This is supposed to be a good day. There's no way this can be real—that I can be sitting here, soaked in coffee and rain, and looking like I've been on a journey to the inner ring of retail hell in this beautiful car. Fate couldn't possibly be so cruel as to have my dream guy show up in a literal chariot when I'm like *this*."

Her voice started soft and dreamy, but her words ended cracked and broken. She covered her eyes and whimpered, "There's just no way I'm that cursed."

"I'm your dream guy?" I meant to tease her, but my voice was hoarse and far too full of hope to be playful.

She sniffled and lifted her left hand off her face to present a middle finger to me. I breathed a laugh and shook my head. At least her weeping stopped.

Too soon, I turned onto her dead-end road and swung into the driveway beside a one-story brick house.

At least she didn't tuck and roll out of the car.

I blew out a breath. "I hate that you think this is a nightmare. Can we talk for a second?"

She rubbed her eyes. "You were supposed to remember me in sexy dresses and bikinis. That's the fairytale. Not—*this*." She gestured to her body. Her upper lip curled in disgust.

My throat tightened, roughening my words. "I'm a lot of

things. I'll admit that. But I'm not a big enough douchebag to give a shit about what you're wearing. The only thing I care about is the fact that, my god. *You*—you, of all people—are sitting beside me right now. Do you have any idea what that means to me?"

Just saying it made me lose my breath. I made a fist and pressed it to my lips. "Please don't leave," I begged, unable to finesse it in the least.

She sat, silent and motionless, hidden in her hood. Finally, she took out her phone and began to type. "Give me your number."

I recited it. "And my name is James. You can call me Jay if you—"

Her hood bobbed with a nod. "I heard you the first time. At Starbucks." She pocketed her phone and reached for the door. "I'll call you."

"When?" I asked before she could open it.

"Don't wait on it. Seriously, don't. It won't be soon. I've got too much going on right now. Too many changes. I can't deal with... I can't. But I will call sometime. And you can tell me about your fantastic life. How you hate that our timing is so awful, but you've just started seeing someone and..." She trailed off and shook her head. "Whatever. It's all fine. Goodbye—*James*."

"No, Jae, wait. I—"

She popped the door open but then paused. Suddenly, she shoved her hood off and squared her shoulders to me. My gaze combed her face, thirsty just to look at her again. She took a deep breath and adjusted her coat, tugging the zipper a little lower.

Revealing the flash of blue stone at her throat.

The necklace I gave her. My head swam. I wanted to grab her by the shoulders and lick her mouth until she couldn't see straight. But all I could do was stare at that gorgeous face.

Her words almost didn't register, I was so overwhelmed. I scraped enough brain cells together to hear her flat, dead tone say, "My name is Juliette. I'm a real-life person with a real-life job. This coffee-soaked, humiliated, exhausted woman who's getting out of this *un*real car is called Juliette. Please don't romanticize me."

"No, but I—" Whatever ended my sentence didn't matter. She was gone.

Her front door shut with a thud that I could hear inside the car. I crashed back in my seat and palmed my eyes, hoping she'd come back and knowing she wouldn't. At last, shell-shocked, I drove away.

21

JULIETTE

I unlocked the door with shaking fingers. Mercifully, Mom was in her office, and Ivy was napping. I whisper-shouted that I was getting a shower as I passed Mom's office door. As I went, I managed to type a mostly coherent text to Liv that I was sick and would miss the party that night.

In the bathroom, I stripped out of that fucking uniform and threw it in the trash. Still shaking, I reached up and unclasped my necklace. *Dammit, he saw it. I know he did... I'm gonna throw up. Oh, god, what just happened? He was supposed to be a memory. Okay, a memory I ache for sometimes, but still. He sure as hell wasn't supposed to witness my coffee-soaked, sleep-deprived ass get yelled at for losing a fucking Americano order. Oh, god, I am so embarrassed.*

Before I lost it, I put music on the Bluetooth speaker we kept in there and cranked the shower on full blast.

Then, I crawled into the tub and bawled my eyes out.

22

JAMES

East Nashville was my old stomping ground. I'd never gone down Juliette's street, but she lived just a few minutes from Ben and Celeste's house that backed the river. Hell, she lived just a few minutes from *my* old apartment.

What were the odds?

I was way too early for the party, but I couldn't think of anywhere else to go. No way could I make the drive home in my condition and this weather. I stumbled up Ben and Celeste's walk and stabbed the bell. Celeste opened up. Her brows drew together at the sight of me.

"James? What's wrong?"

"Ben's not home yet?"

"Not yet. Come in."

She took my coat and hat and guided me to the decorated living room. I paced like an animal in a cage for a few laps, finally coming to stand in front of her. My eyes slowly focused on her worried face. Hesitantly, she put a hand on my arm. "James?"

I bit my lip and realized I was shaking. My eyes burned. I couldn't breathe right. If this was a panic attack, I was most definitely having one. "Celeste," I begged with no idea how to verbalize this.

The next thing I knew, I collapsed in her arms. She was over six inches shorter than me, but I bent down and let her wrap me in a hug while I buried my head in her shoulder. Never in my fucking life had I felt so *overwhelmed*. So helpless. I held onto my sister-in-law and tried to control my breathing. For all the flirty lines I'd teased her with since we met, there was nothing but platonic comfort in her embrace.

"Hey. Come sit down." Her voice was muffled in my chest, but I stepped back and let her lead me to the sofa. She disappeared for a moment and returned with mint tea that I promptly put on the table. I needed to stop freaking out before handling a hot beverage.

Celeste cocked her head. "So... who is she?"

I huffed a laugh. "What makes you think it's a she?"

Shrug. "Why else would you look like that? If it were about the company, I'd have an idea of something. This is out of nowhere. So if it's not scandalous ruin, it's heartache."

"Fair. It's not scandalous ruin. Production is on schedule and the agreements all look good."

"Great. But screw that for now. What's going on? Was I right at Thanksgiving? Sad, right?"

I shoved a hand through my hair. "I... don't know how to explain this. It's so unbelievable. I can't..."

"There you are." Ben walked in while I fumbled for the story. He frowned at me. "What's wrong? You freaked me out earlier."

My brother never freaked out. I cringed. "Sorry. Just... yeah, I can't explain this right now. Sorry, guys."

"You almost look sicker than Nick when he and Mel were separated," Ben said lightly, and Celeste chuckled.

"Hopefully not as shitty as you did when you two broke up," I replied with a twist of my lips.

Ben rolled his eyes and sat down, pulling his wife into a hug. "That never happened."

"Bullshit." I laughed again and calmed down a little. We were talking ancient history on both accounts, but damn. I remembered well my guys in their dark moments. It was not a pretty sight.

Shit, do I really look that bad off? I sucked in a deep breath and reminded myself I was a fucking boss. A boss who had no reason to melt down over this woman. She wasn't mine. She was a stranger.

She still had that damn spell over me.

I stood up to go take a piss. "How can I help with the party? Put me to work. I'm fine. I swear."

I was very fucking far from fine.

This was painfully clear by the time Nick and Mel arrived with Liv and Will not far behind. I was in the kitchen, surrounded by my favorite people, and all I could think about—*all I could fucking think about*—was having her sit beside me. How ridiculous it seemed to be talking about music and TV shows when she was just a couple miles away. What the hell was I doing, going through the motions of life when I was this wrecked?

The whiskey called my name big-time, but I knew if I got started, I wouldn't stop. And I had to get home that night. Besides, there was a non-zero chance that a few drinks would loosen my lips in a way I was *not* prepared to experience at the moment. How in the holy hell could I ramble out this unbelievable story to my pals? Where would I even begin?

This girl stole my lunch down in Aruba, see. And, funny thing. This morning at Starbucks...

No. Way.

As the place filled up, Liv walked up to me with a drink in her hand. She frowned. "Are you sick?"

"A little, I think."

"Hm. Something must be going around."

I didn't ask for more on that.

She tried again. "If you're sick, get out of here. No cooties for Christmas, thanks."

I laughed. "Good point. You're probably right. I better beat it before I bring the rest of you down with me." *Into my existential crisis. Are those catching?*

She held up an elbow for me to bump. "I've got your date for the gala, by the way."

I groaned and walked toward the door. "Yeah, yeah. Fine. Whatever. Pimp me out. I'll see you then, if not before."

"Merry Christmas, James!" A bunch of people chorused at me as I headed for the door. I gave Celeste and Ben a Look that told them enough. They frowned and nodded at me, but we'd see each other the next day.

The cold air braced me and sharpened my senses. The streets were dry by then—no snow had fallen. I wound slowly through Ben's neighborhood and out to Gallatin Pike. My playlist was on a random classic rock shuffle. I was nearly at the ramp to Briley Parkway when "Beautiful Boy" by John Lennon came on.

Life is what happens...

"I will call sometime."

While you're busy making other plans...

"And you can tell me about your life. How you hate that our timing is awful."

"Goddammit."

I jerked the wheel to the left. The car behind me let me know exactly how much of a piece of shit he thought I was by laying on his horn. I couldn't blame him, but I also didn't give a fuck. I spun the car in a hard arc, tires squealing. I nearly spun out but kept control, bringing the wheel back to a straight line at precisely the right moment to wind up in the left lane, facing the opposite direction.

"God*dammit.*" I flexed my fingers on the wheel and gunned the engine.

It was nearly dark when I pulled up in front of her house again. The windows glowed warm and yellow, with a Christmas tree in the front. I cringed and said a silent apology to Max. *Extra pets tonight, buddy. I'll be home soon.* With a deep breath, I killed the engine and hurried up the walk before I could wuss out.

There was no doorbell or peephole. Just an old-fashioned knocker, which I rapped three soft times. No response, so I tried again and heard a faint "Coming!" from inside. The door cracked open, and I stood up straighter and adjusted my collar.

A woman peeked out from behind a chain lock. "Who is it?" Her voice was loaded with suspicion.

"Um, sorry. Is Juliette home?"

She eyed me again. I saw her brows arch, and then she shut the door and reopened it fully this time. The woman could only be Juliette's mom. She had the same oval face and delicate but sharp jaw. Her hair was a softer brown than my girl's. It didn't have those honey-blonde streaks, either, but still. Most definitely an older Jae.

Juliette. Right.

I adjusted my cap and wondered why I was fidgeting. "Sorry, ma'am. I know this is weird. I hope I'm not interrupting. I... I just... needed her. Um, to see her. Juliette, I mean."

Her brows ticked up at my bumbling. "Do you?"

All I could do was nod.

She shook her head. "Lord, where are my manners? Come inside, young man. It's freezing out."

I removed my cap and stepped inside so she could shut the door. The living room was to the left and the kitchen to the right. The hallway extended back to other parts of the house.

A little girl appeared from the living room, staring at me with saucer eyes. I sucked in a sharp breath because if the woman was her mom, then the girl could only be Jae's child.

Juliette, dammit!

How many kids do you have? ... Just the one... I'd known then she wasn't joking. But damn if it wasn't a jolt to see her child in real life.

A jolt, yes. But it did absolutely nothing to stop the fluttery, crawl-out-of-my-skin longing I had to see her again.

"Nana?" the girl asked without blinking.

Juliette's mom took the girl's hand and pulled her closer as she spoke to me. "Be comfortable... sorry, what was your name?"

"James, ma'am. Nice to meet you." I shook her hand.

Her cheeks went pink. "Annette. It's a pleasure, James. Please, go have a seat. I'll get Juliette." She pointed to the couch, so I wandered in and perched on the edge.

I sat for a moment in my overcoat before realizing I was sweating. I shrugged the coat off, but sweat still tickled my spine. I heard holiday music in the distance and smelled something wonderful cooking in the kitchen. Then, I heard her voice from a distance, calling to her mother. Even muffled and far-off, her tone was different than I'd ever heard it before. Relaxed and casual. Real, but not sad.

This is a mistake.

Life is what happens...

"What do you mean, go to the living room? I was about to check on the lasagna."

She appeared in the doorway. I was a trainwreck all over again. She wore candy-cane socks, black yoga pants, and a black shirt with holiday gnomes on it that said, *Rolling with my gnomies.* She smelled like a shower, and her hair was in a high, messy ponytail. She wore glasses. I didn't even know she had glasses. The only thing missing was her necklace.

She looked so... normal. So perfect and normal, and it blinded me with an ache deep, deep inside my soul. I wanted to see that face every day for the rest of my life. I wanted those socks in my lap while I tickled her feet and teased her about that silly shirt.

I wanted it so bad, a thrill of panic shot through me. I knew for sure I was about to fuck this up.

"What the hell?" she hissed just before I bolted for the door. "What are you doing here?"

I got to my feet and reached for my coat. "I don't know," I admitted. "I'm sorry. I shouldn't have come."

"That's for sure."

Something about that saucy comeback made me drop the coat again. Instead of booking it out of there, I walked to her, standing close enough that she tipped her face up to look at me.

She wet her lips. "For damn sure," she repeated, but her tone was softer this time.

"I'm sorry," I said again. "I can go."

"You should."

But her words were practically drowned out by the energy that snapped between us. The temperature in the room skyrocketed. I wanted to throw myself at her feet and... I wasn't sure what followed that. Beg her to touch me. Beg her to see me. Ask her a thousand questions.

It didn't matter. I knew better than to be so bold in that moment.

"I just wanted to say..." I started, but I couldn't concentrate. I couldn't do anything but stare at my beautiful, fairy-tale girl. Right in front of me, here in the real world.

"You don't need to say anything."

Her words pulled something useful together in my brain. I blinked and shook my head. "No, but I do. I really do. I don't want you to—"

A timer beeped and cut me off. Her mother shouted, "I've got it!" from the other room, but it broke the energy between us. Juliette crossed her arms and sat on the couch, glaring up at me.

I ignored the glare and ran a hand through my hair. "I don't want you to call me 'sometime.' I was a fool to let you walk out of my life back in March without any way to find you. And now, here you are, and you're telling me *someday* we can talk again. I'm not good with that plan. Life clearly wants us to talk now."

She scowled. "Don't throw my words at me... I can't believe you even remember that."

"Yes, you can. You can believe perfectly well that I remember every single thing."

That softened her frown lines. "Well, but... but what do you want?"

"I want to throw plans out the window and see where this goes. Come with me."

"Where?"

"Anywhere."

"When?"

"Now."

She scoffed. "Nope, no can do. I have responsibilities."

"No! No, she doesn't! She is completely free!" Annette

burst into the room wearing an apron. Her cheeks were flushed under bright eyes. "I'm so sorry to interrupt—I was coming to say the lasagna was ready—but she is free as a bird, believe me."

Juliette slapped a palm to her forehead. "Oh, my god. I'm in *Pride and Prejudice*."

I twitched a smile. "Of course you are. You turned down my proposal in the gazebo that afternoon in the rain, remember?"

She bit down on her lip, but I saw the hint of a smile. "You proposed with a ring pop. What the hell was I supposed to do?"

"Guess it should've been an onion ring."

"Only if you had ketchup."

"Always, m'lady."

We stared at each other, and every single part of my being screamed *yes.*

Annette was clearly lost, and I couldn't blame her. But Juliette shook her head. "I can't go anywhere. Mom has a date, and—"

"I'll call Martin and cancel. It's fine."

"It is not fine! This is a competition and a holiday party. You've been practicing for months. You're going. I'm staying. Easy. If he wants to stay a while, well. I guess that's alright." She jerked her head toward me, avoiding eye contact. Good thing. After that ridiculous exchange, I was ready to pick her up and pin her to the wall.

Annette and I hesitated until Juliette pointed to the hallway. "Go on, get!" she drawled with a grin at her mom. Annette scurried away, and Juliette gestured toward the kitchen. "Follow me if you're staying."

"Wild horses couldn't drag me away, love," I murmured

as I followed behind her. Chills broke on her neck, and I bit back a wicked smirk.

Yes.

Her daughter sat in a booster seat at the kitchen table, coloring and singing to herself. I guessed her around the same age as my sister's daughter, so maybe first grade. Her brown hair was in two ponytails, head bent over the coloring page. When we entered, she looked first to Juliette and then to me. She grew still, put down her crayon, and fidgeted shyly.

"Mommy, the lazana is ready," she said, eyes on me. "I helped butter bread. Nana put it in the oven."

Juliette went to the oven and pulled out a tray. "Good buttering, little one. Are you hungry?"

"Mm-hm."

Juliette left the bread and came to kneel in front of the girl. She cut me a loaded glance and then said, "Ivy, look at me. This man is my friend. His name is James, okay? Do you want to say hi?"

I liked that she gave her the option. Pro parenting move, according to my sister. Ivy looked from Juliette to me and back again. At last, she nodded.

I slid into a chair at the table when Juliette gestured. "Go on, then," she coaxed the child.

Finally, Ivy's whiskey-colored eyes—just like her mom's—turned to me. "Hi," she said shyly.

"Hello, Ivy. I'm James."

She frowned. "Ja-aims."

"You can call him Jay."

Ivy and I stared at Juliette. Her cheeks were pink, but she smiled at her daughter. "It's easier to say, right? Try it."

"Jay. Do you like lazana?"

"Very much."

Ivy nodded at this and then picked up her crayon. Juliette rose and crossed her arms, staring down at me. "My daughter." Two words that dared me to say something.

"You told me you were a mom."

"I said I was lying."

"I didn't believe you."

She narrowed her eyes, then spun to march back to the oven. I rose and followed her, leaning on the counter while she plated the food. At last, she said softly, "Aren't you freaked out?"

"About what?"

She snorted. "I have dated a total of two men long enough to have them meet my daughter. Once they did, I didn't see them much afterward."

"You really ought to stop dating mouth-breathers then."

That got her. Her lips clamped closed, but a giggle burst out. She cut those eyes to me again. I arched my brow and wandered back to the table. Juliette followed with three plates of food. Ivy recited the "God is Great" prayer, so we all bowed our heads. I thanked her, took one bite, and moaned, my eyes rolling back in my head. Ivy giggled, which was entirely the goal.

"Stop that," Juliette said.

"It's fu-fantastically delicious." I liked kids, but I had to remember my language around them.

"So good, Mommy!" Ivy made a moaning sound.

Juliette tried to roll her eyes, but she didn't get far.

Annette appeared while we ate. She was dressed in a black turtleneck with a long skirt and red shoes. She kissed them both and flashed me another grin before hurrying out the back door.

"Where is she going?" I asked.

"Dance competition."

"That's awesome."

Finally, I got a little smile. "It is. I'm super proud of her." That smile flattened fast. "So, what did you want to talk about?"

"Hmm?"

"You said you wanted to see me. About what?"

"I wanted to *see* you. Which I'm doing right now. Did you want to talk?"

She looked down, but I saw the pink on her cheeks. Her lips opened and closed twice before she muttered, "So should I assume 'come with me' was a double entendre?"

I coughed on my iced tea. *Fuck. Yes.* "If you want it to be," I said as calmly as I could for Ivy's sake.

"Stop that."

"You started it."

"Yeah, Mommy, you started it!" Ivy was too happy to chime in on that one.

Juliette groaned again. "You're horrific," she said to me as she cleared our plates. To Ivy, she said, "Well, missy, I guess I'll finish it, too. Time for the dishes."

"I'll do those," I offered.

"Not a chance are you doing housework. I'll be five minutes."

So, I sat with Ivy while she washed up. Ivy told me all about her favorite holiday movies, what she wanted from Santa, and how she'd given a present to Toys for Tots at school. Juliette drifted over and stood beside her daughter while I took in this info.

When Ivy paused her chatter, Juliette said, "Ivy and I were going to watch a movie. Ivy, should we invite James to stay?"

Ivy nodded, but I held up both hands and rose from the

table. "I'm honored, ladies. But I have to get home. My dog is way past his suppertime."

Ivy gasped. "You have a *dog*?"

This was clearly a goal for her, so I nodded and kept my mouth shut about her meeting him. Juliette certainly would've murdered me for that one. The message was reinforced by her death stare.

"Fine. I'll see you out. One moment."

We drifted to the living room. I fetched my coat and hat while Ivy got settled in with *Rudolph*. Juliette set the remote on the coffee table and nodded for me to go to the front door.

In the hallway, she crossed her arms and gave me a one-shoulder shrug. "Without skimpy beach dresses and fruity cocktails, I'm dull as dirt. Got the picture yet?"

"I'm getting one. But we can continue this conversation Sunday."

Her head jerked up. "Sunday?"

"Are you available tomorrow? Felt presumptive with the holiday."

"I'm... yeah, I'm busy tomorrow."

"Are you busy Sunday?"

She pressed her lips in a line. "What do you want from me?"

Her voice was so full of fear and dread that it squeezed my heart. I cocked my head. "Why do you sound so afraid?"

"I am afraid," she whispered. Her eyes shimmered. "I don't know what to make of you being here. I don't believe this. And I don't understand what you could possibly want from me now."

I wet my lips and scrubbed my face. A hundred responses tumbled in my head. At last, I dropped to the bench by the door with a sigh. "I don't know what I want."

Liar. Try again. "I know exactly what I want. But what matters to me is what *you* want."

"I said I'd call you sometime, and you showed up at my house a few hours later."

I had to laugh at that. "Fair point."

She kept her arms crossed but stepped closer to me. A line cut between her brows. "So tell me what you want."

"I... I... I just don't want to walk away from you again. Not without knowing it's the right thing to do."

Those eyes shimmered again. At last, she nodded. "I think it's the right thing to do. But," she added quickly, "I can admit that I'm saying that out of fear and disbelief. Trying to control the plan, if you will."

Finally, finally, she let herself flash a little smile. A ton of tension fell off my shoulders. I stood up so that we were inches apart.

"So can I see you Sunday morning?"

"Yes." The word was barely audible.

"If I tell you that I'm back in this neighborhood tomorrow, can I see you then, too?"

"No."

I smirked. "It was worth a shot. I'll see you at nine on Sunday, then. We'll do breakfast. Sound good?"

This time, the glint in her eyes was a warm light. "Yes. It does."

23

JULIETTE

Christmas was a cozy snow globe of a day. Gifts, food, and playtime with my two favorite girls. It was almost enough to keep me from thinking about him every few minutes.

Almost.

When we were piled on the sofa watching movies that night, Ivy asleep between us, Mom whispered, "So? You haven't said a thing about that handsome caller last night!"

I cringed. "That was deliberate. But, um... you're taking Ivy to church tomorrow, right?"

She nodded. Mom liked taking Ivy to church for holidays and occasions. I had no objection, but I usually stayed home.

"Well... I guess I've got plans."

Her eyes gleamed. "Okay, you must tell me everything."

"I will. Promise. Just... please, let me get past tomorrow morning first, okay? I'm... it's a lot." I rubbed my forehead.

"But that is the guy, right?"

My head jerked to her. "What guy?"

"Aruba guy. He looks like the photo you showed me."

"Wow. Good memory. Uh, yeah. That's him."

"I have so many questions," she hissed.

I giggled. "For sure. I promise to tell all. Just let me get my head around it, please?"

Mom reached over and stroked my hair. "Of course, sweetie. You have twenty-four hours."

I giggled again.

I changed clothes four freaking times the next morning. With every sweater that landed on the floor, I got angrier at myself. "Why are you trying so hard? This is a mistake. I'm not going. I hate this guy. Damn him and that smile. He's probably not coming."

He'll come. After Friday? Yeah. He'll come. Dammit.

At least I'd gotten two full night's sleep in a row. The luggage that usually sat under my eyes was a little improved. Sleep had helped take the nauseous edge off the memories of Friday's coffee disaster.

It had not, however, stopped the bubbly giggles that tickled whenever I thought about that silly *Pride & Prejudice* exchange. Or the stomach-on-the-floor feeling from seeing him in my living room.

I shook my head and finally chose dark rinse jeans and a white sweater. My long hair was getting cut midweek, but I left it down anyway. After I slipped in a simple pair of earrings, I stared at the necklace on my dresser.

All these months, wearing it out of... what? Nostalgia. Not hope. Never hope. How could I have begun to *hope* to see him again? And if I ever once had entertained a glimmer of that thought, it sure as hell didn't feature me soaked in coffee and humiliated beyond belief.

Wearing it had been a reminder of the best time of my life. A reminder of a side of me that didn't have a place in this reality—but that I loved anyway. Outside of running, I wore it all the time.

Now, I debated whether to put it on or not. It would look nice with the sweater. It was mine, and I liked it.

Don't lie. You want him to see you in it.

My mental boss had a point. I sighed and clasped the damn thing around my neck. Then, I stepped into ankle boots and headed to the kitchen. Mom was there, brewing coffee. She smiled when she saw me. "Beautiful."

"Hardly."

"*Totally,*" she insisted. "But he already knows that."

Ivy shuffled in, wearing her Santa pjs. "Mommy? Pretty." She yawned.

I lifted her into her chair at the table. "Mommy's going to see Mister Jay. You're going to church."

"Church? With chicken?"

I laughed. Mom's church always held a potluck afterward. Apparently, there was a lowkey but vicious battle for the best fried chicken in the congregation.

"Yes, with chicken," I said.

Mom groaned. "The message is a bit lost, isn't it?"

"She remembers time with you. That's what matters to me. So you two have—"

A purring engine interrupted me. Mom and I traded a look and went to peer out the front window together. Ivy followed close behind. The door opened on that gorgeous blue car, and that gorgeous man stepped out. So cool in that coat and flat cap. His hair was shorter than in Aruba. Darker without the sun's highlights. He was so different than I remembered—and so the same, too.

Mom gasped. "What is that car?"

Ivy copied her exactly.

"I don't know," I muttered.

"Jules. What does he *do*?"

I straightened up and pushed my hair back. "I'll tell you everything later. Please, Mom. I'm so nervous."

Tears pricked my eyes, and Mom hurried to squeeze my arms. "Shh, shh. Don't stress."

I kissed hers and Ivy's cheeks, grabbed my coat and purse, and opened the door while he was still halfway up the walk. Sucking in a deep breath of cold air helped sort me out.

Nothing could cool the tingles I got when he stopped walking and stared at me.

"I woke up almost three hours ago," he said in greeting.

"For extended tantric meditation, or to practice what ridiculous lines you'd try on me today?"

He made a confused face. "Aren't those the same thing?"

"Fair. They pretty much are."

He grinned and crooked his finger so I'd approach. I walked until we were nearly toe-to-toe. My heart rioted at the scent of him. No salt water and sunscreen anymore, but still deliciously familiar somehow. He gazed down at me with that same searching expression as Friday.

"It is so good to see you," he said at last. "You have no idea."

"Yeah. I really do, though."

That made his brows arch and a light spark in his eyes. I was doing everything I could to stay rational and grounded, but how could I pretend that wasn't true? How could I deny how badly I wanted him to bend down and kiss me, even though I was sure my mother and daughter were still watching?

But he kept his hands in his coat pockets and turned toward the car. "Let's take a drive. I promised you breakfast. Are you okay with that being homemade?"

"I figured you'd be taking me to some exclusive restaurant that only people who drive cars like this have even heard of."

He paused with his hand on the passenger door. "We can do that instead if you want."

"Oh. Uh, no. No. It's whatever. I'm good."

I slid into the seat, and he went around to the driver's side. "Good. I was saving that for dinner tonight."

Dammit, that smile was blinding even in profile. He fired the engine and eased us away from the curb. I kept my mouth shut while we prowled the back roads out to Gallatin Pike. When he took the parkway ramp, I ran my finger along the chocolate-brown stitching on the seat.

"I'm glad it doesn't still reek of coffee in here."

"It didn't for a second."

"What the heck kind of car is this, anyway?"

Another grin, another dip of my heart. "This, m'lady, is an Aston Martin Seven-Seventy coupe."

I wouldn't know until I Googled it later what that really meant. His car was unlike anything I'd ever seen—which, I would learn, made total sense. It started at almost half a million dollars.

I dropped my phone when I read that part.

Unaware of all that, I shook my head and breathed a laugh. "Aston Martin. You really do think you're James Bond —oh, god. You *told me* your name was James." I clapped a hand to my mouth.

His eyes cut to me. "I did better than that, love. I got you to say it."

Electricity shot through me at his unspoken implication. He'd gotten me to *moan* it. "Dirty fucking trick," I muttered.

"Literally, it was."

I couldn't stop my laugh.

We glided along the parkway to the I-65 South exchange.

This time of the morning on a Saturday meant that traffic was light. I debated with myself while he cruised just over the speed limit. When we were well away from the city, I gave up being sensible.

"Is this the fastest this thing will go?"

He snorted.

"Show me."

In a blink, my head was pressed to the headrest, and we were freaking flying. Everything about it was sexy as hell. A grin spread across my face. "Oh, wow."

"That better?"

"Much. If I touched you right now, would we die in a fiery crash?"

He laughed. "While your hands on me would wreck the hell out of me, I've got more self-control than that. I promise you're safe. I took driving lessons when I got this thing. However," he added with another glance my way, "If you want to find out what happens when you touch me, be my guest. Anytime."

I wanted to so bad. So. Bad. But I had a daughter to think of, and the speedometer read 115. So, I crossed my arms and hummed.

We took a ramp about 30 minutes outside of Nashville— at that speed, so probably more like 45 minutes away for normal cars. Right away, we left the interstate behind for country roads lined with bare trees. I gazed at the winter-brown landscape while we wound up a hill. This place was secluded for sure. I'd never once thought of going to a guy's house on a first date. But, just like getting into his car Friday, I trusted him in a way that probably made no sense to anyone else.

And, to be fair, this wasn't our first date.

"Is this where you hide the bodies?" I murmured while

we climbed a hill.

"Nah, it's just where I hide."

We turned onto a long driveway. It ended in a circle in front of a gorgeous cabin made of glass, stone, and wood. Clearly a new build. The garage was built in beside the front door. The side view of the house revealed a spectacular back porch overlooking the hill. I guessed there was a floor below the main one based on that glimpse, but I couldn't be sure.

Jay—*James. It's James, dammit*—parked and shut off the engine. I followed him to the front door, where he paused. "Max isn't going to bother you, is he?"

"I like dogs. Max?"

"For Maximum Effort."

"Like *Deadpool*?"

His face lit with delight. "Precisely. You know that movie?"

"Know it, pissed myself laughing at it, sure."

That light dimmed to a glow. "You are... something else, Miss Juliette."

My name was still strange on his tongue, I could tell. It was weird to hear. Weird, but not bad at all. He looked me over again, shook his head, and pressed his finger to a pad by the door.

Of course he doesn't have keys.

A red-and-white dog with crystal blue eyes sat at the door with a toy in his mouth. His whole body wiggled, but he held the sit until James slapped his thigh. "Good boy. I told you I was coming back."

At that, Max wiggled forward and let James scratch his ears. My heart was doing too many strange things that morning. This little scene melted me about as much as listening to him talk to Ivy the other night.

Being sensible would be so much easier if he wasn't

giving every indication that he was as good of a person as I'd thought him to be back in Aruba.

I petted Max and let him sniff me until he backed off and led us inside. Then, I had to swallow a gasp at the impeccable architecture and décor. Vaulted ceilings, exposed wood, creamy neutral textiles, and a wall of windows overlooking the woods. This place was pure crafts-manship.

He came up behind me and spoke in my ear. "May I take your coat?"

I nodded and hurried to shrug out of it. He put it in the entry closet and told me to be comfortable, so I wandered to stare out the windows. The view was spectacular. Thick forest rolled down below us. The clouds were low, but I could tell that on a clear day, the horizon was far.

Except—"There's no tree in here. No decorations. Do you not celebrate Christmas?"

"No, I do for sure. I was with my family all day yesterday. But Max and I don't have much use for seasonal knickknacks out here."

"That's a shame," I murmured, then turned my attention to the porch. "Is that a fire bowl?"

"Mm-hm. You want me to light it?"

"No, you don't have to."

"Come on."

I followed him to the palatial porch and sat on the sofa where he pointed. He pressed a button, and the fire leapt to life. I hugged myself and leaned toward the flames, but James wasn't done. He opened a storage basket and pulled out an Alpaca blanket for me.

"Wow. This is service."

He hit me with a smirk. "I am a full-service kind of guy. At *your* service, ma'am. How else can I service you today?"

I stared at him, fire building in my chest. "It's been a while since I had a full... tune-up. Been changing my own oil lately."

"Mm. You probably need a complete lube and workup, then."

Neither of us blinked. "If I had a car, I probably would."

"Who said anything about a car?"

I broke first. A nervous giggle escaped, but at least he laughed along with me. He dropped down to sit, close but with space between us, and turned to gaze at me again. "I cannot stop staring at you. I'm sorry. I hope it's not weird," he said through the last of his chuckles.

Bantering with him brought out that other side of me. I tucked my hair behind my ear and leaned toward him a little. My gaze walked up and down him before meeting his stare. "This whole thing is weird. What are you thinking while you stare at me?"

He crooked his lips, and my mouth went dry with thirst. "How honest would you like me to be, Miss Juliette?"

24

JULIETTE

My pulse beat in my fingertips and between my legs. "Brutally, please," I rasped.

He nodded. "I can't stop thinking how random this is. What were the odds of running into you? Hell, what were the odds we both lived in Nashville? Then I think about how much time I've spent regretting letting you leave with nothing but memories to hold on to. I also wonder what *you* think about all of this."

James inched closer, but he didn't touch me. I realized he hadn't touched me once in all of this craziness, and I was aching to feel him. He kept the barrier but leaned close enough that I could see individual eyelashes and feel his breath on my lips.

"And, on top of all of that, I'm thinking about how beautiful you are. How badly I want to touch you. To check and see if you're real because this feels a lot like a dream."

"You regretted that we didn't stay in touch?"

Nod.

"You... thought about me?"

His gaze searched mine. "Jae. Juliette. Every fucking day."

A tear slid down my cheek. I couldn't take this. It had to be a dream. James sat back, frowning while I wiped my cheek. "I'm sorry," he muttered. "I can go make breakfast."

I shook my head. "No, I'm sorry. Safe to say I'm a little... overwhelmed... too. I figured you'd forgotten."

He snorted. "You figured wrong, love. There have been many times I wished I could forget." He paused, then slid me a glance and said, "And you? Dare I ask if you ever thought of me?"

I twined the necklace chain around my finger. "Clearly, I didn't."

He watched my fingers play. "Clearly. So... breakfast?"

"Okay. I'll help."

James waved that off and stood up. "I'll bring you coffee. You just sit and enjoy."

Sit and enjoy weren't really part of my vocabulary, but I gave it a shot. I stared at the fire and the woods beyond the deck. He brought me delicious coffee in a Yeti tumbler to keep it warm. Max jumped up beside me and leaned on my hip, so I petted him and let myself melt into the cushions.

I must've dozed off because I jolted upright when the patio doors slid open. James called my name. Max jumped off the sofa and ran to the door. I yawned and picked up the Yeti from the side table. Inside, the kitchen smelled of baked goods and bacon. My stomach growled.

"Biscuits?" He pointed to a plate of fluffy biscuits on the stove.

"You made these from scratch?"

"No, I popped a can." He shook his head. "Told you I was a good Southern boy. This is my mom's recipe."

I climbed on a barstool in the kitchen. He brought over

plates of biscuits, bacon, butter, and jam. While I picked one up and opened it with a fork, he said, "Tell me who you are by telling me exactly who you are."

Wow. He really does remember a lot. The reference to our last night together was obvious. Back then, it was random details. But now, here, I told him real things. Why I'd been working at Starbucks. Brad's exit from our lives a year ago. How hard the year had been trying to parent a kindergartener and work two jobs. My car wreck. And the fact that I had a full-time job starting in a week.

"Jesus," he said when I quit rambling. "This has been a hell of a year for you."

I paused mid-chew and wrinkled my nose. "It wasn't supposed to be a sob story."

"Not a sob story, but definitely a lot at once. I got the impression back in March that you weren't upset about not getting married. Did that change? Do you regret not moving with him?"

I stared at him like he'd suggested putting grapefruit on pizza, and James laughed. "Guess that's my answer."

"Uh, yeah, that's a huge no. I'm so glad he's gone. For all the stuff that's happened this year, that's one thing I never thought twice about." I took a long sip of coffee and pushed the plate away. "What about you? What has your life been like?"

He nodded. "Busy as hell. Different than it used to be, I guess. I mean, we've been busy for the past three years with the business. But this year, I don't know. I felt a lot more... isolated. Maybe that's just my job, and I'm getting better at it. Maybe I just haven't felt like being as social lately."

"Funny. I'm trying to be more social lately."

"Mm. Dating mouth-breathers, like you said last night."

I laughed. "Um, no. I believe I said I'd brought two

people home since Ivy was born. She's *five*. I meant with friends."

He wiped his hands and set one elbow on the counter to face me. "I see. So... you're... not seeing anyone right now?" His tone was overly casual, but his gaze pinned me in place.

I turned in the chair to face him, too, and put on my saucy smile. I had been about to ask about this business of his, but flirting was more fun. "Mm-mm. And you? Where's your girlfriend this morning?"

James breathed a laugh through his nose, but his gaze didn't waver.

"If you want to find out what happens when you touch me, be my guest." Do it. Do it. It's reckless and dangerous and, god, do I want to touch him.

"When do you have to be home?" he asked.

"Uh, Mom will probably be home from church around one-thirty. So, around then. What time is it now?"

He held up his wrist to show me his watch. Past eleven already. Damn.

"That can't be right." My voice was soft and far away, but that might've been due to my pounding pulse. I held my breath and broke the barrier. My fingers closed around his wrist to pull it closer to my face.

Instantly, the ache between my legs reached new levels. He was warm and so fucking *real*. I hadn't touched anyone like this since our last night together. *How did this happen? How did we find each other?*

The questions wouldn't quit, but they didn't matter in that moment. My gaze stayed frozen over the watch face while I felt his tendons tighten and heard his breath hiss.

"You're right. It has to be a mistake," he said, lips almost brushing my ear. James twisted his hand so that his fingers danced along my palm that held him. Chills sheeted up my arm and all over my scalp. He kept up that slow tickle for as long as I held onto him.

It was nearly impossible to break away. I truly don't know how I managed it. But as soon as I let him go, he stepped back, collecting our plates.

I dug my fingers into my hair and wandered into the living room. He found me staring out the wall of windows. I didn't look at him as I said, "I wish you understood how hard this is for me. I didn't think I'd see you again."

"Didn't think? Or didn't want to?"

"Want to," I whispered with a sad smile.

"Ouch." He flinched.

"No, listen. Try to hear me. I wanted to be perfect to someone. A memory of a wild time. *You* were perfect. I wanted it to stay that way. I wanted to have lived a fairytale of my own, just once. I wish life could've given me that."

"It did." He stared out the window, his voice as soft as mine, like we were in a library. "We got the fairytale. What happened at the beach, happened at the beach. Now, we get to see what comes next."

This whole thing was breaking my heart in the sweetest, most painful way. "But you don't know me."

"Like hell I don't."

"I'm serious. You have to see how different real-world Juliette is versus the carefree vacation version of me you met."

"Sure. You work hard and take care of your family. But you're still you. Don't pretend like I don't know the girl I jumped off a cliff with."

I bit my lip, unsure what to say to that.

"Do I seem different?" he asked.

"Yes and no. I don't think I've seen enough of you yet to put my finger on it."

"You can put your fingers on whatever you want, Miss Juliette."

"Stop that." My voice wavered with a laugh.

He side-eyed me. "Only say it if you mean it."

I threw up one hand. "You know I don't mean it."

We faced each other. He crossed his arms and let his lip curl up. "And you're trying to say I don't know you."

I gestured, trying to get my point across. "Okay, you know a part of me."

"I know lots of parts of you."

"Dammit, listen to me!"

He had the decency to stop smiling.

"I wanted us to be perfect. I wanted the no-names, no-strings-attached fling. I wanted you to think of me as this amazing memory. Now you're seeing the me who buys juice boxes and operates on too little sleep most of the time. You're getting sensible shoes and hair that needs a cut. Messy emotions and horrible, horrible insecurity, especially when I'm riding in that car and you're looking... like *that*." I gestured to his burgundy sweater and khakis. They had no labels on them and obviously cost more than my whole wardrobe.

I swallowed the lump in my throat. "Was that too much to ask?"

James scratched his stubble. "So, what are you telling me? Do you want me to take you home and forget we ever ran into each other?"

"I want a rewind button! To have not lost that stupid coffee order, made it on time, and left it on the counter so we never ran into each other! But I don't get that, do I?"

"No." His eyes glinted like silver at my little meltdown. "So what do you want instead?"

"Isn't it obvious? I want—"

I reached for him. My palms landed on his cheeks, pulling his face down to me. As if I needed to. James bent to me like I was a magnet. His arms swept me up at the same moment our lips crashed together.

I kissed that man like this was my last moment on Earth. My lips pulled, tongue desperate to taste him. I kept his face in my hands even as my whole body shook with emotion. I knew that this wasn't how perfect girls would kiss. That I was far too greedy and desperate to be cool. *Calm down, girl. Calm... down.*

I pulled back with a gasp. "Sorry, sorry, sorry."

"Don't you dare be sorry." James's grunt hit my ears just as my back hit the window. His mouth sealed on mine again, and I realized the frantic tempo wasn't all me. He lifted a hand to my cheek.

He was shaking, too.

My eyes flew open. A line cut between his brows. His cheeks were flushed. I watched him kiss me and felt like I was jumping into that pool again. The rush of adventure. The drop and plunge. *My god, he's so beautiful.*

His tongue coaxed mine to play. I let my eyes flutter shut again. My hands roamed up to his hair, and he sucked in a ragged breath. "What do you do to me?"

"You said I could find out what happens if I touched you."

"Fuck yes," he growled before devouring me again.

James's hands roamed up and down my body. I pressed my shoulders into the window and arched to him while I clawed at his neck. I'm not even sure if I realized it when I wrapped one leg around his, but suddenly, he lifted me in the air. Both legs wrapped around his waist. He slammed me into the glass so hard that I bumped my head.

"Oww," I whined, breaking apart to rub my noggin.

"I'm sorry, baby. Did I hurt you?" His voice was barely more than a gasp.

I stared at him for a long moment, slowly shaking my head no. Then, with a needy cry, I leaned in for his mouth again.

The room spun while we kissed. It wasn't all pheromones. James whirled me around and walked to the sofa. He dropped down, my knees outside his hips. Those broad palms ran up and down my jeans. Oh, his touch. It was heavenly and not nearly enough.

"You... can... kiss me... all... fucking... day," he mumbled.

"Want to," I hiccupped. "Missed you."

He paused to let out a long sigh. Those eyes blinked hard, then slowly lifted to meet mine. "So much, love. So. Much."

My heart couldn't take it. Everything about his tone said this was so much more than lust. Everything about his kiss said that lust had a very healthy place in the moment as well. But that level of affection *and* longing? How could I trust it? Who got both?

Fairytale princesses. That's who.

James cupped my face in his hands. I teetered on the verge of jumping up and running away, but dammit. How could I move when he held me like that? Stared at me like that?

His thumbs stroked and dissolved the tension in my jaw. "If I keep kissing you, I'm going to want to take you to bed. And while I would *very* happily do that, I'm not sure if it's the right next step." His voice was soft. Hypnotic. "I don't want us to move too fast and mess this up."

"Mess... what... up, exactly?"

I held my breath while he studied me. *Do not predict his answer. Do not trap him into saying...*

"Us, of course."

My heart sobbed. My voice was barely audible, even to my own ears. "Do you think there's really an us?"

"I don't know yet. I hope so. And I'm willing to be good to find out." He winked.

"You were always good." I bit back my smile and leaned to whisper against his mouth, "You were the best, Jay."

He sucked in a breath. "You little tease."

"Uh-uh. Not me." I licked his lip, on fire with want.

His kiss was a cup of water on the flames, but it gave me something at least. He gripped my head and held me close, kissing me deep and slow. At last, he pulled away again.

"Fuck," he panted.

"Fuck," I agreed.

I wanted to. But I knew he was right. Going to bed together now would leave me feeling foolish and regretful right after. Clumsily, I tumbled off his lap and onto the sofa beside him. James covered his face with both hands and groaned.

"Should I take you home?" he asked at last.

I studied my hands and nodded.

"Should I kiss you again before I do that?"

"God, yes," I blurted as we reached for each other. He laughed into the kiss, so I tugged his hair. But I couldn't stop my smile from curving, too.

Why is this so easy? It's too easy to be real... right? I mean, I'm out here in a hidden house. It might as well be the princess's palace. Certainly not reality.

Speaking of. My phone rang, pulling us apart with a jolt.

"Jesus Christ," James rasped as I fell over him to reach it on the side table. I sprawled across his lap, face-down, and caught Mom before the call ended.

"H-hello?" The word would barely come out, I was so breathless.

James chuckled and stroked my back, both melting me *and* causing me to clench with tension. Melting won. I lay my cheek on the couch cushion, the phone on my free ear, and gazed up at him.

"... bad chicken..."

"Wait. What?" I blinked and forced my attention on Mom's words.

"Ivy's throwing up. I'm worried it was some bad chicken at the potluck. I don't feel great, either. But I'm okay. Just..."

I sat bolt upright. "Crap. Crap! Okay, I'm on my way home."

James was on his feet with me. I explained as he hurried to get our coats. "Shit, poor kid," he murmured, then called, "Max! I'll be back, buddy!"

We were out the door in seconds and flying down the interstate. I stared out the window and rubbed my forehead. "See? This is what I mean. Making out in a secluded house is lovely. But sick kids and responsibilities aren't us."

25

JAMES

I pinched the bridge of my nose. "Okay, look. I'm just going to say this. What if we're about *both*? Has that occurred to you? You've spent a lot of energy telling me what we were supposed to be. But the way you kissed me tells me you want this just as bad as I do."

"Of course I want it. But look at your house. Your car. You're seriously trying to tell me you're not going to get tired of some lady with a kid after a few dates?"

"What do my house and car have to do with me not being an asshole?"

She blew out a frustrated breath.

I clenched the steering wheel several times and forced my voice to stay calm. "Maybe I wasn't brutally honest enough with you. When I look at you, mostly what I'm thinking is, *my god, I need this woman*. I know you don't believe me. I get why you think your 'baggage' is a problem. It's not for me. Tell me something. Are you wet from kissing me?"

The silence electrified between us until, finally, I heard, "You know I am."

"Precisely. To me, that's worth all the schedule changes, all the complicated things life wants to throw at us. That... and so much fucking more." I breathed a laugh. "The way you make me smile. The light in your eyes. Your head on my shoulder. Your laugh at my ridiculous-ass jokes. Your equally ridiculous jokes."

I wanted to look at her but couldn't take my eyes off the road at this speed. Since she wasn't talking, I went on. "You don't have to agree. That's what matters most. If you don't feel it, then fine. Respect. But I want us clear on what *I* feel. And I feel all that—and more that I can't even name. I want to get to know the real you even better. Maybe we aren't well suited together.

"But maybe, just maybe, we should figure that out instead of trying to map an outdated plan onto the current reality."

"Really?"

Fuck me, the hope in that one word. I nodded.

"Hmm. When you talk like that, it makes it very tempting to put my hands on you."

I smiled. "Not right now. I've got to get you home."

Out of the corner of my eye, I saw her lip poke out, and my mouth went dry. "Are you pouting, Juliette?"

"Maybe," she sulked, arms crossed.

I hummed. "If you want to find out what happens when you put that pretty lip out, then we're gonna need a lot more time alone. Because I will spank that ass red if you want to act bratty with me."

Fuck. Shouldn't have said that. My dick instantly strained my pants. I twitched to turn the car around and play all of that out in my bedroom.

Another long silence before, "Would you really?"

"I guess you can find out sometime if you stop trying to tell me why we're not supposed to see each other."

"Well," she said at last, "I guess that would be an... interesting... reason to see you again."

"Have you been spanked?" I was already hard as a rock. Why not poke the bear?

"No."

"Fuck."

"I... haven't done any of the things you said you wanted from me." Her voice was soft and husky. The car was opaque with tension, and I loved every second of it.

I knew exactly what she meant. Knew, had fantasized about multiple times. Same thing.

"And?"

"And?" she echoed.

"And do you want to?"

"Maybe."

"Fuck! You little tease."

She hummed, but a glance at her revealed cheeks flushed deep pink.

I blew out a breath and put the air conditioner on for a moment. She laughed and leaned her face toward the vent. "Read my mind," she murmured.

"Right, so let's try and focus on the situation at hand. What's wrong with Ivy, and what do you need?"

I felt her look at me. "Mom thinks she got food poisoning. Need?"

"Sure, need. Sprite, saltines, Pedialyte?"

"It's... that's a good question. I'm not sure what we have at home."

I nodded and took the Briley Parkway ramp. "Okay. We'll figure it out. I can go get whatever."

"You? James. You don't need to stay. That's way too much."

I hesitated at that. Was it? Was I being pushy? It hadn't occurred to me that I'd drop her off and leave. Was that a mistake?

Screw it. Do what feels right.

I pulled us up in front of her house and unbuckled my belt. "I'll come in. You can tell me to fuck off whenever."

"I'll just wave my middle finger, and you vanish?"

"Your fingers are magical, so that'll work."

"Stop that," she whisper-giggled as we walked in the door.

Ivy's cries sounded from down the hall. Juliette ran to her like a homing beacon was implanted in her brain. By the time I caught up, she was kneeling next to where Ivy sat in the tub, wearing nothing but underwear and a t-shirt, and hugging a bucket. The room smelled of vomit so bad that I choked, but my girl just pulled her hair into a high ponytail and took the washcloth from her mother's hand.

Annette sat on the toilet, her arms around a wastebasket. The poor woman was a horrible shade of green, but the basket seemed empty. She was speaking to Juliette.

"... been dry heaving for the last twenty minutes, poor thing." She glanced up at me, and a flicker of a smile lit her face for just a second.

"Mommy," Ivy bawled and then retched again.

"I... do you have this? I need... to go..." Annette ran out of the room with the wastebasket and slammed a door down the hall. I cringed as the sound of her vomiting hit my ears.

"Damn," I muttered. "What can I do?"

"I don't know," Juliette said helplessly. "I need to call the doctor. Can you sit with her? See if she'll—ice. I'll get her ice. Hold on."

"I'll get it." I didn't wait for her to say okay before I hurried to the kitchen. They had cubes in a tray, no ice maker, so I grabbed some, put them in a bag, and beat them against the counter to crush them up. Then, I jogged back to the rancid bathroom and pressed the cup to Juliette's hand.

But she didn't take it. Instead, she pressed it back at me. "Try to keep her still while I call the doctor."

We traded places. I knelt by the tub and shook the cup at Ivy. "Hey, Miss Ivy. Tummy hurting?"

She looked up at me, sniveling, and nodded. "Jay."

"That's right. Can I give you some ice?"

Another nod. Except I had no idea how to feed this to her. If I gave her the cup, she'd just tip it all over her face. In the end, I turned her palm up and gave her some chips, which she promptly sucked into her mouth. I handed her some more and left my arm outstretched so she could reach into the cup herself.

She had barely swallowed before she hurled again. Clear liquid with a few chunks of chicken and peas shot out of her mouth, all over my arm and her shirt and bare legs. Ivy sobbed. I cursed under my breath in surprise and scrambled for the cold rag Juliette had left on the counter.

"Hey, shh. It's okay. It's... oh, okay, again, huh? Yeah, I don't love this sweater. Go for it."

"Where's Mommy?"

"She's calling the doctor. Here, let's put this on your forehead. Does that feel good?"

She managed to raise her head and nod at me.

Juliette flew back into the room. I moved to sit on the toilet while she took my place. "The doctor says if she can't keep liquid down in a few hours, we have to take her in. But for now, let's try to get you to rest, okay, Ivy? Are you sleepy?"

"Uh-huh."

I watched in amazement as she grabbed the shower wand and washed Ivy's legs off. Then, she reached for the kids' mouthwash on the sink. She couldn't quite grab it, so I handed it to her. She didn't seem to register me there, but she accepted the bottle, turned to Ivy, and handed a capful to her. "Rinse, honey. Let's get that icky taste out of your mouth."

Ivy rinsed and spit into the bucket, then let Juliette lift her out of the tub. Her vomit-stained t-shirt pressed to Juliette's chest as she whisked her away, singing into her ear.

"Wow," I muttered, stunned at her speed and efficiency.

Juliette was back in the bathroom in under five minutes. Her expression was calm but concerned. "She fell asleep instantly. Mom's puking her guts out, too. Christ."

She blinked at me and cringed. "Shit. Your sweater!"

"Your sweater." I nodded to her pretty white top.

"Forget this old thing. You've got vomit all over you."

I reached back and tugged the sweater off, leaving me in a black t-shirt. "It's fine. I'll dry clean it."

Juliette's gaze flickered from my chest to the sweater in my hand. "I'll... pay... of course."

"Juliette?"

"Hmm?"

"My eyes are up here, sweetheart." I bit back a laugh as she turned pink. "And don't be goofy. I don't care about the sweater. What does Ivy need? Shit, what does your mom need?"

"I'm not sure. Let's see what we have." She turned and jogged down the hall to the kitchen. I followed. She was already in the pantry, peering at a wall of over-the-counter medicines. "We definitely need Pedialyte and Saltines. Probably some grownup and child's Pepto, too... And soup, for when they're able to eat. Ugh, this shirt is gross."

Every single thought about groceries and upset stomachs flew out of my head when she whipped that sweater off right there in the pantry. She wore a lacy white camisole underneath that did nothing at all to stop my feral thoughts.

I hissed in a breath, and Juliette's shoulders went to her ears. Slowly, she peeked at me from over her shoulder. "Oops."

I walked forward until her back touched my chest and bent my head to whisper in her ear. "I'm trying to be good, Miss Juliette."

My little tease shimmied against me. "I told you already. You were the best."

My hands landed on her waist, forehead on her shoulder while I laughed. "Get me a grocery list before I go insane, please."

Her fingers slid on top of mine and squeezed. "Keep your sanity. I'll text you the list if you can go. Oh, let me get my credit card."

That stood me upright. "Please. That isn't necessary."

She bit her lip. "Drug dealer."

"In a way, sure. I deal in dopamine. But that's a story for later. Text me. I'll be back in twenty."

I threw on my coat and jumped in the car. By the time I was at Kroger, she'd sent me a little list. I added her number to my phone and typed back.

> Me: Great. Now send me a selfie.

It took a few moments before:

> Juliette: Sent an image.

"Holy..." I muttered at the phone. It was a down shot of

her in that pantry, dressed just like I left her. Her gaze teased the fuck out of me. Her cleavage had me drooling.

Me: You are fucking stunning.

She didn't reply, but no matter. I was in a hurry to get back anyway. She had thrown on a hoodie by the time I returned, which was probably a good thing. I left the flirtation alone for the moment and took the bag into the kitchen.

Several hours slipped away with her running back and forth between her mother and Ivy's rooms. I stayed in the kitchen, reading about dehydration and prepping cups of ice and, eventually, Pedialyte for both patients.

The first round of fluids for Ivy was a disaster. Juliette staggered out with pink vomit dripping from her hair. I tried to tell her to go for a shower, but she shook that off and accepted a towel instead. The only words I got were quick mutterings about when to go to the hospital.

Thankfully, within the hour, another attempt at fluids stayed down. I leaned in Ivy's doorway with a fresh towel in hand while Juliette held the cup to her little lips. Ivy sat back, and all of us waited. After several minutes, she smiled. "That was good," she whispered. "More?"

Juliette gave her one more tiny sip and then stood up. She had brought an iPad into the room and set it on Ivy's nightstand. Now, she opened the screen and hit play on a cartoon. "Try and be still, okay? I'll be down the hall if you feel sick again."

Ivy nodded. Her eyes were half-open but trained on the screen. Juliette kissed her head and slipped out of the room with me. She went straight across the hall into her mom's room. I hung back for that one, but I could hear them talking. Annette was insisting she was alright, that she had kept the fluids down and just wanted to sleep. Juliette repeated basically the same instructions to her and reappeared in the hall.

When both doors were shut, she sagged against the wall, palm on her forehead. "What a long afternoon."

I hummed.

She looked up at me. Slowly, that glazed, auto-pilot look drained away, and she blinked a few times. "What are you still doing here?"

"Did you forget I was?" I chuckled.

"Well, no, but I hadn't thought about it... Go home, James! My god. You didn't need to stay this long!"

I leaned on the wall opposite her. "I'll go home in a while. First, you should get a bath. I'll keep my ear out if either of them needs anything."

"No way. I can't ask you for that."

"You didn't. Now, go. You're disgusting—and not in the good way."

She huffed a laugh. "True. Okay, I'll be three minutes. Promise."

She stood up straight, but I blocked her path and put my hands on her shoulders. "Hey. Hang on, superwoman. There is no fire. Take your time. I'm here, Juliette. You're not alone, okay? You don't have to do it all yourself. Just go relax for a minute."

That shimmer returned to her eyes. "It's not easy for me to relax or rely on people."

"I'm picking up on that. Then do what you want. If you want to go relax for a bit, cool. If you don't, then sure. Three minutes or whatever."

She took the bath.

Our wards were quiet for nearly the whole half hour she was in the bathroom. Ivy called out for a drink, so I took it to her and waited to be sure she didn't vomit again. Annette cracked her door and asked for ice, so I obliged that, too. She hid in the shadows of her room and rasped a laugh when I came to her door.

"Lord, I'm embarrassed to have you see me like this. Doggone chicken," she croaked.

"Not at all, ma'am. I'm happy to help."

"Thank you." Her voice cracked, and she sniffled. "Ahem. Thank you, James."

I was on the sofa when Juliette appeared in her yoga pants and a tank top. Her hair was in a wet bun. I gave her the update, and she nodded.

"I really don't know how to thank you," she said softly.

"You really don't have to. But you could come sit with me for a minute." I thumped the cushion beside me, pleased when she shuffled over and plopped down perpendicular. Her feet rested on the couch, her back to my side. *Perfect.* I hooked my arm around her waist and pulled her closer, inhaling the scent of her shampoo.

"I can't stay much longer," I said with my lips on her ear. "But I can come back later if you need me. Max can go to my brother's house for the night."

"No, no. I'll be fine. I'm sure."

"Fine isn't the objective. We can do better than fine. If you want, we can be fucking *great.*"

She twisted to hit me with that whiskey gaze. "What if fine is all I get? What if I'm not made for great? What if... we're not... real?"

I stared into those eyes, so many words on my tongue. So many things I fucking *knew* in my soul. And none of them came out. None of them seemed right to say.

So, I kissed her.

"Tell me that's not real," I growled against her mouth.

At last, I stood up and left her on the sofa. "Listen. I have to go. And I have to travel for work this week, unfortunately. But... New Year's Eve. Will you be my date for this party my company is throwing?"

She shook her head slowly. "I can't. I have plans already, and I can't back out now."

"Damn. Okay. So... New Year's Day? It's a Saturday. We could go to dinner?"

"Sure. Sounds good."

She walked me to the door and laid a hand on my arm. "James? Listen. I think it's good we don't see each other for a while. So we can, you know. Breathe. Think. Process all this."

"You're probably right, honestly."

"I promise not to text you so you can have space."

"Text me whenever. I can have space and still hear from you. I've spent the last ten months not speaking to you. If you want to talk, then please. Let's talk."

She hesitated but finally nodded. "Okay. But if... well. If you decide you want to cancel next Saturday, I'll absolutely understand."

I wanted to laugh, but I knew she wasn't joking. "Same, of course. And do me a favor. Kiss someone at midnight next Friday."

"Why?" Her brows knitted.

I held her chin, tilting her face up to me. "So the next time I kiss you, you'll know more about what you want from me. So we're not confused about the magic that happens... right... here."

She sighed when I dusted my mouth against hers, and I smiled. Before she could wrap her arms around me, I stepped back and made myself walk out the door.

26

JULIETTE

Mom and Ivy rebounded by Monday night, thank goodness. That meant that by Tuesday when Liv called, I could say yes to her invitation.

"Winter break vibes, baby! The girls are going to one of those things where you paint and drink tomorrow. Oh, and Megan's down to do your hair in the morning. You in?"

I was most definitely in. I needed things to do to keep my itchy fingers away from the phone. The number of times I had thought of texting James with random thoughts or jokes was unreal.

It didn't help knowing that he'd almost certainly be quick to reply with something that made me giggle, grin, or blush. Or all three at once.

Wednesday morning, I borrowed Mom's car. Ivy and I went to the address Liv gave me for the haircut. It was a house north of Nashville with a salon attached. Megan answered the door with a smile. "Welcome."

She led us inside, where Liv and Maddie were sitting. The girls bubbled with excitement and instantly got lost in playing with their dolls. We coaxed them into the salon so Liv could hang out and keep an eye on them.

"I'm sorry. Investor in a huge company and hairstylist?" I asked Megan in what I hoped was a friendly, not nosey, tone.

She laughed. "I'm a woman of many talents."

Despite that cagey initial answer, while Megan snipped my hair into shoulder-length layers, I got her story. Why she had so much money. How she and Luke got together. It was riveting. Sad, hilarious, and touching all at once.

Then Liv sat in the chair beside me and flashed a little smile. "I never told you why I stopped doing CrossFit."

"You didn't."

"I'll tell you now if you want."

Of course I did. But I was not prepared for the roller-coaster story that Liv spun out. My gut clenched to learn she couldn't have children. The parents on the *Chat Me Up!* group sang her praises all the time for being an incredible teacher. And it was clear how much she loved her niece. But she told me everything with a little smile and finished with, "And here I am." No sobs. No tragedy. She was clearly happy.

I left that haircut with a new perspective on my friends —and a lot to ponder about my own life as well.

It was a quick turnaround to the paint and sip. The studio was across town. They'd booked a 4pm timeslot "because we can this week," according to Liv, and were planning to get sushi after. Mom had offered to let me take her car again, but Celeste volunteered to pick me up since we lived close to each other. I slid into her Mercedes sedan and buckled my belt.

"Is this an EV?" I asked.

"Mm-hm. My new baby. I love it." She stroked the steering wheel and grinned.

"And here I am, excited to get my Mazda tomorrow." I laughed.

"Hey, that's awesome! I'm glad you were able to get a new car so quickly. Sorry I've not gotten to see you lately."

"Nah, that's on me. How's everything?"

We fell into chitchat as she cruised us to the spot. Liv, Megan, Kira, and Mel were all there already, so we grabbed our seats at the round table. A terra-cotta plant pot sat in front of each of us. I'd assumed we'd be painting on a canvas, but no. Fine by me. We had an aloe plant in the kitchen that needed a new home, and Ivy kept us stocked with "art" to hang.

Liv had brought a bottle of rosé. Megan had brought Belle Meade bourbon.

"It's not my brand, but I'll take the whiskey," Mel said.

"Shoot, me too." Liv set the corkscrew down before she'd opened the wine. "Jules? Celeste?"

"I don't usually drink straight spirits, but okay." I held out my plastic cup.

Celeste left her cup on the table. "No, thanks."

Every one of us whipped our heads to her.

She blushed and shook her head. "Not yet. Trying."

They drew the attention of everyone in the room with their shrieks. Celeste waved frantically to try and calm them down. I didn't shriek, but I grinned until my face hurt. When the excitement subsided, we toasted her and Ben and got down to painting. I happily worked on my pot and let them talk.

I just wished my mind would stop going back to James.

Give it a freaking rest. You need to clear your head. That's why you're out.

"Jules?"

I jolted out of my thoughts and looked over at Kira. She

was so kind. It was easy to forget how starstruck I was when we first met.

"I asked how your Christmas was. Did you get to feeling better? Liv said you were sick on Friday."

"Oh. Yeah. But Mom and Ivy got food poisoning." I got them groaning with that little story and finished with, "But otherwise, it was... good."

Megan snorted. "Sound a little less sure about that, Jules."

I winced. "Sorry. Just got some stuff on my mind."

They gave me sympathetic nods and steered the conversation away from me. But as I continued to paint, something occurred to me—I was always making excuses. "I'm so tired... I'm too busy... I've got things on my mind."

Every one of these women worked hard and had a lot on their plates. Who didn't? What made my situation extraordinary? Sure, being a single parent was a huge task, but Mom was so supportive. What right did I have to excuse antisocial behavior? They all made time for each other. They didn't sit around complaining about how tired they were.

"I'm sorry," I said out of nowhere. I set my brush down as they fell silent and looked at me. My cheeks heated, but I repeated myself. "I'm sorry. I don't mean to make so many excuses for why I'm not a good friend."

Celeste, Mel, and Kira hurried to reassure me. Liv's and Megan's eyes narrowed in thoughtful stares. "What do you mean by that?" Megan asked when the other three quieted.

"Y'all invite me to things. Include me in your group. And the best I can give you is a maybe, usually coupled with an excuse about how tired or busy I am. That's shitty, and I apologize. I'm not sure when I became that person, but I'm realizing I don't like being her."

Megan's blonde eyebrow arched. "I respect you for saying that. Massive respect. Funny the things we tell ourselves about our situations, isn't it? The labels we put on ourselves that really don't help anything at all."

"Exactly." She and I tapped whiskeys. I smiled at the other women. "I can be a better friend. I'll work on it."

That got me a round of toasts. I took a gulp of bourbon, picked up my brush again, and blurted, "It's a boy. That's what's on my mind. I have boy problems."

After a single beat of silence, the table erupted in questions and exclamations. My face got even hotter, but I laughed at their excitement.

Liv slapped the table. "Dammit, you minx! How did you keep this from us? I want every filthy detail right now."

Celeste held up her painted pot. "We're nearly done here, though. Save it for dinner?"

Liv groaned and pointed her brush at me. "You are the evening's entertainment. You got that?"

"Yes ma'am," I said shyly.

We finished our pots and relocated to a nearby sushi place called Maru Nations. When drinks and edamame were on the table, five pairs of eyes fixed on me.

"Start at the beginning and don't stop until you get to the end," Liv declared.

Oh, god. How do I really start at the beginning? "I hit on this guy in Aruba..." No. No way.

"I, uh, met a guy last spring. It was a few months after Brad took off—Ivy's dad—and I wasn't looking for anything serious. We, uh. We had great chemistry, but the timing wasn't right.

"Anyway, fast forward to last Friday when I... ran into him again on my last shift at Starbucks. We had a date on Sunday before Ivy and Mom got sick. Breakfast. Anyway, it was... wonderful." I paused and sipped water. "Really wonderful. Like no time had passed. He even helped me take care of Ivy and Mom for a while."

I dropped my head to stare at the table. Silence fell.

"So... where's the problem, Jules?" Celeste asked, and the others hummed in agreement.

Fair point. When I summed it up, it seemed so easy. I waved my hand, searching for clarity. "He's... I'm... how the hell do I trust this? We had this amazing time together last year. Out of nowhere, he's back. Not only that, but he's even more perfect than I thought."

Liv snorted. "No man is perfect, Jules. It's the dick. They can't help it."

I twisted my lips. "His dick was pretty perfect, Liv."

I admired this group's lack of self-consciousness. Yet again, they whooped and didn't give a damn who stared. Kira clapped her hands to her cheeks and shook her head, helpless with giggles. Megan and Celeste, on either side of me, both held up their hands for high-fives. Liv threw her head back and laughed, then jumped up and ran around to hug me.

"You are a freaking legend," she gasped through her laughter. "I'm so glad we met."

I hugged her arm that was around me. "I am, too."

She sat back down, and Megan tapped the table. "Back to the topic, ladies. I'm still not hearing the issue. The man is some degree of amazing. Perfect for you—yes?"

"Yes," I whispered.

"But we don't trust him? Is that it?"

"I think I don't trust me." As soon as I said it, everything made sense. "I think he sees me as something I'm not. Fun. Sexy. I don't know."

A chorus of hums met those words. I looked around, and

Liv said, "You are those things, goofball. You're hot AF and know how to have a great time. What? Do you think because you have a kid, you're not allowed to be sexy, too?"

I sucked down a gulp of water. "Kind of?"

Another round of disapproval.

I tried to explain. "I don't know. He feels perfect for me, but my life doesn't really do perfect. So... it feels dangerous."

Liv crossed her arms. "Really, Juliette Reid? Your life doesn't 'do perfect'? Is your daughter not perfect?"

"No, she is. An absolute angel."

"And your job. Is exercise physiologist not a perfect job for someone who runs marathons and wants time for her family life, too? Your mother. Is she not a *perfect* mom who's got your back on everything? Do you not live in a *perfect* city with too much traffic but every type of music and food you can imagine? And let's talk about your friends. You are sitting among a *perfect* group of flawed, gorgeous women who're all doing their best to balance life and self-love every damn day. But your life doesn't 'do perfect,' hmm?"

My eyes burned as the truth of her words sank deep into me. I opened my mouth but closed it again without speaking.

Liv leaned forward and propped her chin on her fist. She flashed me a gentle smile. "Perfect is only ever what you say it is, Jules. Believe me."

"Sage," Megan whispered.

No joke.

∼

Liv's words followed me home. Celeste was gracious enough to let me reflect on the drive. When she pulled up in front of my house, she turned to me.

"Jules. I know about trying to control the narrative. About protecting your heart. Everyone is different, and I'd never tell you what to do. Only you know what's best for you. But I will say, you don't gain if you don't risk. So roll the dice if it feels right. Even if it hurts, you'll learn new things about yourself from taking the leap."

I gazed into her green eyes. This "perfect" woman with a high-powered job and seemingly blissful home life. Something in her words told me that she had worked her ass off for where she was—just like they all had.

"Thank you," I whispered before exiting the car.

"I'll see you Friday at the gala, right?" she called.

"You bet."

27

JAMES

I was walking up 5th Avenue to my hotel with "One More Night in Brooklyn" playing in my headphones. The late great Nashvillian, Justin Townes Earle, singing about New York. Felt right for the evening. My phone vibrated in my pocket, but I didn't check it until I was on the elevator at the hotel.

> Juliette: I got a haircut. No more wild woman mane.

> Juliette: (I know I promised not to text. I hope it's okay.)

My god. The way my heart *inflated*. I was smiling and didn't even realize it until I glanced in the mirror.

> Me: Ignoring that 2nd message—let me see!

> Juliette: Sent an image.

The photo was her face, lips pursed, brow arched. But the shot was too close, so it just looked like her hair was sleek and straight. I chuckled and let myself into my hotel room. Then, I hit the video icon.

She answered. That alone surprised me.

"What do you want?" she snipped with a smile.

"Sassy. I wanted to see. Show me."

She extended her arm and looked up at the camera. "Is that better?"

I whistled low. "Hell yeah it is. Smoke show."

Her hair was just to her shoulders, sleek and sexy as hell. I loved that long mane of hers and had fantasized about wrapping my whole damn arm around it more than once that week. But this new look worked just as well.

The camera moved closer to her face again. "I didn't mean for you to call."

"Then you should've sent a better photo." God, I could not stop smiling when I talked to her.

"Are you enjoying being vomit-free and not having my nervous worrying to distract you?"

I shook my head. "I don't enjoy much about being away from you, love. Not sure how to make you believe that."

She chewed her lip. "I believe it," she said softly.

"Good." I shrugged out of my coat, and she cocked her head. "What are you doing?"

"Getting comfortable. Just got back to my room."

"Oh, gosh. I don't even know where you are. What time is it there?"

I checked my watch. "Nine. I'm in New York, so an hour ahead of you."

"I've never been there. Do you like it?"

"Yeah, it's alright. My sister-in-law used to live here. That I can't really imagine, but it's a good place to visit." *I'll take you someday.* I left that thought in my head.

She nodded, but her gaze drifted down when I unbuttoned my collar. I smirked. "Want me to strip for you?"

Her head bobbed up and down. "No."

I laughed and propped the phone against the lamp on the table. "So," I said as I stepped away and began undoing my cuffs. "How's your week going?"

"Not bad. Had a girls' night just now and... um..."

Once the buttons were undone, I began to shrug out of the shirt. "Yes?" I drawled.

"Oh, shut up and take it off."

Done. I whipped the shirt through my legs and flexed my hips, then threw it aside and blew her a kiss. "Happy now?"

She ran her finger along her lower lip. "Not mad, that's for sure."

Retrieving the phone, I stretched out on the bed. "There's more where that came from. But first, you've got your assignment for New Year's Eve. Unless you've changed your mind and are coming to my party."

"I can't."

"Okay then."

She hesitated, then: "Are you going to kiss someone at your party?"

"Do you want me to? I hear I'm being set up with a friend of a friend."

"If you want to, I guess. I don't know. I wouldn't want to stand in your way if you like her."

I laughed. "You do realize you've been standing in my way for nearly a year, right?"

"What?" she yelped.

"I haven't dated anyone, love. Slept with anyone, either. Just so we're clear."

"Because of *me*?" Her eyes seemed ready to fall out.

I shrugged. "One of several factors. Others being work and... work. But after our weekend together, nothing else seemed as..."

"Appealing?" she guessed.

"Exciting."

"Amusing."

"Thrilling."

"Satisfying," she whispered, nodding.

"So goddamn satisfying," I said through clenched teeth.

"I don't like this new year's plan." Her voice was soft and rough all at once.

"I don't either."

"Maybe we don't plan it, then. Maybe we just go with the freaking flow and see what happens?"

"You mean... like sneaking off together in the middle of our respective parties?"

She held a finger to her lips. "No plans, silly. Just keep your phone on and your options open."

"Ooh, yes ma'am." We stared at each other for a long moment. Finally, I shifted my hips and opened my pants. "I'd better tell you goodnight."

"Why?"

"Because I'm going to come in about ten minutes, and I'd hate to keep you on the line for that. And by hate, I mean I would fucking love to."

Nod. "Then goodnight, James."

"Miss Juliette."

But she didn't hang up. And neither did I. I stroked myself and stared at the mischief in those whiskey eyes. She blinked and smiled, all angelically innocent, and I breathed a laugh.

"I thought you were hanging up."

"Shh. I told you goodnight. I'm not here. Got it?"

"Well, since you're not here, suck on your thumb and keep those big eyes on me."

Fuck me. She did it.

I clenched my teeth and held back from saying all the filthy things in my head. In Aruba, our talk had been natural and fun. But this was different, and I didn't want to push too hard. So I spit into my palm and kept stroking.

"Does it feel good?" she murmured as I got closer to the edge. I gave a quick nod. "Are you thinking terrible things about me?"

"Horrible. Disgusting," I gritted out.

She gave me the most angelic smile. "Oh. Good."

Done. I threw my head back and groaned a laugh. "You little fucking tease."

When I went slack and looked back at the screen, she puckered her lips into a kiss. "Goodnight, James. Call me again sometime."

And then, she was gone.

Luke and I were on the morning flight Thursday. We rode to the airport in silence. Just before we got out at the terminal, he lowered his phone. "Megan says everything is ready for the party tomorrow."

"Does that mean we can take an actual break until Monday?"

"Obviously, there will be people to meet at the gala. But otherwise, I believe so." He flashed a relieved smile.

The driver opened the door, and I nodded. "Great. Let's put that on the agenda."

I finished emails on the flight and put my out-of-office auto-response on. When I got to my house, I took a shower, paced in the kitchen while I ate lunch, and finally grabbed my phone.

> Me: WYD?

It took a few minutes to get a reply.

> Juliette: not much. Mom & Ivy left for the weekend.

> Me: Oh, really?

I sent the peeking eyes emoji. She tapped back a laugh.

> Juliette: Yeah. NYE cabin with aunties. I'm missing out for this party tomorrow.

> Me: Poor baby. I could take you to dinner. In case you're lonely.

Bubbles floated on her side for a moment.

> Juliette: LOL, do you think I ever get alone time? I was going to eat takeout in my robe and watch trash TV. That's a freaking SPLURGE, baby.

"Damn," I muttered at the phone. I'd have loved to see her, but I wanted to respect her alone time.

But then my phone lit up again.

> Juliette: Pick me up at 6?

> Me: You sure??

> Juliette: Yes, Mr. Bond. I'm sure. ;)

She wore a navy-blue corduroy skirt, tights, boots, and a gold sweater that sat off her shoulders and made her cleavage magnificent. I blinked at her several times while she buttoned her coat.

"What?" she asked.

"You look amazing."

She wrinkled her nose. "I didn't know how fancy to be."

I took her hand and walked her out. "You're perfect."

Our hands unlaced as she stopped dead. I whirled around to see her staring at me, mouth open. "What's wrong?"

"Oh. Uh. Sorry. Just... am I?" Her voice was far away, like she was asking herself. I didn't answer, and she eventually crooked a little smile. "Maybe I am some kind of perfect. I'd like to be. Thank you. I'll take that compliment."

A thrill shot through me. That level of confidence was sexy as hell. She'd had it in Aruba. To see it radiate from her now got my blood pumping. *Take it all, Juliette. Grab life by the balls. And by life, I definitely mean me.*

I grinned and led her to the car. "The real question is, what kind of food would you like? Do we go for exclusive and upscale? Or do we—"

"Eat barbecue," she blurted.

"Wow. I was going to say get beers and barbecue."

"I haven't gone out for 'cue in ages. That sounds really fun if you're into it."

I picked up her hand and kissed her knuckles. "I'm into all kinds of things, love. If you want to fill your mouth with meat... that's exactly what we'll do."

She'd always tried to keep her amusement reined in, or at least dialed down to a giggle. Hearing her unfiltered laugh shot another thrill through me.

"That's *exactly* what I hoped we'd do when you texted,"

she teased. "The only debate is what kind of meat I'm craving tonight."

"Allow me to suggest you have as much as you want. I will be your sampler platter—ah, I mean, I'll get you the sampler."

"You always were so obliging when it came to my protein intake. Such a gentleman."

"That's me, baby."

She laughed again. "Let's go, silly. All this talk has me famished."

Something was different about her. She seemed more open than I'd ever seen her. More relaxed. I hesitated, then told her as much.

Juliette hummed and pushed the button for her seat warmer. "I'm trying to appreciate my 'perfect' life more. I had a talk with my girlfriends yesterday. It, ah, it helped me realize how much time I spend worrying. I'm trying to do that less."

"Sound like good friends."

"They're pretty awesome."

I took her to Martin's. She hummed as we walked up. "I was hoping you were a pulled pork kind of guy."

"There is definitely a joke here about pulling pork that shouldn't be missed," I murmured while I opened the door.

"Stop it. We're in public," she hissed through a giggle.

"Now you're just adding to the joke."

We walked through the order line laughing. Juliette calmed down enough to place her order, but she couldn't get "pulled pork" out without another laugh. Pretty sure the cashier thought we both needed to be evaluated. I put my hand on her lower back and guided her to the bar. She got a hefeweizen, and I went for a Belgian triple. We wandered upstairs to find a table and wait on our food.

"How old are you really?" she asked.

"Turning thirty-five in two weeks. You?"

"Twenty-seven. That's a bit of a spread."

"Not as bad as nineteen and... how the fuck old did you tell me you were? Forty?"

"Forty-*two*," she said with a smirk.

I shook my head as our food arrived. "Damn, woman. You're hotter than ever when you smile that much."

"How about when I do this?" She shoved a forkful of pork into her mouth.

I stared at her while she chewed. "It's a little embarrassing how turned on I am right now. But, ah, you've got barbecue sauce on your lip."

She wiped the wrong side. "Did I get it?"

I exhaled hard, stood, and rounded the table. She looked up at me, but I bent down and sucked her lip into my mouth, licking the sauce away. Without a word, I returned to my seat and took a bite of my own food.

"Yep, you sure did."

My god. The sparkle in her eyes.

We spent the meal trading lines, laughing, and talking about Aruba. I had planned to tell her about my business that night, but it simply didn't come up. She didn't talk about work or her family, and neither did I. We finished eating and went to play darts in the corner.

"You throw a dart like it's a baseball." I laughed as she launched another toward the board.

"Yeah, but I hit it." She shook her shoulders in a saucy little move.

I threw mine and waved her to me. "Like this, love."

One hand circled her wrist. The other splayed on her stomach to pull her close. Slowly, I lifted her throwing hand

and showed her the correct motion. "Got it?" I asked in her ear.

Juliette got still in my arms. "No. Show me again."

That's my girl. I arced her arm again. "And release."

She threw the dart. It bounced to the ground, but neither of us cared. She put one hand over mine on her belly and turned her head. "James," she whispered.

I kissed her.

She melted into me. Her now-empty hand wrapped around my neck and laid in my hair. I felt her breath quicken as my tongue teased her, and blood surged my groin.

Juliette broke us apart. "We're in public, James."

"We could fix that." I licked her flavor from my lips and held my breath until I heard:

"We should."

28

JULIETTE

James's eyes were nearly black with lust. "My house is too far. Let's go to the Four Seasons. It's just down the block."

But I shook my head. "No. No hotel rooms. I want real life. And poor Max will be so lonely."

He hummed. "If we get pulled over, I'm blaming you."

"I'll take that risk."

We were at his place within an hour. Neither of us spoke much on the drive, which only heightened the tension. James damn near did a hockey stop with the car in his drive. We were both out in a blink, walking hand-in-hand to the door. *Oh, god. Oh, my god. I'm here. This is... we're going to...*

I cut a glance at him while he opened the door. My mouth went dry.

If tonight is the end of our road, I don't care. This connection is impossible. It makes no sense that we ran into each other. So if tonight is the end of this fairytale, it'll be enough. It'll still have been "perfect."

"I want you so bad," I whispered.

James kicked open the door and hauled me inside. He

pulled me close as Max danced around us. "You have no fucking idea how bad," he growled.

But I tugged his hair. "Yes, I fucking do," I growled right back.

"Max," he commanded. "Be a good boy. Go—dammit. Hold on, Juliette." I whined while he jogged away to the kitchen and returned with a huge bone.

I smirked. "Is that for me or the dog?"

James dropped his head, laughing. Meanwhile, Max spotted the bone and bolted to his side. James gave it to him and scratched his head. "Okay, boy. I'll see you in six hours."

"Six?" I yelped.

But he just took my hand and led me downstairs. "Fine. Seven, if you're going to complain about it."

"I'm going to have to ice my pussy if we go seven hours."

He rumbled a laugh. "Just don't use menthol cream. Burns something wicked on the private bits."

"Oh, my god. Is that a kink of yours?"

Another laugh. "Hell no. That was an accident playing baseball in high school."

I giggled and shook my head.

We were walking down a hallway to a door. One side was all glass, looking out at the night. I guessed we were under the porch but couldn't really tell. The other side held closed doors along the way.

"I'll give you the tour later," he said as we went. We reached the door at the end. James turned to me and stroked my hair. I purred while he worked down my neck and collarbone.

"You get chills everywhere when I touch you."

My eyes fluttered. "I guess I really like being petted."

No one had ever petted me like this. Mom and Dad used to scratch my back and stroke my hair when I was a child, but I'd never had a lover whose touch unwound me like his. If I weren't so eager to feel him, I could've let him do nothing but this for ages.

"Noted," he whispered. "But that's for later. Now, would you like to open that door, Miss Juliette?"

I would. I did.

He followed me inside. I took off my boots while he lit the fireplace and turned on a lamp. Then, he met me in the middle of the room. We stared at each other.

"I never thought I'd get to touch you again," I whispered at last.

His lips twisted. "Thought, or wanted to?"

"Definitely thought. I wanted to... so many times."

"Then Juliette?"

"Hm?"

"Just fucking do it, love."

I lunged for him. He caught me with a grunt as I wrapped my arms around him, pulling him down for a kiss. We stumbled around the room until he dropped down onto the bed. I jerked away from his kiss. "I can't straddle your lap in this skirt."

No words. James just yanked the zip on my hip and let the skirt fall to the floor. Still in my pantyhose, I landed on top of him. His hands roamed over the nylon. "Goddamn, this is pretty sexy."

"It's a cock block," I said between kisses.

His laugh trickled down my spine. "Fucking try and stop me, pantyhose. I dare you."

I laughed and pushed him to lie down. We rolled across the bed in a frantic tangle of lips and hands. The way his breath shook made my toes curl, but then I knew I trembled whenever he touched me somewhere new. He whispered between kisses about how good I felt and how much he'd missed me. I believed it. I felt it right back.

But it was all a little too *nice*.

Then change the mood. You can, you know.

I pushed his shoulders and flipped so I was on top again. Catching his lip in my teeth, I said, "Are you always this sweet in the real world?"

Thundercloud-gray eyes slowly opened. "Hmm?"

I released his lip with a pop and sat up, arms crossed. "You're very sweet, telling me how much you want me. How you've missed touching me. It's all very nice."

He put his hands behind his head and stared at me. "And my little tease doesn't want it nice. Does she?"

My cheeks heated. "Well, of course I do. What kind of girl would I be if I wanted... um, to be..."

"Yesss?" he drawled.

Oh, just do it. I stuck out my lip. "I don't want to say it. I don't want to tell you how filthy you should be with me."

He stared at me for another eternal moment. I squirmed against his cock between my legs. Then, in a flurry of movement, he sat up underneath me, grabbed my hips, and turned me across his lap. His palm hit my ass with nothing but the stockings as a cushion.

"Ohh," I moaned shamelessly when he did it again. "Fuck!"

"Hush that petulant mouth. I'll tell you exactly how filthy I'm going to be with you. Is that what you want?"

Holy shit. He cracked his palm against me again and again, and I could not believe how wet it made me. "James," I whined.

"Yes, love?" he purred, eerily calm.

"Harder."

"Fuck," he growled before obliging.

I wailed with each repetition until he stopped abruptly and pushed me off, leaving me a panting mess on the bed.

"Get up and take off my clothes."

Still gasping, I stood on shaky legs and met the smoldering fire in his eyes. But his lips quirked in a classic James smile, and that made him even hotter. My heart would've melted—if my panties weren't totally dissolving at the moment. I undid his button-down and pushed it off his shoulders, then opened his pants.

"Good girl."

I pouted again. "I want to be your bad girl."

James flashed his teeth in a wolfish smile. "You're about to be. Take your sweater off."

Done.

"Now, turn around and let me watch while you strip out of those pantyhose."

Slowly, I turned and hooked my fingers in the waist, then rolled them off until I was bent in half, hair swinging upside-down. I had just peeled them off my feet when James's palms gripped the backs of my thighs. Between my legs, I saw him slide to his knees behind me, push my legs apart, and run his tongue from my ass all the way to my clit.

I nearly collapsed. He met my gaze between my legs, not blinking as two fingers sank inside me. "How's that?"

"I'm gonna fall on my head. I can't stand like this."

He laughed at me. "No one said you had to hang upside-down."

Standing upright wasn't much better. James fingered me and pressed his thumb backward until I howled. "I want this ass to be mine. Will you let me be that filthy with you, *Miss Jae*?"

"I would let you do anything to me," I breathed, eyes closed.

"What was that?" His hand stopped. I shook my head, and he spanked me with his free hand.

"I would let you do *anything* to me." My shout bounced around the room.

"Say it again."

It came out as something between a vow and a sob. "Anything, James. Whatever you want. Please."

My feet flew out from under me. James had got to his feet and scooped me into his arms. He carried me to the bed and sat me down, kneeling between my legs. God, his eyes were electric.

"I want to," he said softly. "I want to ruin you for anyone else. I want to be your best, your filthiest, your most fun. Because, Juliette, you are mine."

I sniffled and nodded. "I'm sorry. I don't know why I'm teary."

He crooked a smile. "Because you just got the hell spanked out of your ass?"

"Maybe," I laughed. "Or maybe because you won't get fucking on with it."

Those beautiful eyes rolled—just before he dove between my legs. I groaned and fell back on the bed, gripping the sheets. "James," I wailed.

"Mm-mm. Don't you call my name until you come. Say anything else, but when you get there—when you're coming all over my face—that's when I want to hear it."

His tongue swirled around my clit, and I hissed. James ate me like I was his death row meal, alternating between merciless intensity and maddening little licks until I was squirming and frustrated.

"I can't," I groaned. "I can't get there. I've been too close for too long. Stop. Just—"

But he laid his palms on my abdomen and glanced up. "Shh. Relax. You don't have to come."

"But... but you're..."

"Having fun, love. That's what I'm doing. And you should be, too."

I stared at him. "Fun?"

James's knuckle glided between my lips. "Fun. Tasting you? Finding out what you like best? There's not a damn thing I'd rather be doing. You are my fucking playground, Juliette. I would play with you all night long." He glanced up and quirked his brow. "May I?"

"Uh... uh-huh." *Play with me?* No man had ever put it that way before.

But then, no man had come close to making me feel like he did.

James leaned into me again. This time, he found the sweetest rhythm and kept his tongue exactly where I wanted it most until...

"Oh, fuck. James. James, please. Please, I... I..."

He pressed the flat side of his knuckle against my perineum, and a whole new level of pleasure rocketed through my body. "Fuck," I screamed. "James, James, please don't stop, don't stop."

"Mm-mm," he hummed with his lips around my clit.

I completely shattered.

James sat back on his heels. I blinked my eyes open in time to see him grin broadly and wipe his face. Then, I collapsed on the bed again. My body surged with pheromones. As soon as I could see straight, I propped up on my elbows and looked at him.

"Wow."

He laughed, and I blushed. "Are you going to... I mean,

do you want to... have my ass tonight?" Saying it made my face melt.

"No. It's better if you work up to that."

My brows knitted. James climbed over me, kissing me slow and deep. "Plugs, baby. You want to get used to it so you really enjoy it. And lube, of course. Sorry, I don't keep a stock of sex toys or supplies handy."

"Oh. Silly me. And silly you. I'm kind of surprised."

He kissed me again, shifting to cage me between his knees and hands. "I told you you've been cock-blocking me."

I reached between us and gripped him. "Speaking of said cock." I stroked, loving how he responded to my touch.

"Yours," he hissed, eyes shut tight. His hips flexed to my rhythm. "Fuck. Yours. Do with me what you want. I am fucking *yours*—and yours for fucking."

I laughed even as I met him in another kiss. James flipped us over so that I was on top. "I do have condoms," he said before I could lower down.

I sucked on my lip. "No, thanks."

"Jesus Christ," he bellowed when I lifted my hips and sank down on his cock. "Juliette, what the hell—"

"Shh." I put a finger to his lips. "Neither of us has been with anyone. I have an IUD—have since after my C-section. I think... I want... oh, fuck."

My sentences crumbled at the exquisite feeling of him bare inside of me. I swiveled my hips and hissed.

James forced his eyes open as I sat up straight again. His palms rested on my thighs. "Now who's ruining who?" he muttered.

29

JAMES

But that was bullshit because I was already ruined. Had been since Aruba. If I had to put my finger on a specific moment, it probably would've been after our first time. When we were lying there after, and she put those eyes on me and said, "Hi." Right before I suggested we spend time together all weekend.

I knew she'd fucked me even then.

Now, with her pussy squeezing around my bare cock, I threaded my hands in my hair and tried to remember to breathe. My hips flexed, and she moaned.

"James... if this is all we get... I won't be sorry."

I froze. "What does that mean?"

She shook her head, eyes closed.

I sat up underneath her. "Look at me. What do you mean?"

"I just, mm, mean that if... if it's not... if this is all just part of the fairytale, I don't care. I won't regret this. No plans," she whispered with a smile. "Just living."

My hands gripped her hips to keep her still. I waited

until she looked at me. "You know it's not, though. You know tonight isn't all."

"I don't know what comes next."

"But." I wouldn't move, no matter how good she felt.

She squirmed and huffed. "But I hope it's not all. But I want more."

Good enough. I pushed her off me. "Hands and knees, you little tease. You want to talk nonsense? I'll fuck you until you forget how to talk."

"Yes," she moaned, switching her hips.

I took her hard and rough. No matter how hard I thrust, she moaned for more. The sheets twisted and knotted in her hands. I turned her ass red with my palm. And she just got wetter and wetter for me. When her thighs started to shake, I pulled out and lay on my back. I had to help her climb on top of me, she was so spent.

"James," she slurred.

"Hush. A girl like you can take a lot more than that. Can't you?"

Fuck me, that wicked grin curled her lips. She forced her eyelids open. "Mm-hm."

Juliette sank down on my cock and leaned over me, tits brushing my chest. "A lot more."

30

JULIETTE

Good god. I was sore, brainless, and absolutely blissed. I could've slept for a week, but I had a claim to back up. So, I sat up and rolled my hips, hissing at the change of angle. "Is that what you wanted, Mister Bond?"

He teased my nipples. "Yeah. That's what I fucking want," he rasped in his bourbon-on-the-rocks voice.

"James, I'm gonna come if you keep touching me like that."

"That's the point, love. Come all over my cock. Let me feel that pussy clench on me."

My eyes slammed shut, face on fire. "Keep talking."

"Such a bad fucking girl, riding me with those thighs sweating and your juices dripping all over me. Shame on you, Miss Juliette, for being so wild. Getting off on how I touch these tits. Grinding my cock like 'it's the last time.' Silly girl. You know damn well there's no way this is enough."

"It wouldn't ever... be... e-enough."

"Damn fucking right. Now, come for me, you filthy little tease."

"J-James, I..."

He pinched me. Hard. "I said *come*, Juliette!"

Oh, fuck. The stern command in his tone absolutely undid me. Waves of pleasure crashed down on me. Sweat rolled down my back, and I screamed from the bottom of my lungs.

At last, I fell forward onto his chest and into his arms. "Good girl," he whispered, kissing my hair.

"I like bossy you."

He rumbled low in his chest. "I could tell."

"Your turn to finish?"

He inhaled. "You know what I want to do, Juliette. Is it okay?"

My fatigue cleared. A blush warmed my already-flushed face. I wet my lips and nodded. "How?"

He disappeared into a door that must've been the en suite and returned with a bottle of lotion and a towel. "Like this. Lie against the pillows."

I propped against the pillows, breathing shallow. He walked over. Asked again if I was sure. I nodded, and he squirted lotion all over my chest. His palms smeared it everywhere, turning me on all over again.

"Your tits are incredible," he growled as he straddled me and gripped the headboard. "Tell me to stop if you hate it. I'm going to come all over you if you don't stop me."

"Okay." I held my breasts together and tried not to hold my breath at the same time.

His cock slid between my cleavage, and he hissed. "Okay?"

"Shut up and do it."

That made him laugh. It also made him fuck. I dug my heels into the bed to stay still and tipped my head back. Staring up at him staring down at me, my heart fluttered.

This felt... well. It felt sexy as hell but also challenging. But the glint in his eyes and the sight of his body above me made it even hotter.

James fucking Bond fucking me.

I grinned.

"What?" he huffed, so I said it aloud.

James threw his head back and laughed. "Fuck, that's going to make me come."

"Good. I want you to. Come for me, *James.*"

He reached down and gripped his cock as his hips went erratic. I held my breath. His was ragged. "Juliette—*fuck!*"

Ropes of hot come laced my chest and pooled in the hollow of my throat. James flexed a final time and fell back on the bed with a groan.

"Goddamn."

I stared at my body, fascinated. I was covered in him. It was filthy.

It was so not me. And it was so completely, totally me.

It's us. This is part of who we are together. And I want all the parts.

James struggled to sit up. He eyed me. "Fuck, that's hot."

I looked up at him. "I know."

His eyes rolled. "Fuck, *you* are hot."

"Hot and sticky. What a way to go through life." I giggled.

He grabbed the towel that I'd forgotten about and wiped the worst of it off me. Then, he helped me stand and walked me into the bathroom. It was as gorgeous as every other part of his house, creamy walls and state-of-the-art amenities. Soft yellow light glowed from the mirror. James tapped the glass, and music began to play. Without speaking, he led me to the shower and batted my hands away to wash me himself.

Ooh. If I liked being petted, I freaking *loved* being washed. "Mm, can you just be my full-time body washer?" I sighed.

His hands paused. "Hell yes, I can."

I sucked on my lip. "About that."

"About what?"

"About... full time."

But James kissed me softly. "We don't have to know tonight, love. It's enough."

Enough. It is more than enough. I nodded.

We finished showering. He handed me a towel. While he dried off, he said, "So, it was more like two and a half hours than six. Should I take you home now, or would you want to stay with me?"

"Oh. You can—"

He spun to me, towel around his hips, jaw set. "I want you to stay. So we're clear."

My shoulders dropped. "Then I'd like to stay."

He loaned me a t-shirt and insisted I sit by the fire while he ran upstairs. I heard Max's nails on the deck. After a while, the door opened. Max ran into the room and sniffed me all over. James appeared, holding a tray of crackers and cheese.

"I'm starving after all that. You want?"

My lips twitched. "Are you suggesting that you wouldn't kick me out of bed for eating crackers?"

He had to put the tray down, he laughed so hard. "You are the perfect woman."

Perfect is what you say it is. "Maybe I am." I skipped to him and plucked a cracker.

James hummed. "If you're going to skip around without a bra, we're going to go for another two or three rounds before you get to sleep."

I turned wide eyes to him. "I'm both incredibly agree-able and unsure I can physically do it."

He pointed to the bed, and I crawled on. James handed me a glass of iced tea and sat down, putting his arm around me. Max immediately stared at us from the floor, emitting little whines now and then.

"Hey. No. You stay down there." James snapped his fingers, and Max feigned laying down. He popped back up in a heartbeat.

"Oh, it's okay. He could come up if—"

The words left my mouth, and the big dog was right between us. He was really well trained, though—he didn't take one bit of the food.

So, James tossed him a cracker. "I'm not giving him cheese," he said while Max crunched loudly. "Not if he's sleeping in here tonight."

I giggled.

Conversation dwindled, though. We were clearly both exhausted, so after a little snack, James took the food back to the kitchen. When he came back, I followed him into the bathroom and brushed my teeth with my finger. Then, we climbed into the sheets while Max curled up at the foot of the bed.

James pulled my back to his chest. I drifted off while he petted my arm. I had never felt so safe. So worked.

So perfect.

31

JAMES

It was the first time I woke up next to her. And, dammit, the first thought I had was, *Please don't let this be the last time.*

I'd had women sleep over before. Okay, not at this house, but still. I'd dated the same person long enough to have them sleep over. This did not feel the same. This hit different. But then, everything about her hit different. And it had since the moment we met.

She stirred in my arms and clutched my wrist, and my heart did strange, fluttery things. I gazed down at her, wanting her to sleep the whole day just to keep holding her.

Well. I guess if she woke up and we did half of what we'd done last night, that would've been okay, too.

I stirred just thinking about that marathon fuckfest. She squirmed, and that exquisite ass pressed against me. I swallowed a groan, but her eyes opened. "Someone's up already," she said thickly.

"Shh. Sleep some more. I'm good."

Oh, but she wasn't. The next thing I knew, I was sending Max outside and running back to pin her down on the bed.

I came inside of her. And while I knew we weren't at risk

of pregnancy, it unlocked yet another level of the depths of my feelings for her. There was something primal about it—and I had thought coming all over her had felt like claiming her. The light in her eyes as I unloaded only furthered the feeling.

When we were lying on our backs side-by-side, she looked over at me.

"Hi."

"Hi."

"Have we met?"

I shook my head. "I don't think so. But then, I think you've fucked all my brain cells out of my head."

She rolled to snuggle against my arm. "You smell familiar, though."

"Maybe we met at the blindfolded speed dating event."

She laughed. "What a disaster. Works much better as an app, doesn't it?"

I jolted. "What?"

"That app. *Chat Me Up!*. It's kind of the premise, isn't it?"

"Yeah. How did you—"

"Ugh, be right back. Leaking." She rolled off and hurried to the bathroom. "I'm going to shower, okay?"

"Go for it." I got up to let Max back in.

When she emerged, I'd dressed in jeans and a hoodie and changed the glass walls of the bedroom from "night-time" to transparent. I loved tech like that. Until I hit the button, you wouldn't have known it was full-on daytime.

Juliette blinked when she saw the wall of windows. "Oh, my god. That's amazing. Also—what time is it?" Her forehead wrinkled as she dove for her phone. "Oh, shit! It's almost noon?"

"We were up until after two a.m."

"I have to go. I have a mani/pedi at one-thirty. Oh, god. I'm never going to get ready in time."

I went to my dresser. "Just put on these sweats. I'll get you home in no time."

She walked out to my car wearing my clothes, hers in her arms. As we zoomed along, she said, "So. Big party tonight?"

"Mm-hm. I wish you'd join me."

"I told you. No plans. Just see what we feel like doing."

I squeezed the wheel. "Okay, but about that. What was that last night about 'if this is the last time?' Why did you say that?"

She took a deep breath. "I want to have plans. I like knowing where I'm going. And, as you remember, I make terrible plans and wind up on my ass all the time.

"I'm afraid of that with you, James."

"What exactly are you afraid of?"

"The... the improbability of all this feels... like a fairy-tale. It feels so unreal that surely, I must be mistaken. Surely there is no way someone like you fits in my life. You're too big, James."

I snorted a laugh.

She paused and then giggled. "Not like that."

"Hey."

"Okay, like that. But I'm trying to be serious! I've put all my stock into plans before, just to end up working at Star-bucks and taking the bus. You and I feel *perfect*. I hope it's okay to say that. But how do I trust it? How foolish would I be to wrap my arms around a connection like this?"

I rolled to a stop at her house and parked. Frowning, I turned to her. "We do feel perfect. And I want to tell you not foolish at all—or maybe perfectly foolish. I don't know. Anytime you fa—hmm." I clamped my mouth shut and gave her a wry smile. *Anytime you fall in love* had just about fallen out of my mouth, and this was not the moment to toss the L-word in the mix.

Not that I didn't feel it.

Juliette's eyes widened, but a little smile hinted at her lips, too. "What?" she whispered.

I gave her a playful glare. "Anytime you *embrace a connection*, you're vulnerable to playing the fool. I think we've all felt that sting. I know I have.

"And I know you've been through it, Juliette. I understand. I've got my share of experience to make me doubt relationships, too—not like you, I'll admit, but still. We're a crazy story. Unlikely as hell. Shoot, I tried to explain it to my sister-in-law the other day. Wound up saying nothing because I couldn't figure out how to make us make sense. But I'm not asking you to put your plans on hold. I'd just... like your life to include me. And I guaran-damn-tee you won't be working retail unless it's what you want to do. What's the worst thing that could happen if you *did* wrap your arms around this? If you gave us a shot?"

She wrinkled her nose. "Heartbreak. Devastating heartbreak."

My head swam with points to make—and the underlying knowledge that no argument would win this debate. The decision had to be hers. So I rubbed my jaw and nodded. "Then I guess you have to decide if the reward is worth the risk."

"I guess I do."

"*I* think it's worth it if that has any impact on your thinking. I very much think this impossible story is worth the risk."

Her smile flickered. "That has a lot of impact."

I leaned over. At least she leaned in to kiss me. Before

she could pull away, I said, "I want to be the one you kiss at midnight, Miss Juliette. I would love to see you later. Let me send a car for you. They'll drive you to your party—but all you'll have to do is say, 'Take me to James' if you want to find me. They'll know where to go."

"We'll see what life has in store."

I laughed and shook my head. She blew a kiss and got out—but she doubled back before I could drive away. I buzzed down the window, and she rested her arms on the sill.

Her eyes sparkled with a playful light I knew well. "No plans... but I'd bet money I was kissing you at midnight, sailor."

I laid a hand on my heart. "Then I'm staking my entire net worth on it, love."

God, her smile. "Later," she whispered before running inside.

Five hours later, I gave Max his food and scratched his head. He looked at me with sad eyes, and I sighed. "It's almost a new year, buddy. I promise to start bringing you more places with me, okay? Perk of being the boss. Sound good?"

He pressed his wet nose to my palm. We had an agreement. But for the time being, I left his dog door locked and set the perimeter security. This far out, I wasn't worried about fireworks scaring him, but I didn't want to take chances.

My usual driver, Lauren, rolled up right on time. I slid into the back of the Escalade and said hello. She nodded at me in the rearview, confirmed the car service was dispatched to "Ms. Reid's house," and buzzed up the privacy partition.

I spent the ride toying with my phone and thinking about the wild twists of the past year. The company. That clusterfuck with my ex and her boss. Five weeks in Aruba. Expanding the product—and then expanding into merchandise as well.

And, of course, Jae/Juliette. Changing my whole fucking heart. Forever redefining my perfect woman. Falling into my life, out of it, and impossibly back into it.

I was on top of the world. I could buy damn near anything I wanted. But no money would buy her trust, her willingness to take a leap with me. That, I could only hope for. No plans. No amount of "maximum effort" would make that happen.

The next move was hers.

32

JULIETTE

My gown was red and shimmery. It sat on my shoulders and plunged into a deep-v and low back. The thigh-high slit showed off my three-inch black heels. Honestly, I looked sexy as fuck. Sweaty sex had ruined my blowout from the cut on Wednesday, so after my mani-pedi, I dropped into a salon for a touchup. By the time I was home, dressed, and had done my own makeup, I was running late.

A black SUV sat on the curb when I peeked outside. Just like he'd said it would be. *Prince Charming is also my fairy godmother*. The thought made me roll my eyes at myself. I took one last check in the mirror, touched up my lipstick, and blew a kiss at my reflection. "Bibbity-bobbity-boo, bitch."

The driver opened the door for me when I walked up. He gave me a formal nod. "Evening, ma'am. See this button on the door handle? You'll just push that if you need me. Where should I take you?"

"Oh, uh..." I checked my phone to find the party's address.

His brows knitted. "You mean the gala."

"Yes? Is it that big of an event?" I laughed lightly.

"Oh, well... Yes, ma'am, I understand it sure is. We'll get you there right away."

He helped me in and shut the door. I looked around to find a hibiscus flower on the seat beside me. The same color as the one on our dinner table in Aruba.

Oh, my heart.

The car began to move, and I glanced at the glass partition. "Can you hear me?" No response, so I FaceTimed Mom and Ivy. Ivy gasped and called me a princess. Mom shook her head and murmured how I was "So lovely."

"You two make me feel pretty special," I said with a lump in my throat. "Miss my favorite girls tonight."

"We miss you, Mommy! There's a *big*, big, big playground, and we saw deers! And Emily and I had a fight but it's okay because we're friends again."

I laughed at this report. "Sounds like I'm missing all the fun."

"Are you?" Mom asked with an arched eyebrow. "Or are you having fun, too?"

"I'm doing okay. I went out with James last night." My cheeks warmed at the gleam in her eye. "Don't look at me like that."

"I'm glad you're going with your friends tonight, but I think you should see him again ASAP. Like, tonight."

"Too saucy to be a mom," I sighed with a headshake.

"You should be a little saucy, too!" She laughed.

I blew her a kiss. "Well, maybe I'll give it a try."

"That's my girl."

"Apparently." We laughed and said goodbye.

I tucked the phone in my black sparkly clutch and gazed out the window. *Impossible odds, and yet here we are. He's too perfect for me... Or, okay. He's just perfect for me. Is the risk worth the reward? I've never met a man who made me feel like I was in free-fall* and *totally safe all at once. Never really wanted to. But if I leap into this and it fails... it'll hurt so bad.*

I blew out a breath. "And if I walk away from this without trying, it'll hurt worse."

Okay then. Leap it'll be.

But I wasn't going to ditch my friends.

We rolled to a stop in front of a gorgeous, rustic-chic venue. The sprawling old mansion glowed with twinkling lights. People in glamorous clothes stepped out of cars and made their way to the entrance.

"Wow," I breathed while the driver opened my door. He helped me out and gave me his card, saying to text him whenever I was ready. I tucked it in my clutch and made my way to the stairs. Megan and Luke stood side-by-side, greeting guests. Megan beamed when she saw me.

"Jules! You look *fantastic*. And, wow, who does your hair?"

I laughed and flipped the ends. "Best stylist in town."

She stepped away from Luke. "We're on door duty, but everyone should be here in just a few. Here, stand by the heater with me."

"Good plan." I hung back and let her say hello to people.

Within moments, Will's Audi rolled up. He and Liv emerged like a pair of models. She was in a vampy black dress with old Hollywood hair and a red lip, and he was sharp as hell in his tux. But their air of mystique vanished the moment she spotted us. A smile broke on her face, and she scurried over to kiss our cheeks and compliment our outfits.

Nick and Mel arrived next. His bowtie matched her emerald gown. The cool jewel tones were a perfect contrast to her stunning red hair, which was in a classic French twist.

They'd just clustered around us when David and Kira arrived with Aaron and his date. By then, it was clear that each couple had a thematic color. You & I were in silver. Aaron and his partner both wore plum bowties.

I looked down at my dress with a sad smile. It wasn't that I minded being solo. It was that I wished I was with *him*.

I'll leave at eleven. No excuses. I'll just tell Liv. She'll understand.

"Let's go inside," Aaron declared with a shiver. "It's too cold out here."

Luke turned to Megan. "Go on with them. I'll be in shortly."

She slipped her arm through his. "I'm with you, Agent Paris."

I hadn't been around Luke much, but I was sure that was the first time I saw him smile. "Bien, Pearl."

"Where are Celeste and Ben?" I asked as I fell in step with Mel.

"Inside already."

Indeed, they were the first people we saw when we walked in. A small group of people were asking them lots of questions, but they excused themselves quickly and joined us. Celeste kissed our cheeks while we complimented her royal blue mermaid gown. She hugged Nick, who said something in her ear that made her laugh.

Cousins. Right.

"Jules, you look amazing. Thanks for coming," she said when she got to me. "Hey, Ben. You remember Jules from Thanksgiving, right?"

She tugged his sleeve, and he turned from Nick to me. "Jules, yes. We only met for a moment, but I remember. Good to see you again."

His gray eyes crinkled in a smile, and my stomach

clenched. I gaped at him, then shook my head. "Sorry, got lost for a second. Congratulations on the expansion."

"Thank you so much for your input. You have to meet—oh. One moment, sorry."

Who? Who do I have to meet? Why is my heart racing?

"Come on, girlie. Let's get a drink." Aaron linked our arms and walked me to the bar. I ordered a signature cocktail and clinked with him. We started chatting about music while the venue filled up. David and Kira joined us, followed by Nick and Mel, and I forgot the weird jolt Ben had given me.

Celeste walked up with a woman in tow. The woman's layered pixie haircut was super cool, but she wore a simple wool sweater dress and an expression that told me she felt out of place. "Friends, I want you to meet one of my favorite people—outside of all of you, of course," Celeste said with a broad smile. "Sarah Rose, meet my friends." She pointed and named us all in turn.

Nick grinned and walked to shake Sarah's hand. "I remember you, Sarah. From Celeste's TennStar days. How have you been?"

Sarah smiled, clearly relieved. "Good. And you?"

Celeste slid between Mel and me while they talked. Under her breath, she said to me, "Sarah and I used to work together before I left to start the company." I nodded while she leaned toward Mel. I wasn't trying to be nosy, but I heard her say, "I think Sarah would be perfect for what you're looking for."

Mel lifted her drink to her lips and spoke behind the glass. "You're sure? She's reliable enough? I need someone who won't let one single thing slip. He's got to keep his shit together, and he needs help."

Celeste nodded. "I vouch for her. She'd be great. And she needs something new."

Mel chuckled. "This would be that."

Celeste hummed and drifted back to Sarah's side while I tried to forget the conversation that clearly wasn't meant for me. We made space for Sarah at the high-top table. She leaned her elbows on it and puffed out a breath. "I feel so out of place here. Everyone is so fancy."

My heart twisted for her. I certainly knew about feeling out of place. "You look great," I said, and everyone was quick to agree.

Aaron affirmed. "And anyway. It's all about the confidence you exude. Chin up, girl. That's all you're missing."

The chitchat resumed, and I excused myself. A passing waiter pointed me down a hallway off the main ballroom. At the end of it was a trio of doors, two of which were marked as restrooms. One was marked "PRIVATE." I ducked into a restroom. When I'd washed my hands and reapplied lipstick, I stepped back into the hall at the same moment the private door opened.

My heart stopped.

James froze, then broke into a wide grin. "You're here."

"I'm... what? No. You're here?"

He stepped closer and took my hand, his gaze traveling over me. "Holy smokes, love. You're more stunning than ever."

"James... wait. Why are you here?"

He cocked his head. "Because this is my party?"

"No. This is my party. Or, my friends' party."

"Really? Well, there are like three hundred people here, but that's still a pretty big coincidence." His eyes cut up, then back to me. "So you didn't tell your driver to take you to me?"

I stared at the delicious pout on his lips. At his impeccably fit tux. At his styled hair that I itched to ruin. At last, I blew out a breath. "I was going to leave in a while for yours. But, ah, if you're going to pout like that..."

He backed me against the wall, so close I could feel his warmth. "Then what?"

I puffed out my lips. "Then I'm going to need another spanking."

Those gray eyes went black. "Goddamn. I will give it to you right now."

Bubbles raced up my spine, right to my head. I gave him the saucy smile that I'd patented in Aruba. "It's a fancy party. I can't go around looking wrecked." I slipped out from under his arm and swished my hips, glancing over my shoulder. "You'll just have to wait."

This is so us. And I love it.

James was beside me in a blink. He dragged his fingers down my bare back and leaned to my ear. "I'm interpreting that to mean you'll be mine at midnight."

"I told you it was a safe bet."

He hummed. "Listen. I have to go talk to a lot of people right now. Business. Boring shit. But I'll find you in a while, okay? And then... I want you on my arm for the rest of the party. As a start."

"'Hi, this is my escort' kind of vibes?"

"Just don't fellate any food, and no one will think that."

We stopped walking and leaned into each other to laugh. "I will forever be embarrassed about that," I admitted.

He shook his head. "So am I. What a fool I was. I should've let you drag me to your room right then and there." I hummed, and he tilted my chin up. "Okay, gorgeous. I'll see you shortly. Got it?"

My cheeks warmed. "Sounds good. And, um, James? I'm ready to—"

But a woman in a suit with an earpiece ran up just then. "Sorry, sir. We need you to come to the terrace now."

James glanced backward and gave me a nod as she all but raced him away.

And again, my stomach clenched. This was all too coincidental to make sense.

"There you are!"

I jumped out of my thoughts as Liv hurried toward me. She guided me back to the ballroom, where our group—minus Luke, Celeste, and Ben—were at a table with small plates of food. Liv had made me a plate, bless her, so I slid in and tried to focus. Mel and Sarah seemed to be in a side conversation while the rest of them bantered about New Year's resolutions. Aaron, Kira, and I volunteered to get a dessert spread for everyone, so we rose and went to the adjacent room where the buffet waited. The whole time, servers kept our champagne topped off. I didn't drink too much, but between the good friends and bubbly anticipation, I was damn near floating anyway.

Liv leaned over. "You look *so* happy."

I sipped my drink and nodded. "I'm pretty happy, yeah. I, uh, well. I'm waiting for—"

"Oh, hey. They're saying we can meet them in the lounge," Megan said suddenly, waving her phone. "Let's go. It's loud out here."

33

JAMES

I rubbed my temples as the interview wound down. Of course talking to the press would be part of this event—as would talking to shareholders, people interested in the stock, politicians, and damn near anyone else who had the mind to grab our ear. Part of the point of a gala was exposure. We were building momentum for this new stage. Obviously, this was a work party.

It's just that I wanted to go find Juliette, drag her into the lounge, and do unspeakable things that would certainly ruin her gorgeous dress.

Well. I also wanted to hold her and stroke her hair until she melted into my arms. *Freaking sap.*

Yes. I sure as hell was when it came to her.

The four of us were finally alone on the terrace. We traded a look and filed in behind the head of security. As we skirted the perimeter of the ballroom, I scanned the crowd for Juliette. I didn't see her, but we were moving quickly. As soon as the lounge door closed, Ben and I headed for the bar. Luke dropped onto an overstuffed leather sofa, and Celeste perched on a barstool.

"I miss parties at the old apartment," I said in the quiet.

Ben grinned. "Me, too. To be fair, your ass has been MIA at gatherings all fall."

I cringed and left my drink on the bar to sit on another sofa. "Yeah, yeah, I know. But this is off the ground now, so... yeah. Balance and all that shit." I rubbed my eyes. "Someone text the crew. Tell them where we're hiding. I can hang for a minute, but then I've got to go."

"Go?" Ben asked. "Where?"

"Never mind. I'll tell you in a bit."

Luke pocketed his phone. "They're on their way."

"Great. Ben, grab a stick. Rack them up, and I'll even let you break. I'll still kick your ass, though."

He laughed and headed to the pool table. "Bet."

34

JULIETTE

Our group drifted through the ballroom, back toward the hallway with the restrooms. Liv and I walked arm-in-arm. "I'm so excited," she said once we were out of the middle of the noisy party. "No pressure, of course. I'm not actually setting you up. I'm more like... encouraging a meeting I think will go well."

"Liv," I groaned.

"I know, I know. You have a situationship with the boy."

I cut my gaze at her. "It was a little more than a situation last night."

Liv squealed. "You minx! Tell me everything!"

"We, uh, went for barbecue."

"And dessert at your place?"

I smiled at my hands. "His."

"He was as good as you remember?"

"Oh, god. Even better." I fanned my face, and she squealed again. "And, uh, he's here tonight. Somewhere. I'm supposed to meet up with him in a little while."

"Wait. He's here? Arg, okay, cool. Then *really* no pressure."

"No pressure on what—oh. You mean the mysterious CEO." My tone was playful. So why did my pulse start thrumming in my ears? *What was his name again? Friends-giving was too many long shifts and so many names ago.*

Liv nodded, so I refocused. "Yeah, sorry he's been such a ghost lately. But come on. If it weren't for your comment about shared experiences, we wouldn't be here tonight. *Chat Me Up!* wouldn't be unveiling a whole product line to go with their website."

"Which was *your* doing, I believe."

"Exactly. Together, we're masterminds." She blew me a kiss. "So I'm not saying you have to fall in love with James or anything, but—"

I almost ate the floor.

Liv grabbed my arm to keep me from pitching forward. "What?" I strangled.

"Are you okay, hun? Take a wrong step?"

Clearly, I had. My stomach was about to crawl out of my mouth. And, somehow, we were still going forward. "W-what did you say?" I tried to ask. "*Who?*"

"James Addison. Ben's brother? The head of the company? I thought we were talking about the same thing."

Ben's brother.

Those eyes.

His car and house.

My party.

His fucking party. Literally.

And we were walking right back to that door marked PRIVATE. His private lounge.

This was not happening.

The head of the fucking company. Of fucking Chat Me Up! "I deal in dopamine." Oh, my fucking god, I cannot go into that room. This is too wild to be real.

"Liv. I... I'll join you in a sec. Let me just... restroom?"

"There's a private one in here," Megan said behind me, stepping around to open the door.

"Well, no but I..."

Liv squeezed my arm. "You're gorgeous, girlie. Follow me."

The room was an opulent lounge decorated in dark reds and greens. An unmanned, fully stocked bar lined the corner. A pool table sat in the center of the room. Ben leaned on the short edge. Another man bent over the long end to sink a ball in the corner pocket. He stood up, grinning.

That grin vanished the second he saw me.

What is happening? What is... how is this happening?

A nonsensical laugh lodged in my throat. I covered my mouth to keep it in, but a loud "Ha!" slipped out anyway.

James dropped the stick on the table and strode to me. He tilted his head, eyes narrowing. "Hey. I was coming to find you. Is everything okay?"

Okay is not how I'd define this moment, no. Extraordinary? Surreal? Sure. I shook my head. If I took my hand from my mouth, only god knew what might come out.

"James? Do you know Jules?"

His head whipped to Liv. "What? Who?"

She gestured to me. "This is my friend Jules, who I've told you... uh... about. Okay, you're looking like you want to murder me."

"*Jules*?" he barked, then whipped back to me. "What the hell is happening?"

I made myself lower my hand and stick it out to him. "James—Addison, is it? I'm Juliette Reid. My friends call me Jules. On your lovely new platform, I'm Jules Twenty-Seven —not that I'm sure you're part of all of those details."

"I've seen that handle," he gritted out, gaze lasered on me.

"Fantastic product you created, truly. It's been such a great resource. I feel so fortunate to have met Liv and all her lovely friends thanks to it as well. Oh, excuse me. All her lovely friends—except for you, all this time." My voice was weirdly low and husky, but I was working hard not to dissolve into hysterical giggles at the absurdity of the moment.

"You don't say." It was clear to me that a clenched jaw was his version of holding it together, but I couldn't interpret his emotions in the least. His jaw worked side to side, eyes a steely gray.

Finally, he blew out a breath and shook his head. That light I knew so well sparked. "Tell me, *Jules*. Have we met before?"

Warmth exploded in my chest and brought tears to my eyes. I bit on my lip to keep all this mess inside. "I don't think so."

"Funny. You seem very familiar."

He cast a look around at all his—*our*—dumbstruck friends. Then, he smoothly stepped forward and leaned to my ear. "I'm pretty sure I can spark your memory if you give me a chance."

"Dare you to try," I whispered back.

"What is going on?" Liv yelped just at the moment his fingers tickled up my forearm.

James withdrew and turned to her. He threaded his hands into his hair, utterly ruining the style. "You have some explaining to do. What's all this about?"

She huffed. "That's my question. I told you I was setting you up with Jules tonight. I've been trying to get you two in the same room for—"

"Months." He and I both finished for her. My head spun again at the implication.

"Months," James repeated softly. He cast another glance at me and began to pace. "She's the one? The one who gave us the product idea? The one with the awesome daughter? Who's funny and... and whatever the fuck you told me? *This* is fucking *Jules*? I need a goddamn drink. Someone get me a whiskey. Get her one, too."

Ben and Celeste headed for the bar without a word. The rest of them edged around us and took seats. It was clear we were the show of the moment. I gripped my little clutch and fought the urge to run out of the room. I wanted to laugh and cry all at once, and I wasn't sure why, exactly.

"Why are you so freaked? What did I do wrong?" I'd never heard Liv so upset.

James spun back to her and put his hands on her shoulders. "Nothing, dear Liv. I'm sorry I snapped at you."

She looked at me and pursed her lips. "Who are you, Jules?" she asked softly.

My heart dropped. How could I explain this impossible situation to my new friend? Emotion choked my words. "No one, Liv. I'm not..."

"Yes, you are. Don't say that." James shook his head, but he didn't look at me. "Tell her who you are."

"I'm... James and I have met before. That's all."

He snorted. "That's very fucking far from all, love."

Celeste gasped as she pressed a glass into his hand. "Oh, my god!" Her eyes went wide as she looked between James and me.

"Shh," he hissed.

"I tried to explain us to my sister-in-law..." Celeste. He meant Celeste. Megan's phone call at the bar about Liv getting a cut of the business—that was him. *My brain is going to explode.*

The connections, the veins and arteries that now tied our stories together, they all swam in my head. All the moments we'd nearly connected. All the stories Liv had told now had a face to them—a face I knew so damn well.

I guess I don't need to call the chauffeur.

That silly thought made a giggle burst out of me. "Too much. This is too much," I managed through my laughter. "I'm sorry, but... yeah."

Liv looked at me as if I should be committed, but James grinned. That grin was enough to simmer my emotions. This wasn't a disaster. Wild, yes. But that fear I'd had before we walked in here melted away. Why be afraid? We were here.

I shook my head. "Excuse me, y'all. I need some air."

"No, Jules, hang on. I'll come with you," Liv said, but I held up a hand.

"No, I promise. I'll be back. Five minutes, tops."

I nodded at her and James, then spun and hurried outside through the nearest exit. It was a terrace overlooking rolling fields. A wall of windows meant that plenty of light from the party spilled out onto the patio stones. The night was cold as hell, but I didn't care.

What the hell happens now?

But I already knew what was going to happen. How this fairytale could end, if I just let it happen.

35

JAMES

The door shut behind her, and my friends let out a collective breath. Liv pointed at me and glared. "Alright, Addison. Tell me what the hell is going on!"

I opened my mouth and closed it again. A weird humming filled my brain, like this coincidence had its own frequency. Finally, I said, "I... don't know how to explain it. I'm not totally sure. *Jules*? *She* was the one you've been on about all fucking fall?"

"Yes, dammit! Who is she to you?"

"Everything, Liv! She's fucking *everything*!"

My shout hung in the room. Liv's dark eyes widened. Her lips fell open. "Well, shit, James."

Luke cleared his throat. "This feels very personal. I think I'll give you all some space. Megan? Shall we go dance?"

"Good idea," Kira murmured, and before long, it was only Ben, Celeste, Nick, Liv, and me in the room. Even Will and Mel murmured excuses and stepped out.

I looked at my four closest people in the world, shook my head, and went to the bar to pour five Blanton's single barrel reserves. I left theirs on the bar and took a gulp of mine while they drifted closer.

Nick and Ben were the first to approach. Their shit-giving grins were firmly in place. "So, what was that about?" my little brother asked, clearly trying to lighten me up.

I shrugged. "I told you. We've met before. And by met, I mean..."

But I didn't wink or grin. I looked down at my drink and shook my head. "Fuck off, guys. I'm not in the mood."

"Oh, my god. The mighty James has fallen." Nick laughed and slapped his leg. "It's about time someone brought you to your knees."

"Oh. She definitely did." Again, I wanted it to be an innuendo. Again, it just came out lovesick and pathetic. I scowled and gulped the whiskey. "Was it the 'fuck' or the 'off' y'all didn't hear?"

"It was the bullshit." We all looked up as Liv sauntered toward us, Celeste following close. "It was definitely the bullshit, James Addison. I'll ask one more fucking time. How do you know my girlie, and why did I not know anything about this?"

She picked up her drink and handed one to Celeste while I groaned and flipped back to March in my camera roll. I held up the photo of us by the natural pool. "We've met before. As I said."

Liv let out a muffled shriek and snatched the phone. Of fucking course, she flipped to the one of me kissing her. She issued another little shriek while my guys laughed.

"Oh, my god! James! These are the cutest pictures!" Celeste said as she peered around Liv.

I grabbed the phone back. "Yeah, whatever. We met in Aruba and reconnected randomly last Friday—at Starbucks." I cut Ben a loaded look.

"*Oh*." Realization hit him quickly.

"I knew it!" Celeste squeaked. "I freaking knew it!" She jumped up and down, waving her fists in the air like a cheerleader.

But Liv clapped a hand over her mouth. "Ohmygod. *Oh. My. God.* It's you! You're her boy!"

I rolled my eyes. "I'm all man, baby."

She cringed. "Oh, god. I know too much about you now. Oh, god. *Way* too much."

Celeste froze. Her green eyes went wide, and she gripped Liv's arm. "At sushi. She—oh, *no*. She said that thing about... *ohh, no*."

She and Liv hugged each other, eyes shut tight. Ben and Nick doubled over laughing.

I smirked. "It's about time y'all knew I was more than just talk."

"I *never* needed to know that, and I can never un-know it. Ugh." Liv shook all over, and the guys laughed harder.

I punched Nick and Ben on their arms. "Stop that, you children."

"Fucker," Nick said, wiping mirthful tears away. "It's not my fault your girl likes to gossip."

"I'm gossip-worthy. Girls can't help it."

Liv shook her head. "Mm-mm. *Your* girl took a lot of coaxing to get her to open up. Icky details aside, the gist was she's fucking crazy about you. Like, deep-end crazy to the point that she's terrified." She pointed to the door. "And it's been five minutes, and she's not back. Your move, Addison."

"Shit, you're right." I left my drink on the counter and skirted them all to run for the door.

36

JULIETTE

It took more than five minutes to get my head to stop spinning. I stood on that terrace and thought of the full moon on the ocean on my last night in Aruba. Sitting there while he slept, thinking so many things and nothing all at once. This was very much the same. Just a good forty degrees colder.

"Why does everything have to be so *much*?" I whispered to the full moon.

So big. So difficult. So incredible. The goods and bads of life felt too potent. Couldn't I have just a normal little existence? Why was I the princess in this weird fairytale?

Perfect is only ever defined by you. Maybe well-planned and neutral just isn't your brand of perfect.

"James Addison." I sighed his name and rubbed my forehead. "James fucking Addison."

"Juliette fucking Reid."

He leaned in the doorway, gazing at me. I stared at him, so unbelievably sexy in that tux. *Well done, Megan.* The thought was wildly out of place, but hey. Why not?

"It's Annette, actually. Like Mom."

He twitched a finger at his chest. "Alexander. And, for the record, when I was in college, my friends did call me Jay."

"No one ever called me Jae. Except you. But lots of people call me Jules."

He stuck his hands in his pants pockets and walked toward me. "I'm not going to be one of them. I like Juliette. It fits. Although I'm sure I could have fun working up lines about what *jewels* your eyes are or something. How you're the *jewel* of this party, you stunner." His gaze walked over me, and chills broke out that had nothing to do with the cold night.

"Not so bad yourself, Mister Bond."

He stepped closer. "My friends call me—"

"I know that now," I chuckled, then shook my head. "What were the odds? I mean—none. Right?"

"Not as far as I can figure. From a beach chair in Aruba to a Starbucks in Brentwood seemed like one in a billion. To learn I could've met you—re-met, I guess—months ago? I'm kicking myself for not making the time this fall. But as for the odds? I... I really don't know."

He looked so baffled, and I realized it was a foreign expression on him. Made sense. The head of a company as successful as *Chat Me Up!* probably didn't get stumped too often.

"You made that app?"

He nodded. "I wasn't trying to keep it from you. I fully intended to mention it, but ... I don't know. It just didn't come up."

"I know. I can't believe you really made it, though. You're famous, James. Like, a genius."

That got me a brief smile. "Shocking, isn't it?"

"No." I smiled back. "Not really."

Silence fell. I shivered, and he shrugged off his jacket and handed it to me. I wandered around the terrace with it around my shoulders. "You do realize that we're back in some kind of fairytale, right? At the ball. You're the king of the night."

"I want to deny it. But you're right," he admitted. "Except..."

"What?"

He shrugged. "This means we were always going to meet. One way or another, you were going to come into my life. At the beach or on a Friday night with my friends. Either way, we were..." he breathed a laugh, "fucking destined."

"Fucking destined. You think so?" I climbed up on the low stone wall that edged the perimeter and began to walk it.

"Mm-hm. Careful. Don't fall."

"Oh, please. After all my years on the trapeze? Do you think I'm really about to fall?"

That earned me a laugh. I stopped in the middle of the wall and faced him, crooking my finger so he came closer. My heart had crawled back up to my throat.

"I am, though," I said softly.

James cocked his head in a silent question.

"About to fall." I forced my lips into a smile. "Well, no. I already did."

And because it was him, I could see right away that he knew where I was going. His jaw clenched again, but the look in his eyes was anything but angry. It was damn near *hopeful*.

"Did you?" he asked, so soft. So calm. It didn't match the energy snapping between us.

"I did. But I think you know that already."

"I've been telling you, love. What you want matters. I know what I want. What I think."

"And what's that? What do you want, James Addison?"

"I want you to fall."

"Oh?"

"Hard."

"Oh?"

"As fucking hard as I have."

He didn't blink. I didn't breathe.

"I love you, Juliette. I've never met a woman who lights me up like you do. We fit together, as far as I can see. And if you decide to give this a shot... I will work every damn day to make you feel like my queen. I don't know if the risk is worth the reward, but I've taken some pretty big swings in my life. And *nothing* has ever made me feel like I fucking *won* like when I'm with you."

My lip trembled. "There were no odds."

"None."

"No way we could've planned this."

"No way."

"There was only..."

He crooked a smile. "Life."

Thirty seconds to midnight!

A mic'ed up voice from inside startled me. I tore my gaze away from those thundercloud eyes. Inside, the partygoers were holding noisemakers and champagne, getting ready to toast.

But a group of very familiar faces had gathered in the doorway. Liv and Celeste stood at the front of the crowd. They stared at me, hands clapped over their mouths, eyes screaming with anticipation.

James turned his head to follow my stare. He grunted a

laugh and shook his head. Immediately, his attention was back on me. "Ignore them. They have no manners."

I laughed, and a tear leaked out.

"Ten! Nine! Eight!"

My lips moved, but the noise from inside grew louder.

"Seven! Six! Five!"

James cocked his head. "What did you say?"

"Four! Three! Two!"

That was it. The final moment of a crazy, improbable year. The year I learned what happened when I let go of planning and just freaking lived. Hard work happened. Exhaustion happened. But *friends* happened. Music. Adventure.

Love. Love happened. In so many unlooked-for ways.

But none more than this.

"One! Happy New Year!"

I took the leap. Literally.

I jumped off the wall and right into his arms. My feet didn't even touch the ground. James caught me and spun me around while I laughed.

"I said I think I remember you now, James Addison. You're the one I fell in love with last year."

He lowered me down only to thread his fingers in my hair and claim me in a kiss.

Our friends cheered us on. James and I both lifted our middle fingers to them, but we didn't stop kissing until laughter got the best of us.

EPILOGUE

JULIETTE

I'm blind. No big deal. Just keep breathing. Bubbles rolled up my face while I lined the rubber lip against my forehead. I blew out hard through my nose, fit the rest of the mask on, and blinked my eyes open. The murky green water didn't give me much visibility, but at least I had my sight back.

Okay, now it's time to lose your air supply. I pulled my regulator out and let it float while the dive master nodded. With a broad sweep of my arm, the hose hooked at my elbow. I put the mouthpiece back in and puffed out the remaining air in my lungs, then sucked in a grateful breath.

The checkout test went on. I happily ran through all the required skills—skills I'd been learning for the last two months in a pool and classroom. When we were done, I trudged back up the ramp from the quarry to the picnic area. My gear was heavy, but I declined the instructor's offer to carry it for me. I wanted to do it myself. *Dad, can you believe it?* I smiled at the mask with a lump in my throat. I had no doubt Dad would be cheering me on.

At the top of the ramp, all my poignant thoughts scattered at the sight in front of me. James and Ivy sat on a bench in the shade, playing My Little Ponies. Max spotted me and jumped up to come dry me off with his tongue.

"That neoprene can't taste good, buddy," I said with a laugh as he worked on my wetsuit.

"Great job, Juliette," Larry, my instructor, said with a grin. "You're officially a diver. Come to the shop this afternoon, and I'll take your picture and print your certification card."

I squealed and promised I would. He loaded the air tanks in his truck, and I went to the bench to set my gear down.

James grinned as he watched me approach. When I set my BCD on the table, he stood up and clapped. "Way to go!"

Ivy looked around and hurried to jump onto the bench and clap, too. "Good job, Mommy! What did you do?"

I laughed. "Something I've wanted to do forever. I passed a test."

She clapped again.

James helped me unzip my wetsuit. I pulled it off my legs, and he wrapped a warm, dry towel around me. "Lunch?"

"That's service."

"I know how ruthless you get if you miss lunch." He winked at me and opened the picnic basket.

"Max! Come eat lunch!" Ivy bellowed. She and Max had fallen into insta-love when they met in January. Six months later, I felt sure that dog would've laid down his life for my daughter.

The amount of treats she liked to give him definitely helped.

Six months of a real-life fairytale that only got better. Ivy and I stayed with him more and more, especially now that school was out. James had changed one of his guestrooms to a little girl's hideaway that she was obsessed with. Maddie had even come to play a few times when Liv and Will joined us for dinner. Mom missed us, but we got plenty of time with her, too—and she insisted on keeping Ivy at least once a week so James and I could have "date night."

Date night meant I got to be louder than when Ivy was down the hall. But I definitely appreciated her support of my love life.

Love life. No joke. I *loved* this life. And I adored this man. He worked harder than anyone I'd ever known. But he always made time for us. He was never too busy to hear how my job went, what Ivy was learning in school, or how cute Mom and Martin were together. We easily found a rhythm for our relationship that worked for everyone.

As we ate, I gazed down at the glittery water in the quarry and let my mind drift back over the year.

On New Year's, when we were all back in the lounge, Liv had pulled me aside. All of the women circled me while the guys shot pool. James had caught my gaze and rolled his eyes, but he was clearly amused.

"First, I hate you for telling me *anything* about my brother-in-law's sex life," Celeste said with a huge grin. "Second, *ohmygod*, I am so happy for you two!"

Liv snapped and pointed at Celeste. "Exactly what she said."

My face had nearly melted off. "I promise never to tell you anything again. Especially the part about how he likes to..."

They all shrieked, just like I'd wanted. Across the room, the guys laughed.

"Tell them everything, love," James shouted at me. "Every. Damn. Thing."

"Even the part about the ketchup?" I called back, and they shrieked again.

He caught my eye and winked, and I nearly swooned.

Liv shook her head. "I really never imagined James in love. I always figured he was all BS, given his corny lines. Who knew he could be so romantic?"

Those lines are genius. I couldn't see why they didn't see it. James was hilarious. But I'd never met someone as imaginative as he was. He couldn't have invented such a successful product—and then expanded it—without being incredibly clever. The innuendo jokes and well-timed silly lines were small, in-the-moment outlets of creativity. A way of making something fun at random. All part of the brilliant way his mind worked.

Oh, god, I am so in love.

The thought had hit me and made me giggle just when James cut through the circle. He took my hand and kissed my knuckles. "Ladies. I'm stealing my queen for a dance. You may have all our filthy details later. M'lady? A dance?"

He'd walked me out of the lounge to the dance floor and spun me into his arms.

It had only gotten better from there.

∽

James

Juliette sat on the picnic blanket, staring off into space, munching on a chip. I sat down behind her, my bent knees outside her hips, and wrapped one arm around her shoulders. "What are you thinking about?"

She stirred and snuggled into me. "How much I love this. And by this, I mean *you*."

"And by me, you mean my..."

"Shh." She glanced over to see Ivy and Max eating on the picnic bench, then whispered, "I mean your cock. Your tongue. Your hands. That's what I mean."

I growled and pulled her closer. "I don't like competing for your favor. Even with myself."

She laughed. "Fine. Then by this, I mean *us*."

"I'll take that."

"I thought that was my job."

I buried my face in her shoulder and laughed. "Dear god, I adore you."

"Are you ready to adore me on vacation in two weeks?"

"Hm, yeah, although I'll be adoring you many, many times between now and then."

She bit into a chip and hummed.

"You sure you don't want to take Ivy?"

Her spine straightened. "We did the weekend in New York back in April. She was over the moon. That was a blast, but no. I want two weeks of *diving,* wearing bikinis, sipping umbrella drinks, and sweaty nights with my fella."

"That's the plan?"

She laughed. "No. That's the idea. We'll see what else we find."

My breath quickened. "Sounds good. But, uh, what if we added one more thing to the agenda?"

Juliette half-turned in my arms to look at me. Her whiskey eyes narrowed, assessing me. She knew me too well not to sense my struggle to stay cool here.

"What if we got married?"

My question hung between us. Her eyes got huge and blinked rapidly. "You're kidding."

I stroked her cheek. "You know I'm not," I murmured.

She puffed out a breath. "I know. But it's only been six months, and we're still working on a rhythm, and our friends would kill us if we just got married without telling them."

I nodded along.

"And yes."

My hand froze on her face. I cocked my jaw. "Do what now?" I drawled.

Her smile damn near blinded me. "Yes. That sounds... perfect."

I leaned forward and stole a quick but deep kiss from those lips. "Does it? Because I'm serious. I want to—"

She put her finger to my lips. "I want to, too. That's all the plan we need."

"Miss Juliette? Have I told you I love you?"

She narrowed her eyes. "That's not familiar. Maybe you should jog my memory."

I kissed her.

Her cheeks got pink. "Oh. Right. Actually, you have. In so, so many ways."

I hummed, and she closed her eyes with her forehead against mine. Whiskey-colored eyes opened to gaze at me. "So, an island elopement. That's how this fairytale ends? Happily ever after with a beach sunset?"

"No."

Her grin deepened, and I could tell she was with me. "No," she agreed.

"A beach sunset is just another chapter. Because, baby, we are just getting started."

~

Have you read all of the Anti-Belle Series? Celeste, Mel, Liv, and Megan's stories await! READ THE SERIES NOW.

Done with Nashville? Game on, baby. *SCORELESS* starts a fire-on-ice hockey romance series!

ACKNOWLEDGMENTS

First, I'd like to thank Lincoln, my Aussie pup, for inspiring Max in the book—and for lying beside me during long hours at the desk.

It's easy to get lost in writing. Easy to overthink every plot point. Easy to wonder if your book is decent or a dumpster fire.

My gratitude is to the people who keep my tunnel vision in check.

Dawn, my friend. You're there for a text about anything. Thank you so much for reading this book in a day, for working the blurb with me, and for being your brilliant, wonderful self.

To the king of innuendo jokes. Thanks for letting me ramble about this one.

And B. You try to keep me balanced, even when that's nearly impossible. Thank you for being my scuba buddy, my thought partner, and my missing piece.

Thank YOU, readers! If you've made it this far with me, I'm excited to get you to the end of this series—we're nearly there!

ABOUT THE AUTHOR

Skye McDonald writes books that will make you laugh, cry, and swoon. She believes that falling in love with yourself is the real path to happily ever after.

Skye's first novel, *Not Suitable for Work*, won the Linda Howard Award for Romance in 2019. Her co-authored Unlikely Pairings series (written with Sarah Smith) have been Amazon bestsellers and #1 New Releases. Skye writes about living life with your heart open in her "A Bit Much" Substack.

Born in Nashville, Tennessee, Skye spent years teaching English in Brooklyn, New York. Now, she lives in Montclair, New Jersey, where she writes and facilitates a women's group. In her free time, she hikes with her dogs, runs Spartan races, travels, Scuba dives, and is learning to ski. Someday she'll take a break and chill out, preferably on a beach. But not yet. There's so much life to live first.

MORE BOOKS TO BINGE

Click to Get on Skye's Newsletter Now!

The Connecticut Commodores Series

Book 1: Scoreless

Book 2: Scored On

Book 3: In the Crease

The Anti-Belle Series

Prequel: The Not So Nice Girl

Book 1: Not Suitable for Work

Book 2: Off the Record

Book 3: Nemesis

Book 4: Just Your Type

Book 5: What Happens At the Beach

As Sarah Skye

The Unlikely Pairings Series

www.ingramcontent.com/pod-product-compliance
Lightning Source LLC
Chambersburg PA
CBHW070637260626
47161CB00007B/2737